W9-BVZ-424

A House Divided

KIMBERLA LAWSON ROBY

GRAND CENTRAL
PUBLISHING

LARGE PRINT

Copyright © 2013 by Kimberla Lawson Roby

All rights reserved. In accordance with the U.S. Copyright Act of 1976, the scanning, uploading, and electronic sharing of any part of this book without the permission of the publisher is unlawful piracy and theft of the author's intellectual property. If you would like to use material from the book (other than for review purposes), prior written permission must be obtained by contacting the publisher at permissions@hbgusa.com. Thank you for your support of the author's rights.

Grand Central Publishing
Hachette Book Group
237 Park Avenue
New York, NY 10017

www.HachetteBookGroup.com

Printed in the United States of America
RRD-C

First Edition: May 2013
10 9 8 7 6 5 4 3 2 1

Grand Central Publishing is a division of Hachette Book Group, Inc. The Grand Central Publishing name and logo is a trademark of Hachette Book Group, Inc.

The Hachette Speakers Bureau provides a wide range of authors for speaking events. To find out more, go to www.hachettespeakersbureau.com or call (866) 376-6591.

The publisher is not responsible for websites (or their content) that are not owned by the publisher.

Library of Congress Cataloging-in-Publication Data
Roby, Kimberla Lawson.
  A house divided / Kimberla Lawson Roby. — First edition.
     pages cm. — (The Reverend Curtis Black series; 10)
  ISBN 978-1-4555-2606-2 (hardcover) — ISBN 978-1-4555-2956-8 (large print hardcover) — ISBN 978-1-4555-2607-9 (ebook) — ISBN 978-1-61969-464-4 (audiobook) 1. Black, Curtis (Fictitious character)—Fiction. 2. African American clergy—Fiction. 3. African Americans—Illinois—Chicago—Fiction. 4. Domestic fiction. I. Title.
  PS3568.O3189H68 2013
  813'.54—dc23
                                        2012051204

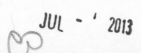
JUL - ' 2013

GRAND CENTRAL
PUBLISHING

GC

LARGE
PRINT

Also by Kimberla Lawson Roby

The Reverend Curtis Black Series

The Reverend's Wife
Love, Honor, and Betray
Be Careful What You Pray For
The Best of Everything
Sin No More
Love & Lies
The Best-Kept Secret
Too Much of a Good Thing
Casting the First Stone

Standalone Titles

The Perfect Marriage
Secret Obsession
A Deep Dark Secret
One in a Million
Changing Faces
A Taste of Reality
It's a Thin Life
Here & Now
Behind Closed Doors

CONELY BRANCH

To all my readers everywhere.

Thank you for everything.

CONELY BRANCH

A House Divided

Chapter 1

What a witch. For months, Vanessa Anderson, the *other* grandmother, had been working Charlotte's last nerve, and Charlotte wished this heifer would vanish into thin air. Ever since hearing the news just over seven months ago about Matthew's girlfriend, Racquel, being pregnant, things had turned pretty ugly. At first, Vanessa had seemed like a decent enough woman, and her husband, Neil, a noticeably good man, but once Matthew had left for Harvard last fall, Vanessa's attitude had changed drastically. Now, though, it was the middle of January, and things had only gotten worse. Vanessa no longer answered Charlotte's phone calls or attempted to return them, and Racquel had suddenly begun answering a lot less, too. Racquel did talk to Charlotte every now and then, but mostly when Charlotte and Curtis received updates about Racquel's doctor visits, her ultrasound testing, and any other information relating to their grandchild, it came directly from Matthew. Of course, when Charlotte had asked Matthew why Vanessa was treating her like the enemy, Matthew had told her it was because Vanessa had begun feeling as though Charlotte was trying to take over and control every decision relating to Racquel and the baby. Charlotte had been stunned, to say the least, because whether Vanessa liked it or not, Charlotte was going to be just as much a grandmother to Matthew and Racquel's baby as she was, and Charlotte had every right to ask as many questions and make as many suggestions as she wanted. This was going to be Charlotte and Curtis's very first grandchild, and she wouldn't back down for Vanessa, Racquel, or anyone else. It was the reason Charlotte was sitting front and center at this pathetic little baby shower, even though she knew Vanessa didn't want her there.

"Oh what a precious little christening outfit," one of Racquel's cousins said.

"It really is," a couple of other women commented. Other ladies cooed over the gorgeous little satin two-piece pant and jacket set, too.

Charlotte cast her eye at Vanessa, who was boiling, and then smiled at Racquel. "As soon as I saw it, I just had to buy it. It'll be perfect when Curtis christens the baby."

Vanessa set her coffee cup down on the small table next to her. "Hmmm. Well, I guess Racquel hasn't told you."

"Told me what?"

"That *our* pastor will be the one doing the christening. Pastor Collins has been our minister for more than twenty years, and he and his wife are Racquel's godparents."

Charlotte took a deep breath. She didn't want to show her behind in front of all these women, but if Vanessa didn't watch herself...

"No, actually," Charlotte said, "the subject has never come up. I just assumed that since Curtis is a pastor and since he's the baby's grandfather, this was a done deal."

Vanessa smirked at Charlotte. "Wow. Then, I guess it's a good thing we got this all cleared up. Now there won't be any misunderstandings."

It was all Charlotte could do not to fire back at Vanessa, but instead, she scanned the drab-looking family room they sat in. It was a shame they were bunched so close together. At least that's what it felt like to Charlotte, because had the shower taken place at her house, they'd have had a lot more room—not to mention the atmosphere would have been far more beautiful. Vanessa's decorating skills were average at best, and Charlotte was tempted to recommend a professional to her.

"Thank you so much for buying this, Mrs. Black," Racquel said nervously. Her tone was awkward, and Charlotte knew it was because Racquel was hoping this christening topic wouldn't spiral into a heated debate.

"You're quite welcome," Charlotte said. "I know we still don't know if you're having a boy or a girl, but I'm praying for a grandson, of course."

"Me, too," Racquel said, smiling and stroking her shoulder-length, thick brown mane to the side.

Charlotte wanted to ask her again why she didn't want to know the sex of the baby, because to her that was just ridiculous. Racquel had gotten Matthew to agree to that nonsense, too, and this had ruined Charlotte's plan of having a huge family get-together where everyone, including Matthew and Racquel, would find out the sex all at once. A couple of years ago, Charlotte had gone to a baby announcement party, where the ultrasound technician had written down the sex of the baby on a piece of paper, given it to the parents in a sealed envelope, and the parents had taken it to a bakery. The cake decorator had then told them that if they were going to have a girl, she'd make the inside of the cake pink, and if it was going to be a boy, she'd color it light blue. That way when they cut into it, it would be a surprise to everyone. Charlotte had loved that idea—but again, Racquel had spoiled everything. Charlotte's feelings toward Racquel had always been lukewarm at best, and this latest harebrained decision of hers hadn't helped. In fact, the only reason Charlotte tolerated her and stayed in contact with her was because she was carrying her precious little grandchild.

But Charlotte smiled as genuinely as she could. "Oh and hey...those other four boxes are from Curtis and me, too."

Racquel opened each of them, one by one. The contents included: an Elsa Peretti silver baby spoon from Tiffany, a silver frame for the baby's birth record, a five-hundred-dollar gift card from Target for disposable diapers or whatever else the baby needed, and another five hundred dollar gift card from Toys"R"Us.

"Thank you for everything," Racquel said. "This really was very kind of you and Pastor Black."

"Anything for our grandchild," Charlotte said, glaring at Vanessa. "Anything at all."

Racquel opened at least another twenty gifts that others had brought, and while not all of them would have been items Charlotte would have chosen for any baby, some of them were very thoughtful and in some instances very cute; especially some of the little onesies. Still, as Charlotte sat watching and trying her best to pretend as though she were happy to be there, she wished her mom or her best friend, Janine, had come with her. At least then, she wouldn't feel like some outcast and would have had someone familiar to talk to. But her mom and best friend not being there was all Vanessa's fault because, as it was, Charlotte hadn't found out about the shower herself until three days ago. Her mom had certainly wanted to attend, but since she was chairing a luncheon over in Chicago, she wouldn't be finished in time to make it. She and Charlotte's dad lived ninety minutes away, and as for Janine, she and her husband and daughter were away for the weekend in Wisconsin. Even now, Charlotte wanted to go off on Vanessa, because while Vanessa had claimed she'd mailed Charlotte's invitation two weeks ago along with all the others, Charlotte knew she was lying. Had it not been for Matthew asking her why she hadn't RSVPed, Charlotte never would have known about it, period. But that was okay, because even though Vanessa didn't want Charlotte in her home or anywhere near her, Charlotte was there, anyway, and she was planning to be around all the time as long as her grandchild was living here.

"So have you thought about names?" Laura asked. Laura, Racquel's great-aunt, was a classy, elegant woman with gorgeous white hair, but Charlotte could tell she was just as devious as Vanessa. It was clear, too, that she didn't care for Charlotte.

Racquel smiled. "Actually, Auntee Laura, we have. If it's a girl, her name will be Madison, and if it's a boy, Matthew Jr."

"You mean, Matthew the Second," Charlotte chimed in.

"No," Vanessa said, frowning. "She means Matthew Jr."

Charlotte stared at Vanessa. "I realize he'll be a Jr., but Matthew the Second sounds a lot more prestigious...and I'm sure we all want what's best for the baby. Especially when it comes to his getting into the right schools, colleges, and graduate programs, let alone when it's time for him to write a résumé."

Vanessa stood up. "You know what, Charlotte? We don't care about any of that nonsense. If my daughter says her son's name will be Matthew Jr., then that's exactly what it's going to be."

"Is that how you feel, too, Racquel?" Charlotte asked.

"Matt and I are both fine with Jr. We know how you feel, Mrs. Black, but Jr. is traditional, and that's what we've decided on."

"That's what you and my son have decided, or *you* and your *mother*?"

"Now, you wait just a minute," Vanessa said, stepping closer and pointing her finger in Charlotte's face. "Don't you ever speak to my daughter that way. And as a matter of fact, I want you outta here! We never wanted you to come in the first place."

Charlotte got to her feet and slapped Vanessa's finger away from her. "I knew all along you didn't want me to come, but I'm here, anyway. And for the record, you've got one more time to wave that decrepit-lookin' hand of yours in my face." Charlotte guessed Vanessa looked okay to be in her forties, which was about ten years older than she was, but Vanessa sure had a lot of wrinkles and she needed to do something about them.

"Mom...Mrs. Black," Racquel begged. "Please don't do this."

Vanessa stepped toe-to-toe with Charlotte.

"And if you ever touch me again, you'll regret it for the rest of your life."

Laura rushed toward them. "Ladies, please. This isn't the time or place for this, and you're upsetting Racquel."

"Why can't you guys just get along?" Racquel asked in tears. "At least for the baby."

"Because this witch," Vanessa spat, "is out of line and is always trying to control everything. She thinks because she and her husband have a lot more money than we do that she should have a say-so in everything. But sweetheart," she said, turning back to Charlotte, "I've got news for ya. It ain't happenin'. My husband is a successful neurosurgeon, I have my own business, and we don't need you."

"Honey, whether you feel like you need me and my husband or not, you're stuck with us. That baby Racquel is carrying is just as much ours as it is yours—and if you push me, I'll be your worst nightmare."

Vanessa took her finger and jabbed it into Charlotte's shoulder. "Get out of my house! Get out or I'm calling the police."

Charlotte squinted and wrinkled her forehead. Then she pushed Vanessa. "You must be crazy, putting your hands on me."

Vanessa slapped Charlotte so hard the sound of it rang throughout the family room. Charlotte smacked her back, and Vanessa grabbed the side of her face.

"You're going to jail!" Vanessa yelled.

No one moved or made a peep until Racquel stood up, grabbed her stomach, and screamed loudly. "Oh God, please don't do this!"

Racquel didn't look so well, and Charlotte hoped she was okay.

Vanessa wrapped her arm around her daughter. "Honey, why don't you sit back down."

But as soon as Racquel went to grab the arm of the chair, attempting to do just that, she grabbed her stomach and yelled at the top of her lungs. "Oh God, something's wrong," she said, doubling over. "Oh God, Mom...it hurts, it hurts, it hurts."

Vanessa helped her daughter over to the sofa, and Charlotte noticed how wet the inner parts of Racquel's pant legs were. Charlotte feared that her water had broken, and her heart skipped multiple beats.

"Oh no, Mom...dear God, please don't let me be losing my baby. Please, please, please," Racquel said, screaming.

"Someone call 911!" Vanessa said. "Now!"

Charlotte looked on, unable to move or say a

word. She hoped this episode wasn't her and Vanessa's fault. If only Vanessa hadn't approached her the way she had, threatening her and trying to throw her out of their house. Charlotte prayed that Racquel and the baby were going to be fine, because she just couldn't lose her new grandchild. Not now. Not when he or she was so close to entering the world. Not when Charlotte had already lost a child of her own a few years ago. She simply couldn't bear the thought of going through that kind of pain again.

Worse, if something happened to Matthew's baby, and he found out that Charlotte and Vanessa may have been the cause, he would never forgive her. When Charlotte had had those two affairs on his dad two years ago, it had taken Matthew a long time to get over it, but with something like this, there would be no coming back from it. All the apologies and explanations in the world wouldn't be able to fix things, and Matthew would be done with her for good. He would likely disown her completely and never speak to her again.

Charlotte watched Racquel twist and turn on the sofa, moaning and crying, and her heart beat faster than before. *Oh God, please, please let Racquel and the baby be all right…especially the baby. I'm begging you.*

Chapter 2

As soon as the automatic ER doors opened, Curtis, who was dressed casually in a black turtleneck, black pants, and a black leather jacket—perfect for the mild January temperatures they were having—quickly strutted through them. Charlotte left everyone in the waiting area and rushed toward him. She hugged him as though her life depended on it, and she wished she never had to let him ago—she prayed this nightmare wasn't actually happening.

"So is there any news?" Curtis asked. "I got here as fast as I could, and I called Matt while I was driving. He's worried to death."

"I can only imagine, and no, so far we haven't heard a thing. Vanessa and Neil are in with Racquel, though."

"Well, we may as well have a seat," he said.

Charlotte really didn't want to, not with some of Racquel's relatives and her mother's friends still waiting. They'd been gawking at her and whispering the whole half an hour they'd been there, and not one person had tried to console her. She could tell they blamed her and not Vanessa, and that they didn't care one bit how she was feeling. They acted as though they hated her.

But since there was nowhere else to go, at least not where they'd be able to receive in-person updates about Racquel and the baby, she went along with Curtis and sat back down in the room with them. Curtis said hello to a few of the women, and Charlotte wanted to slap two of these jezebels because of the way they were staring at him. Women. They knew full well who Curtis was and that he was very married, but that certainly hadn't stopped them from smiling at him like teenage schoolgirls. Charlotte almost laughed out loud, though, because neither of them could hold a candle to her in the looks or class department, and what she wanted to tell them was that Curtis would never have either one of them; not even if he was single and desperate.

Another half hour passed, and Curtis's phone rang. It was Matthew.

"Hey son," he said. "No, not yet...I know, but everything is going to be fine. I've been praying like never before, and my staff members are praying, too. It's Saturday, so no one is working at the church this afternoon, but Lana is going to ask one of our administrative assistants to post it on Facebook and Twitter. A lot of the members follow the ministry, and I know everyone will be praying for Racquel and the baby."

Charlotte looked on as Curtis tried to calm their son and reassure him that everything was going to be okay. But while she loved Matthew, she was hoping he didn't want to speak to her. She didn't want to have to answer the kind of questions she knew he would ask.

"Your mom?" Curtis said, looking at her. "She's right here. Hold on."

Charlotte swallowed the huge lump in her throat but then took the phone. "Hi, son, how are you?"

"Not good, Mom. What happened? Why did Racquel go into labor? I've been trying to call you."

Charlotte knew he'd been trying to call, but she'd pressed Ignore each time his number had displayed. She'd wanted so badly to hear his voice, but she just hadn't been able to do it.

"Honey, I don't know," she lied. "One minute Racquel was opening her gifts, and the next she was screaming out in pain and her water had broken. It's all a mystery, and I'm so sorry."

"I'm sorry, too, and if I don't hear something soon, I'm taking the last flight out of here."

Charlotte had known this was coming, and she had to talk him out of it. "Sweetie, I don't think that's a good idea. I mean, I know how worried you are, but you just started your second semester. You really don't need to miss any classes this week."

"But what about Racquel and the baby? They really need me, Mom. They need me to be there."

"Your dad and I are here, and your grandparents will be, too. Plus, we may be worrying for nothing because there's a chance that Racquel and the baby will be fine. Babies come early all the time with no problems."

"Still, I really need to be there. I'll bet Racquel is terrified."

"Why don't you just wait until we hear more?" she said, trying to appease him. "Then, if you still think you need to come, we'll make a reservation for you."

"Whatever, Mom," he said. "I just don't understand this, though. Because with the exception of Racquel's blood pressure being a little high, she'd been doing fine, and so was the baby. I just don't get what went wrong."

Charlotte didn't say anything.

15

"Can I speak back to Dad?"

"Of course. And honey, I love you."

"I love you, too."

Charlotte handed the phone over to Curtis.

"Son, don't worry," he said. "We just have to trust and believe that God is going to protect Racquel and the baby. We have to stay prayerful."

Curtis chatted with Matthew for a few more minutes and then told him he'd call him back as soon as they knew something. Charlotte phoned her mom and dad, her friend Janine, and then her aunt Emma to let them know what was going on. Curtis had dropped their daughter, Curtina, off at Aunt Emma's before heading to the hospital, so Charlotte had wanted to check on her, too.

Finally, after another twenty minutes or so, a thirty-something nurse walked into the waiting area. "Hi, I'm looking for the Anderson family."

Racquel's aunt Laura spoke up. "We're the Anderson family."

"And the Black family, too. We're the baby's other grandparents," Charlotte said matter-of-factly, but when Curtis glanced at her disapprovingly, she regretted it.

"It's good to meet all of you," the nurse said. "I'm here because Racquel wanted me to let you know that she's fine, and that she just gave birth to a beautiful baby boy."

Everyone blew a sigh of relief, and tears streamed down Charlotte's face. Everyone hugged the person sitting next to them, and Charlotte squeezed Curtis as tightly as she could. "Thank you, thank you, thank you, Lord," she said.

The nurse smiled at everyone. "Okay, well, I just wanted to give you the great news, and Dr. and Mrs. Anderson will be out shortly."

"Thank you for the update," Curtis said.

"No problem. We all love Dr. Anderson here, so we sort of feel like little Baby Anderson is our baby, too."

You mean little Matthew Curtis Black the Second. Charlotte wished she could yell those words out loud for the whole world to hear, but she knew Curtis wouldn't like it, and that it would likely infuriate Vanessa's friends and family members, so she didn't.

"We really do appreciate everything you've done for my great niece and great-great nephew," Aunt Laura added.

"You're quite welcome. You all take care now," the nurse said, turning and leaving.

Curtis pulled out his iPhone, preparing to dial

Matthew. "Wow, God is good all the time, and all the time God is good."

One of Vanessa's friends—one of the ugly "teenage schoolgirls" who'd spoken to Curtis when he'd first walked in—said, "You are so right, Pastor, and I just know it helped having a true man of God like yourself praying the way you were. A man like you must have the absolute best relationship with Jesus, and I'm sure that's why He answered your prayers so quickly."

Curtis smiled, and Charlotte was glad Matthew had answered his phone on the first ring because had this woman continued her flirtatious looks and comments, Charlotte would have had to set her straight, and the scenario would have been worse than it had been between her and Vanessa. Charlotte hated feeling this way, but she just couldn't stand it when women blatantly came on to her husband, letting him know they wanted him and that they didn't care whether he had a wife or not. This woman acted as though Charlotte wasn't even sitting there.

"Hey, son," Curtis said. "Great news. You have a beautiful little boy, and Racquel is fine, too....Yes, they're both doing well. We're just waiting for Racquel's parents to come out to give us more details....No, I really don't think you need to come, unless you maybe just want to fly in tonight and then right back out tomorrow. That way you won't miss your classes on Monday.... Yeah, that would work, too, so just let me know what you decide once you speak to Racquel. I'm sure you'll be able to talk to her soon.... Okay, I love you, too, son."

"What did he say?" Charlotte said. "And why did you say, 'that would work, too'?"

"Matt was saying that since Racquel and the baby are fine, maybe he'll just wait and miss class on Friday only. That way, he can fly home Thursday night and stay until Sunday."

"He really shouldn't miss any classes at all."

"I know, baby, but he has a new son, and I totally understand why he wants to see him. He's a father now, and if I were him I'd want to get here right away, too."

"I realize that, but Matt worked hard to get straight As all the way through high school. I just don't wanna see him ruin his scholarship. It's not every day that any child receives a four-year academic scholarship to Harvard University, and the last thing he needs is to be missing classes. Not to mention jeopardizing his grades."

Charlotte looked over at Aunt Laura, along with the hussy who was still gawking at Curtis, and wished they'd mind their own business. They'd been listening to her and Curtis's entire conversation, and there was no doubt they would take every bit of it back to Vanessa. They'd twist and exaggerate Charlotte's words and have Vanessa thinking Charlotte didn't want her own son to fly home to see his new baby, when in reality, all Charlotte wanted was what was best for Matthew and her grandchild.

After an hour had passed everyone started to get worried, and finally Vanessa and Neil came out to the waiting area and led them all to a large executive conference room. Charlotte assumed that since Neil was on staff there, he could use whichever room he wanted.

"Everyone, please have a seat," he told them. "Overall, Racquel and little MJ are fine. But I figured it would be better to speak to everyone in private instead of disturbing the other families."

Little MJ? Charlotte kept her mouth shut, but if she'd said it once, she'd said it a thousand times. Her grandson's name wasn't Matthew Jr., it was Matthew II. Matthew...the...Second. Matthew...Curtis...Black...the...Second.

"The reason it took us a while to come out here," Neil continued, "is because little MJ stopped breathing two different times, and they had to intubate him, start an IV, and place him in an incubator."

Charlotte covered her mouth with both hands. "Oh no."

Curtis shook his head with sadness, and everyone else's spirits dropped dramatically.

"I know this sounds bad, but when babies are born prematurely, even with only a month to go like little MJ, sometimes they're not able to breathe on their own and need more time to develop. But the good news is that I believe with everything in me that little MJ is going to be fine."

"Can we see him?" Charlotte asked.

"I'm going to arrange for the incubator to be moved close to the window so that all of you can see him there," Neil said. "But for now, I think it's best that not a lot of people go into the actual room where he is. Maybe in a few days when he's better."

Curtis nodded in agreement. "Totally understandable."

"We just have to keep praying for little MJ is all," Vanessa said.

What is it with everybody and this "little MJ" nickname? It was as if everyone was calling him that because they knew Charlotte didn't want them to. What was so wrong with calling him "little

Matt"? Or "little MB"? And why on earth did Racquel and Matthew want such a common suffix as Jr. when they'd both been brought up with a certain amount of class and culture? She knew most everyone she'd mentioned this to likely didn't understand why it was such a big deal to her, but it *was* a big deal, because it was like she'd been thinking all along: the end of his name would make a difference for him when it came to schools and certain levels of employment. It was just the way things were, whether folks wanted to admit it or not. Sometimes a certain kind of name preceded you, and it was the reason you got your foot through various doors, even if no one had ever laid eyes on you before.

"Do they know why Racquel went into labor so early?" Aunt Laura asked.

"We all know why," Vanessa spat, then glared at Charlotte. "This never should have happened, and it's all your fault."

Charlotte raised her eyebrows. "Excuse me?"

"You heard me. This is all *your* fault. You just had to show up at the shower, even though none of us wanted you there, and then you started all that drama. You completely disrespected me and my daughter in our own home, and then you had nerve enough to push me."

"Only after you poked me in my shoulder."

Vanessa moved closer to the side of the table where Charlotte was sitting. "And that was only after you slapped my finger away. You had no business touching me, and when I told you to get out, that's exactly what you should've done."

"Whatever, Vanessa. You're just mad because you can't get rid of me. You're mad because I have just as many rights as you do." *You're mad because when I'm around your husband, he can barely take his eyes off me.*

"Rights?" Vanessa said. "Hmmph. Think that if you want."

"And what is that supposed to mean? Because if you even think about trying to keep my grandson from me, I'll have you in court so fast you'll—"

"Ladies, ladies, ladies," Neil said. "That's enough. Our grandson is fighting for his life, and our daughter just gave birth, so let's keep things in perspective."

"Exactly," Curtis said. "Ladies, this really does have to stop."

Charlotte turned away from Curtis and stared at the wall. Vanessa folded her arms and turned in the opposite direction.

Charlotte was so livid, her head ached. That witch, Vanessa, clearly didn't know who she was dealing with, but if she kept taunting Charlotte and trying to dismiss her like some child, Charlotte would show her a thing or two. If Vanessa forced her, she would make Vanessa's life a living hell. End of story.

Chapter 3

Charlotte stepped out of the shower, drying herself with a velvety, oversized bath towel. Finally, she sawed her back from top to bottom, smoothed shea butter across her skin, and slipped on a full-length, floral satin robe. It was Sunday morning, and while she was thankful to see another day, she was slightly exhausted because she'd barely slept a wink. Partly because she'd worried about her grandson and wondered how he was doing, and partly because she hadn't had a chance to hold him or even get close to him. It had been a blessing just to see him, even through the maternity ward glass window, but what Charlotte had longed for was to at least touch him and look into his eyes. She did understand Neil's suggestion about everyone allowing the baby some time to get better, but this was her grandson and she wanted to be there for him; let him know how much she loved him and how she couldn't wait to do everything she could to keep him happy.

Charlotte walked toward the bed and saw Curtis standing in front of the dresser mirror, buttoning one of his custom dress shirts, and it was at that moment that she decided she was skipping church. "I think I'm gonna head over to the hospital."

Curtis looked at her reflection but never turned around and never said anything.

"Did you hear me?"

"I heard you. Just don't know if that's a good idea. Why don't you wait until I get back from church, and we can go together?"

"That'll be hours from now. And why don't you think it's a good idea?"

Curtis wrapped his tie around his neck, but he was silent again.

"Hello?"

"Because the last thing I wanna see or hear is you and Vanessa going at it again. Racquel doesn't need that, neither does little MJ, and the hospital isn't the place for it."

"First of all, the only reason Vanessa and I don't get along is because of her. She hates when I come around, and she treats me horribly. And let me ask you something, Curtis: why are you calling the baby 'little MJ'? You know what we discussed."

Curtis sighed. "Baby, I just don't understand you sometimes."

"Why?"

"Because if Racquel and Matt want to name their baby Matthew Jr., then everyone should be fine with that. We should call him what they want us to call him. Either Matt Jr. or little MJ, since that's what Racquel called him last night before we left the hospital. That's also what Matt called him on the phone. Baby, it's their child and their decision, and we should honor that. Plus, there's not a single thing wrong with having Jr. at the end of your name. It's tradition."

"That's all fine and well, but I like what I like and for good reason."

Curtis laughed and shook his head. "There's just no getting through to you, is there?"

"I don't see what's so funny. Matthew the Second sounds so much more prestigious and important, and I wish all of you realized that."

Curtis shook his head again.

"Oh, and did you know Vanessa has already chosen someone else to christen the baby?"

"No, but if that's what Matt and Racquel want I don't see anything wrong with it."

Charlotte scrunched her face. "Baby, he's your grandson. You're the only person who should even be considered."

"But whether I christen him or not, he'll *still* be my grandson."

Curtis was frustrating her to no end, and Charlotte couldn't understand why he was so calm about this. Couldn't he see that if they didn't stand up for themselves now, Vanessa would push them completely out of their grandson's life?

She opened her mouth to say just that, but there was a knock at the door.

"Who is it?" Charlotte asked.

"It's me, Mommy," Curtina said.

"Come in."

Curtina walked over to her father. "Good morning, Daddy."

"Good morning, pumpkin." Curtis leaned down and kissed her on the forehead. "How are you?"

"Good."

"Good morning, sweetie," Charlotte said.

Curtina embraced her. "Good morning, Mommy. Are we going to church or to the hospital?"

Charlotte had known the hospital question was coming, because this was all Curtina had talked about last night when Charlotte had picked her up from Aunt Emma's. "Well, I'm going to the hospital, but you and Daddy are going to church. Daddy's going to be leaving soon, and then I'll drop you off when we get dressed."

"Why can't I go to the hospital with you? Why can't I see the baby?"

"Because you're not old enough to visit mothers and their newborns."

Curtina's lips curved into a pout. "That's not fair. I wanna see little MJ."

Even Curtina was calling her nephew by that name. She'd only heard Curtis say it a couple of times, but it had obviously stuck with her. "You'll get to see him when he comes home."

"When will that be?"

"When he's a lot stronger."

Curtina didn't argue any further, which was a bit unusual, but Charlotte was relieved. "Let's go pick out something for you to wear," she said.

"Okay," Curtina groaned. "But can we call Matt first? I wanna talk to him."

"We'll call him on the way to church. You can talk to him while I'm driving."

"Is he coming home?"

"Not right away."

"I miss him."

"We all do," Charlotte told her.

"He'll be home again soon," Curtis said.

When the landline rang, Charlotte glanced over and saw that it was Matt. "I guess we talked him up....Hey, son, how are you?"

"I'm good, Mom. How are you guys?"

"We're good, too. Have you spoken with Racquel this morning? How's little Matt?"

"Just got off the phone with her. She's doing fine. And so is little MJ. He's hanging in there very well."

Charlotte debated whether or not this was the time to bring up this name dilemma, but she took a chance. "Honey, I know this isn't my business, but are you really going to name your son Matthew Jr.? I mean, remember what we talked about?"

"Mom, are you still trippin' about that? We told you months ago that if we had a boy, we weren't naming him Matthew the Second."

"I know, but—"

"Mom, please! Listen to me. The baby's name is Matthew Curtis Black Jr., and that's that. So, you can call him 'Matt Jr.' or 'little MJ' like everyone else."

Tears filled Charlotte's eyes. His tone was so curt. "I'm sorry. I didn't mean to upset you."

"You're upsetting me because even though little MJ's lungs haven't fully developed, you're more worried about his name than his health. It's so petty and shallow, Mom, and I'm tired of hearing about it. All I want is to see my son and for him to get well."

Charlotte swallowed hard. "I won't bring it up again."

"Is Dad there?"

"Yes."

"Then I'll talk to you later," he said.

Charlotte passed the phone to Curtis and the tears she'd tried holding back flowed across her cheeks. It was official: everyone was against her when it came to little Matt—or little MJ, the name Matthew had basically demanded she call the baby. Yes, everyone was dead set against her. Even her own son.

Chapter 4

*C*harlotte strolled through the hospital's main entrance, dressed in a pair of skinny jeans, a pure white, wrinkle-free, button-down shirt, and a brown and tan cashmere wool blazer. It wasn't overly cold, but she also wore her brown lambskin leather gloves and Burberry scarf that her mom had given her for Christmas. She walked into the elevator, rode up to the maternity floor, signed in, and headed toward Racquel's room. She'd hoped Vanessa wasn't in there visiting with her, and thankfully she wasn't.

"So how are you this morning?" Charlotte said, walking in and hugging Raquel.

Racquel smiled, but it was obvious she wasn't ecstatic about seeing Charlotte. "Pretty good. How are you?"

"I'm fine. I'm so glad you were still able to have the baby naturally, because a C-section would have meant a ton of pain."

"I'm glad, too."

"So how's my grandson?"

"About the same, but his doctor says he's definitely a little fighter, and he's already made progress. He's down there now examining little MJ and going over more test results."

"He's going to be fine, and it will be great when we can finally hold him."

Racquel smiled. "I know. I can't wait, and neither can Matt."

"So when are they letting you go home?"

"I'm not sure, but I really don't wanna leave little MJ."

"Understandable. I wouldn't want to, either."

Racquel looked up at the flat-screen television, and now the atmosphere felt awkward again. Charlotte wondered if Racquel blamed her for what happened yesterday, but she didn't dare ask her.

"Is there anything I can get you?" Charlotte finally said.

"No, I'm fine, but thank you."

Charlotte looked at the TV screen, too, but then turned when she heard someone walking in. To her regret, it was Vanessa. Although, the good news was that Neil strutted in behind her.

"Good morning," Charlotte said, smiling.

"Good morning," Neil said, but, of course, Vanessa pretended Charlotte was invisible and that she hadn't heard her speaking to either one of them. Now Charlotte felt even more out of place, but she tried to make small talk. She still couldn't stand Vanessa and never would, but she would put on a happy face to keep peace. For the moment, anyway.

"I just thought I'd come see how Racquel and that grandson of ours is doing. Curtis will be here, too, when service is over."

"Sounds good," Neil said.

Charlotte looked back at Racquel. "Actually, I was hoping to see the baby now. Is that okay?"

Vanessa tossed Charlotte a dirty look. "I don't think that's a good idea. My grandson needs his rest, and too many visitors aren't good for him."

It was all Charlotte could do to hold her tongue.

Neil seemed out of sorts and hurried to say, "I need to see a couple of patients, but I'll be back soon, sweetie." He clearly didn't want to witness any trouble, so he kissed Racquel on the forehead and left.

Charlotte grabbed her handbag from the chair. "Racquel, I think it's best I leave, too."

"No arguments here," Vanessa said, taking a seat in the recliner.

"What?" Charlotte said.

Vanessa ignored her.

Charlotte held her tongue again. "Like I said, Racquel, I think it's best I leave. I don't wanna upset you, so I'll see you later."

"Hmmph, you should have thought about that yesterday," Vanessa spat.

Charlotte smiled at Vanessa, all the while wishing she could wring her neck. If only she could give Vanessa a Chicago South Side beatdown and get away with it, she would. But instead, she gained her composure and walked out of the room with total class. She had another plan, anyway.

As she headed down the hallway, preparing to ask one of the nurses to page Dr. Neil Anderson, she spotted him talking to another physician. This was right up Charlotte's alley.

"Charlotte," Neil said, "this is Dr. Koster, little MJ's pulmonary specialist. And Doctor, this is MJ's other grandmother."

"Very nice to meet you," Dr. Koster said.

Charlotte smiled. "Likewise."

"Dr. Koster just gave me some very good news. Little MJ is doing much better than expected."

"How wonderful," she said.

Dr. Koster nodded. "It is. He's doing so much

better already that we might be able to remove his breathing tube tomorrow."

Charlotte smiled again. "What a blessing, and I know Racquel and Matt will be thrilled."

"I was just on my way to tell her," Dr. Koster said, "but then I saw Neil. I could tell early on that your grandson was a fighter, but I guess he's more of a fighter than we realized."

"Apparently so, and thanks for taking such good care of him," she said.

The doctor extended his hand. "Again, it was great meeting you, Charlotte, and I'm sure I'll see you again."

Dr. Koster walked away, and Charlotte didn't waste any time making her move. "Neil, could I speak to you in private?"

"Sure. Let's go in here," he said, opening the door to a small family waiting room. No one was in there, so it was perfect.

Charlotte gazed at him for a few seconds and burst into tears. She hoped this wasn't going too far, but she needed an ally, and this was the only way she could think to get one.

"I am so, so sorry, Neil, for the way things turned out between Vanessa and me yesterday." She sobbed for effect. "That argument never should have happened, and I'm so sorry we upset

Racquel the way we did. I'm sorry for everything," she said dropping her purse onto the floor
and covering her face with both hands…still
weeping.

"Heyyyyy," Neil said, pulling her into his arms
and caressing her back. "Everything is going to be
fine. None of us is happy about what happened,
but what we have to do now is focus on little MJ.
We have to band together for him and Racquel."

"I know, but I just feel awful," she said, stepping back and gazing directly into his eyes again.
"And I can't stop thinking about Racquel and how
she could've lost the baby."

"But she didn't."

Charlotte sniffled and wiped her face with her
hands again, and Neil snatched a few tissues from
the Kleenex box on the table and passed them to
her. She carefully patted her face, so she wouldn't
ruin her makeup any more than she had. "I just
don't want you to hate me."

"Hate you? I could never do that. We all make
mistakes, but the important thing is to move on."

"Thank you for being so understanding," she
said. But this time when she gazed into his eyes,
there was no denying the strong attraction and
obvious chemistry between them. Charlotte had
noticed this very thing many months ago and had

purposely ignored it. She and Curtis were happier than ever, so no matter how intense the attraction was between her and Racquel's father or how undeniably gorgeous the man was, she wasn't interested. Although this still didn't mean she wouldn't take full advantage of the way Neil felt about her, along with anything else he had to offer, if it meant keeping her in the constant presence of her grandson. She would do just about anything to be around him—even call him little MJ. She needed to have a real relationship with him, especially since she was the better grandmother. And no one, not that witch, Vanessa, or even Racquel, would stand in the way of that. It was true that she was the first lady of a very well-known church right there in Mitchell, and that she had deep-rooted Christian values the same as the next person, but there was also another side to her—a side she hoped she wouldn't have to expose anytime soon. She'd gladly and willingly do it, though, if she had to.

Chapter 5

Talk about a turn of events. Charlotte had gone from hoping to see her grandson up close to now actually standing over him inside the neonatal intensive care unit, and she was in pure heaven. She and Neil were dressed in protective scrubs and surgical caps, and thanks to all her tears, apologies, and the pleading she'd done, Neil had agreed to slip her in to see the baby for a few minutes. What a handsome and precious little thing he was, even with a breathing tube and an IV needle inserted into his body, and Charlotte was in love with him already. He even had thick, coal-black hair, the same as Matthew when he was born. Charlotte could hardly take her eyes off him and wished she could scoop him out of his incubator, whisk him away from the hospital, and fly him out to Boston to see Matthew. If she could, she would take little MJ and physically move there for the remainder of Matt's semester.

That way, he'd be able to stay in school and wouldn't have to worry about trying to get home on weekends, something she knew he was planning to do as often as he could so he could be with his son. She totally understood that, but it was like she'd been trying to explain to Curtis yesterday: she also didn't want him jeopardizing his education. What Charlotte wanted was the best for her son, and eventually she would figure out a way to make sure he had it. She would do whatever was necessary to keep him in school, and at the same time make it possible for him to be a good father.

One of the NICU nurses walked over to Charlotte, the one who looked to be no more than in her late twenties. Still, she seemed extremely knowledgeable. "He really is the cutest little thing we've seen in a while. We all just love him."

"Thank you," Charlotte said. "And, of course, I agree with you."

All three nurses laughed, as did Charlotte and Neil.

"We're very happy for you, Dr. Anderson," one of the other nurses said. "We're happy for your entire family."

"That's very kind of you, Donna. How nice of you to say such wonderful things and take such great care of little MJ."

Donna stood next to Charlotte. "You can touch him if you want."

"You sure?" Charlotte asked, and also looked at Neil.

"It's fine," the nurse said.

Neil smiled. "Of course. Go ahead."

Charlotte's stomach fluttered. She didn't know why she was so nervous and excited, but maybe it was because she hadn't felt this overjoyed since the day Matthew was born and then the day when, well…Marissa had come into the world. Charlotte remembered how elated she'd been as soon as she'd laid eyes on her new baby girl. Her daughter's birth hadn't happened without controversy, what with Curtis questioning whether Marissa was actually his daughter and then Charlotte having to work as fast as she could to figure out a way to pay off a DNA technician so the results could be falsified. But once all that had been taken care of, she and Curtis had welcomed their new child and loved her with all their hearts. Even Matthew had loved his baby sister from the beginning, and life had been good.

Charlotte smiled at her latest thoughts, but then sadness overcame her. She always tried to forget about all the ugliness, particularly the fact that Marissa had been a bad seed with serious mental issues and that as she'd gotten older, she'd shown signs of deception. She'd purposely done cruel, evil things on the sly and with a smile on her face. For some reason, Marissa had loved Curtis, but whenever Curtis left for out-of-town speaking engagements, Marissa had always treated Matthew and Charlotte like they were hated enemies. But Charlotte knew she couldn't help herself, and that her actions were a result of her heredity. Aaron, Marissa's biological father, the man Charlotte's first affair had been with, had been diagnosed with serious mental issues and had been institutionalized before Marissa was born. Sadly, though, Marissa had eventually fallen to her death, and ever since then, Charlotte had longed to have another baby. She'd mentioned it to Curtis a few times, only to learn that he didn't think it was a good idea because of all the marital problems they'd been having over the last few years, but even when she didn't talk about it, her desire to have a child never waned. It was the reason she desperately needed to be around her grandson.

"Go ahead," Neil told her again. "It really is okay."

Charlotte looked at the purple latex gloves she'd slipped on before entering the nursery, took a deep breath, and reached her hand through the round opening. She grabbed little MJ's hand and admired each of his tiny fingers. Oh, how she loved this little baby with her entire being. She knew she hadn't given birth to him, but her feelings for him were no different than if she had. She would protect him at all costs and would give her life for him if she had to. He was only a day old, but he was everything to her.

"He's so absolutely beautiful," she said, her voice shaking and eyes watering. "He's just perfect."

"He certainly is," Neil said, standing next to her and admiring his little grandson. "I never expected to be a grandfather so soon, but I wouldn't trade him for anything."

"Same here," Charlotte said, caressing the baby's fingers while watching him stretch his tiny little neck and arms and move his legs. He never opened his eyes, and he seemed to be resting peacefully.

A bit more time passed, but when Charlotte looked to her side and through the glass, she saw Vanessa and Racquel and quickly turned her attention back to the baby, pretending they weren't there. At first she wondered why they hadn't come inside the unit yet, but then she realized maybe they were waiting for her and Neil to come out. But she wouldn't leave her grandson until someone made her. She wasn't planning to move until she was forced. To her regret, though, only seconds passed before they heard a knock on the door.

Neil turned around, as did all three nurses, and Neil said, "Oh, Racquel and Vanessa are here."

Charlotte kept her eyes on the baby. She'd heard Neil very clearly, but she didn't let on.

"I'm sorry to have to end your visit, but I know Racquel can't wait to see her little one," he said.

Charlotte still didn't respond to him but told the baby, "Nana loves you, little MJ. I love you with all my heart, and I'll be back to see you soon, okay? I love you."

Charlotte released the baby's hand and stepped away from the incubator. She so wished she didn't have to leave him, but she also knew it wouldn't be long before Vanessa called in a firing squad if she didn't. Even now, as Charlotte turned and looked at her again, she saw how disgusted she was—although, this actually made Charlotte happy. Not only was Vanessa fuming because Charlotte was spending quality time with the baby but also because seeing Charlotte with her husband was likely making her psycho. It was the reason Charlotte rubbed the side of Neil's arm right in front of her and said, "Thank you for bringing me in to see our grandson. You have truly made my day."

"You're quite welcome," he said.

Charlotte and Neil exited the room, and Charlotte smiled at Racquel, who was sitting in a wheelchair. "He's the most precious thing in the world, Racquel, and Matthew is going to be beside himself."

"I know. I can't wait for him to get here."

"I'm going to call him shortly, but if there's anything you need, anything at all, just let me know."

Vanessa pushed Racquel's wheelchair forward so that she stood directly in front of Charlotte. "I want you to hear me and hear me good. If our daughter needs *anything at all*, her father and I will get it for her."

Charlotte stared at her like she was crazy, but since Neil and Racquel were witnessing this madness, Charlotte forced a smile and said, "I was only trying to be helpful, Vanessa. I know you don't like me, but I really do care about Racquel and the baby. And I hope you and I can eventually become friends."

"Ha!" Vanessa said. "Please. That will *never* happen. And I do mean *never*."

Charlotte feigned another smile, mostly to appease Racquel and Neil, but thought, *You got that right. Not only will it never happen, but it's only a matter of time before you become my worst enemy. And sweetheart, it won't be pretty.*

Chapter 6

Thank God little MJ's breathing tube had been removed as planned. Not yesterday, the way Dr. Koster had anticipated, but about an hour ago. Charlotte was glad she'd decided to call Racquel to see how things were going this morning, because if she hadn't, there was no telling when she and Curtis would have found out. There was a chance Matthew would have told them, but since he had class this morning, he likely would have waited until this afternoon.

"You know," Curtis said, drinking the cup of coffee Agnes had just set on the table in front of him, "little MJ is very blessed, and so are we. The entire congregation was praying for him, and you know how I feel about the power of prayer."

"It really is wonderful to have so many people that care about us," Charlotte agreed.

"We need prayer because the devil is always

busy. But the good news is that we serve not just a sometimes or every-now-and-then God, we serve an every-hour, 365-day God who does all that He says He'll do."

"Wow, you're on fire this morning, aren't you?" Charlotte said.

Curtina laughed. "Daddy, you're saying the kind of stuff you say at church on Sundays."

Curtis laughed, too. "I guess I am, huh? Daddy's just happy, sweetie. Happy my little grandson is fine and thankful for all our other blessings. God is so good to us, even when we're not all that great ourselves."

Curtina ate the rest of her cereal and drank her orange juice. "Mommy, can I go back upstairs to watch Sprout until it's time to leave?"

"I suppose. We're heading out in about thirty minutes, though, so you make sure you have everything packed in your book bag."

"I will."

Curtina skipped out of the kitchen, and Charlotte couldn't help thanking God for her little girl, the same as Curtis had just thanked the Lord for little MJ. Years were passing, and Curtina was almost five years old now, yet it was still hard to believe there had been a time when Charlotte couldn't stand her. She was embarrassed to even think back to those days when she'd treated an innocent child so horribly, but it had only been because Curtis had conceived Curtina with another woman outside of their marriage. He'd had an affair and broken it off, then his mistress had died, and Charlotte's stepdaughter had moved in with them. It had been the worst time of Charlotte's life, or so she had thought, but soon she'd come to love Curtina as if she were her own, and Curtina loved, loved, loved her back. She never even brought up her biological mother, mainly because she barely remembered her, but it was fine, because to Charlotte, Curtina was in fact her daughter. It was funny how things changed and how time truly did heal all wounds, just the way folks always said.

"So are you going to the hospital this morning?" Curtis asked.

"Maybe around noon, and hopefully I won't have to run into Racquel's witch of a mother."

Curtis looked at her and then toward the television. Agnes wiped off the counter near the stove but never said a word.

Charlotte knew they didn't want to hear her ranting on and on about Vanessa, but she was still beside herself because of the way things had turned out yesterday. Charlotte had gone to the hospital first thing, yet Vanessa had said and done everything she could to stop her from seeing little MJ. She'd been downright rude, and since Charlotte hadn't been able to contact Neil, she couldn't do anything about it. She did finally hear from Neil early evening, once he'd finished a ten-hour brain surgery, but by then, she'd been too frustrated to talk about it or drive back over to the hospital. Charlotte wondered when this tug-of-war was going to end, and although she was trying her best to keep things cordial with Vanessa—at least when Racquel and Neil were around—she was growing very tired of this woman. Charlotte had held her tongue more than a few times, but she was also human and knew if Vanessa didn't watch herself, this wouldn't end well.

"Curtis, something has to be done about Vanessa. She's doing everything she can to keep me away, and it'll be even worse once Racquel brings little MJ home."

"Baby, why don't you give her some time? Give her a few more days to get past what happened over the weekend."

"Even a year from now, that woman will still be treating me the same way, so time has nothing to do with it."

"Maybe you could try a little harder to get along

with her," he said. "I know you don't like her, but do it for the baby and Racquel."

Charlotte was stunned. It almost sounded as though Curtis was siding with Vanessa, but she quickly tossed that craziness out of her mind. She ignored it because there was no way her own husband was sitting there defending the enemy. He simply wouldn't do that to her.

Curtis must have picked up on what she was thinking and said, "Baby, I'm not taking anyone's side. I'm just saying that sometimes you have to be the bigger person. Sometimes it's the only way to deal with certain situations."

"Do you feel the same way, Agnes?" she said, but kept her eyes on Curtis. "That I should have to kiss Vanessa's behind? That I should have to tap-dance around that woman in order to see my own grandchild?"

"You want the truth? Because you know that's what I'm going to give you."

"I do."

"Mr. Curtis is right. And maybe you should sit down and try to talk to her. One-on-one and face-to-face. Maybe you should ask her if the two of you can start over. Let bygones be bygones."

"I tried that on Sunday and the first thing she said was how that would never happen."

"Well, why do you think she despises you so much, Miss Charlotte?"

"If you ask me, I think she's jealous."

Now Curtis spoke up. "Of what?"

"Us and what we have. She's afraid we'll be able to give little MJ a lot more than she and Neil can, and that he'll prefer to spend all his time over here when he's older. She hates everything about me," Charlotte said, but she didn't add what she'd figured out a couple of days ago: that the main reason Vanessa couldn't stand her was because of her husband and the way he was attracted to Charlotte. Then, although Charlotte hadn't thought about it all that much for a while now, Vanessa probably hadn't gotten over the fact that Charlotte had purchased the baby's bassinet, crib, and dresser set and then had it delivered to the Andersons without warning. She'd wanted her grandchild to have the best and the style of furniture *she* wanted him to have. So, as soon as Matthew had mentioned how Vanessa was planning to take Racquel to pick out everything in a couple of weeks, Charlotte had rushed over to one of the best baby stores in downtown Chicago. She'd gone that very same day, and because everything she'd chosen had been in stock, she'd paid a ton to have it overnighted so it would arrive the next day. Of course, even if Vanessa had wanted to return it, she hadn't, because at the time Racquel had been very excited about it and so had Matthew. They'd both thanked Charlotte multiple times, and that had been the end of it. At least it had been for Matthew and Racquel, because Charlotte knew it had burned Vanessa to a crisp. She'd never confronted Charlotte, but it was after that when Charlotte had noticed a subtle yet noticeable change in her attitude. Charlotte didn't know what she was supposed to do about Vanessa's jealousy, though, because it wasn't Charlotte's fault that she was in a better position to buy her grandchild whatever he needed or that she had better taste than Vanessa. Charlotte couldn't help that Vanessa was simply beneath her in a number of ways, and that there was no comparison between them.

Curtis stood up. "Baby, I really doubt that Vanessa is jealous of anything. I mean, why would she be?"

"You don't get it. You believe everyone thinks logically, but that's not always the case. Especially when it comes to women and their envy."

"I guess. But hey, I have to get to my meeting. We have a lot to discuss today."

"I wish I could be there, but maybe I'll make it to the next one."

Curtis kissed her on the lips. "See ya later."

"See ya."

"Have a good day, Agnes, and thanks for breakfast."

"You're welcome, Mr. Curtis, and you, too."

When Curtis left, Charlotte went upstairs. She still had a few more minutes before she'd have to drop Curtina off at school, so she sat on her bed, picked up her cell phone, and dialed Matthew. She knew he had class, but she wanted to leave a message for him to call her back as soon as he could. Surprisingly, he answered on the first ring.

"Hey, Mom."

"Hey. Why aren't you in class?"

"I didn't go."

Charlotte frowned. "Are you okay?"

"I'm fine. I'm packing and then heading to the airport."

Charlotte couldn't believe this. She'd been so sure that since the baby was doing much better, Matthew would just wait until this weekend to fly home. "Honey, it's already Tuesday, so why don't you just wait another three days? Why don't you finish out the week?"

"No, Mom. And I never should have listened to

you on Saturday, either, when you told me not to come."

"I was just trying to get you to do the right thing."

"This *is* the right thing. But on a different note, I need to talk to you about something else."

"What?"

"Saturday, and what happened at the shower."

Now Charlotte wished she hadn't called him. "I'm not sure I understand."

"Mom, just stop it. Racquel already told me everything. About the way you got into it with her mom at the shower and the things you've said at the hospital. She said when you and her mom got into it, she got so worked up, she went into labor."

"It wasn't that serious. Vanessa and I had a couple of disagreements, but—"

"But nothing, Mom. When you and Dad were at the hospital, I asked you what happened. I asked why Racquel had suddenly gone into labor, and you claimed you didn't know. You lied without even flinching. You do that stuff all the time."

"I'm sorry."

"You're always sorry. You do stuff and then you think apologizing for it is enough. But it's not, Mom. You caused a scene at that shower, and that's why Racquel went into labor. We could have lost little MJ, and I'm doing everything I can not to blame you for it."

Charlotte's heart beat frantically.

"Are you hearing me, Mom? I could have lost my son."

Charlotte was so shocked, she hadn't even noticed the tears flowing down her face and onto her pants. Matthew was actually blaming her for everything and hadn't said much of anything about that witch, Vanessa. He acted as though she'd been arguing with herself. She needed to make him understand that Vanessa was just as responsible as she was.

"Honey, you do know that it wasn't just about me, right? Vanessa didn't even send me an invitation. Then, she admitted that she never wanted me at the shower in the first place. She treated me like some animal the whole time I was there."

"Mom, you really don't see yourself, do you? You have no idea how controlling and self-centered you are and how you offend people. But you know what? I have to go."

"What time are you getting in?" she said.

"I'll let Dad know when I get to the airport."

"Okay...travel safe."

Charlotte waited for a response, but when she pulled her cell phone away from her ear and looked at it, the call had already disconnected. Matthew had ended the call without so much as saying good-bye. He was beyond angry with her, and she had to fix things when he got home; make him see that she wasn't the heartless, self-centered mother he believed her to be. If necessary, she would smile in Vanessa's face and treat her like royalty the whole time Matthew was in town, but she wouldn't forget any of this. Now she owed that witch more than ever before—she and her tattling daughter. They were both doing all they could, trying to turn her wonderful son against her, and they deserved whatever they got. At this point, they were literally asking for it.

Chapter 7

*E*veryone gathered around the shiny wood conference room table: Curtis; his executive assistant, Lana; his two assistant pastors, Minister Simmons and Minister Morgan; his two lead elders, Elder Jamison and Elder Dixon; his director of radio and TV broadcasting, Riley Davison; his new CFO, Kendra Smith; and Anise Miller, an elder and director of expansion projects, who was also Charlotte's first cousin. There were four other elders and two administrative assistants there as well. It was time for their weekly staff meeting, but today they'd be meeting longer than usual, as they had a lot to discuss. Their congregation of nearly four thousand members had grown so rapidly that a few months ago they'd had no choice but to add on a second service for Sunday mornings. Curtis hadn't necessarily wanted to move forward with this, because it now meant he had to deliver the message at both nine-thirty and eleven, but he also hadn't wanted to turn anyone away. In the beginning, it had been a pretty tough task, but now he was used to it, and he looked forward to giving his sermon twice every week. There were times when he asked either Minister Simmons or Minister Morgan to step in, but mostly that was only when he was out of town speaking.

"So," Curtis began. "I first want to thank all of you for your prayers and for asking others to pray along with you. My grandson is doing exceptionally well."

"Praise God," Lana said.

Elder Dixon nodded. "Amen."

"God is good," Elder Jamison, Minister Simmons, and Minister Morgan said almost in unison.

Everyone else smiled and talked about how happy they were to hear the news.

"Things certainly could have turned out a lot differently," Curtis said. "But the God we serve had a different plan, and I'm thankful for it."

There were more Amens and smiles all around.

"So I guess the first order of business is to discuss our early service on Sundays," he said, looking at his assistant. "Lana?"

"Things are going great," Lana told him, passing a stack of reports to Anise, who was sitting next to her, so everyone could take a copy. "Everything is running smoothly, and so far no one is complaining about the nine-thirty service ending right away at ten-forty. It's shorter than the eleven o'clock, but what we're learning is that folks who have other things to do are very happy about that."

"This is true," Elder Dixon said. "As a matter of fact, some have even started comin' to the early service all the time, mainly because they're like me: they wanna get in and outta here as fast as possible. I mean, you know how long-winded you can be sometimes, Pastor."

It was just like Elder Dixon to get everyone going, and of course, everyone laughed. He was like a father to all who he came in contact with, and no matter how many years passed, he still never gained any tact. Whatever came up, came out, and he never apologized for it. Thing was, though, people loved him for it.

"You should be ashamed of yourself," Lana said.

"Awww, puddin'," Elder Dixon said. "You know I'm just teasin' Pastor."

Lana rolled her eyes toward the ceiling and then down at the report, but everyone knew it wasn't because of Elder Dixon's words to Curtis. It was because Lana still pretended she and Elder Dixon weren't an item. They'd been dating for almost as long as Curtis had known them, but Lana wouldn't own up to it to anyone. Not even Curtis. He wasn't sure why she was so ashamed, except maybe because she was in her late sixties and Elder Dixon was in his seventies. Maybe she thought dating was inappropriate at their ages, but Elder Dixon had told Curtis a long time ago that he'd asked Lana to marry him more than once; however, she'd told him she wasn't ready.

Curtis flipped the document to the second and third pages. "I'm glad this is all working out, but if these attendance and official membership numbers are correct, we're at a crossroad. It's great news because we're still growing at a very rapid rate, but it's also bad because it means we'll be out of room again in no time."

Elder Jamison nodded. "I was thinking the same thing, and that's why I asked Anise to contact the architects again and to get together with Kendra. Need to start mapping out a new expansion project."

"I agree," Curtis said, and then looked at Anise. "So can we get everyone in here fairly soon for early discussions?"

"Hopefully, week after next," Anise said. "Both

the architects who spearheaded the last expansion and our finance guy from the bank."

"Great," Curtis said.

"I'm also going to run some initial numbers to get a better idea of what we have in the building fund," Kendra said. "That way, I can run them by you before our next staff meeting."

"Sounds good," Curtis told her. "We have more than enough land to expand, but I guess what we'll need to determine is how large we want the sanctuary to be this time. Figure out what else we want to add and also decide whether it's worth expanding or maybe just building from the ground up. That would mean buying a new lot, but we may have to consider it."

Minister Simmons leaned back in his chair. "I agree, Pastor. The congregation really is growing, and if we only have so much room to expand, we'll find ourselves having to build again in only a few years."

"Exactly," Curtis said. "That's why we really need to think this through." Then he addressed Riley. "So how are things on the broadcasting front? I know we've been getting lots of positive feedback from viewers, and folks have also been mailing in tithes and offerings."

"It's going wonderfully, and I'm excited about

our talks with TBN. The cost is still a little pricey, but with the way the ministry is growing, we'll be airing on TBN in no time. As it is, we're airing locally once on Saturday and twice on Sunday, and the viewership has increased every month. People are very happy with it, and both the TV and Internet broadcasts are bringing folks here for the live service."

"All good news," Curtis said, looking down at the agenda. Then he looked over at Minister Simmons. "And you wanted to discuss a teen Bible study, right?"

"Yes," he said, leaning forward. "We have a lot of young people here, so I think it would be great if we created a separate Bible study group just for them. Maybe even on a different night."

Minister Morgan looked at Minister Simmons but didn't say anything, mainly because Minister Morgan was a laid-back and very quiet man. But Curtis knew he was likely thinking the same as the others in the room: Minister Simmons had come up with yet another idea that would allow him to lead something. He was very ambitious, and Curtis believed he meant well, but sometimes he came across as pushy to the other staff members.

"We definitely have a lot more teens," Curtis

said. "So let's all take some time to think about it and then revisit this at our next meeting."

"Sounds good," Minister Simmons said, but Curtis could tell he was hoping to discuss his proposal now.

Over the next hour, they reviewed and discussed the rest of their agenda. First up were a couple of letters from two members who had concerns about the parking situation. They weren't too happy because they didn't like having to wait so long to get in and out of the lot. Curtis didn't blame them and looked forward to the expansion or new building that was coming. Then they'd discussed the upcoming church picnic, his and Charlotte's Annual Pastor and Wife Appreciation Day, and a cost-of-living increase for all staff members. Curtis never wanted his people to be unhappy or feel like they could do better working elsewhere, so he made sure this subject was addressed every six months. This was also in addition to annual performance review raises for the administrative staff.

As the meeting adjourned and everyone filed out of the room, one of Lana's assistants walked in with an envelope for Curtis. She was fairly new, and as she approached Curtis, he could tell she was a bit nervous.

"How's it going, Shelia?"

"Fine, Pastor. I'm sorry to bother you but because this is an overnight package, and the words *urgent, please open immediately* are written across the top of it, I wanted to get it to you right away. Lana said we should always do that."

"Of course. And it's no bother at all."

Shelia passed the envelope to him and turned to leave.

"So is everything working out with your new position?" Curtis asked her.

"It is, and I'm really happy to be working here. I appreciate the opportunity."

"Glad to hear it. Is everyone treating you well?"

"Yes, very much so."

"Good. And thanks for bringing me this."

"You're welcome."

Curtis hadn't been expecting any packages or envelopes from anyone, so he had no idea who this was from. But as he ripped it open, his phone rang. It was Matthew.

"Hey son, how are you?"

"I'm good, Dad."

"Are you at the airport?"

"Yep."

"No delays?"

"Nope. Everything's on schedule."

"So did your mom call you?"

"Yeah, and I sort of lost it, Dad. I didn't mean to, but Mom is so wrong for the way she's been acting."

"I wish she'd stop being so overbearing with Racquel and Vanessa, but you know your mother."

"Knowing who Mom is, is what I'm afraid of. She doesn't listen to anyone, and I'm just worried things'll get worse."

Curtis pulled a letter from the mysterious envelope. "Well, let's just pray things get better."

"I don't know, because just like I told you, she even tried to talk me out of coming home again."

"You didn't tell her I was the one who made your reservation, did you?"

"Nope. I just told her I'd call you when I got to the airport."

"She'd be through if she knew you called me while she was downstairs on the treadmill this morning. But I totally understand how you feel and why you want to see your son. School is certainly important, but you're also a father now."

"Thanks for having my back, Dad."

"Anytime."

"Okay, then, I'll see you soon. Love you."

"Love you, too, son."

Curtis set the phone down on the table and nearly broke out in a sweat. He'd been listening to everything Matthew had said, but he'd also been reading the anonymous letter at the same time. This just couldn't be. Not after so many years had passed, and he had moved completely on with his life. But nonetheless, someone was out to get him—again. They were threatening to share some pretty damaging truths, those he'd worked hard to forget and those his new congregation and not even Charlotte knew anything about. The killing part was, Curtis had no idea who was behind all this, so all he could do was trust, pray, and depend on God to fix it. He was so tired of dealing with one scandal after another, tired of hurting his children and tired of paying such hefty prices for all his past sins. There was something else that made him uneasy about this particular letter, too. Whomever had mailed it wasn't doing it for money. They were doing it merely as a way to bring him down from the "pedestal he'd been perched high in the sky on for way too long." Worse, the letter went on to say, "And just so you know, I don't want or need anything from you. I'm simply going to destroy your perfect, little privileged life…because I can…and more important, because you deserve it."

Curtis reread the last line again and finally dropped the letter onto the conference room table. He'd done a lot of dirt in his life, but if anyone ever found out about...

If anyone ever learned that he'd...

Life would never be the same, and he'd be ruined.

Chapter 8

Just watching Curtis stand in a church pulpit—a very large one at that, acting as holy as anyone I can think of and preaching God's Word, was enough to make me puke. To be honest, I'm not even sure why I continue to torture myself this way. Ever since the church began streaming live on the Internet several months ago, I haven't been able to pry myself away from it. I guess it must be sort of like when people watched train wrecks. They always knew how awful it was going to be, but they still couldn't help watching with full attention. But then there was this whole idea of my wanting and needing to monitor my prey. I say this because I was surely going to get Curtis. Not just for me or because of the terrible things he'd done to me but for all the other men and women Curtis has crossed or betrayed at one time or another. And make no mistake about it, there are plenty—and I do mean plenty—of folks who could tell the kinds of stories about Curtis that would embarrass a veteran hooker. Curtis had, in fact, done just that much and so much more for a great number of years. Sure, he claims and appears to be a completely changed man, but I still believe in consequences. You know, reaping whatever you've sown, and from what I can tell, Curtis hasn't reaped even 1 percent of all the terrible things he's done over the years. When I tell you the man was just plain awful, that's exactly what I mean, and all you'd need to do is ask a few people who attended the first two Chicago megachurches he led, shortly after moving there from Atlanta. He was very married while serving as pastor at Faith Missionary Baptist Church and then Truth Missionary Baptist Church, but that certainly never stopped him from whoring around the way he did. Then, don't get me started, when it comes to all the husbands and boyfriends that lost wives and girlfriends because of Curtis, even though Curtis ultimately dumped each and every one of those wives and girlfriends just as soon as he became bored with them. He moved on as soon as something better came along or until something new drove him wild. Some of those disgruntled husbands and boyfriends and dumped wives and girlfriends had been angry enough and bold enough to confront him, but some were cowardly and simply went on their way. As for me, I'm ashamed to say, I fell into the latter bunch—until now, that is. For

70

years, I'd wanted to call Curtis just to ask him why. For years, I'd wanted to travel to wherever he was and take a knife to him. But I never found the courage. I'd think about it, dream about it, and get excited about the possibilities, but I was always much too afraid to do anything. But like I said, that is . . . until now. Today, I have all the courage I need. I've taken months to plan how I was going to bring Curtis down, and it will only be a matter of time before I get total satisfaction. You see, I know a lot. I know more than Curtis would ever expect me to know, and I realized a long time ago that nothing could give me more pleasure than forcing Curtis to his knees. Sometimes when I think about it for more than a few minutes, I get so tickled I laugh out loud. I mean, I actually laugh so hard that I sometimes cry. I think I do this because now the pain I once felt has slowly turned to the worst kind of rage, and laughing about it keeps me calm. It settles my nerves, and it is the reason I am finally able to sleep at night a lot more peacefully. So many others before me have tried kicking Curtis where it hurts— they've tried blackmailing him in the worst possible way and tried exposing him nationally. But in the end, Curtis has always come out smelling better than top-selling cologne and has gotten away with whatever he wants. But not this time. No, after I finish with Curtis, the man will finally fall from grace the

way he should have many, many years ago. He'll fi-
nally receive his just desserts, and life will be better all
around. At least it will be for me, anyway, and for so
many others I now know personally. A truly awesome
day is coming. Finally.

Chapter 9

*A*s Curtis slowly drove his black SUV along the passenger pickup area, Charlotte peered through the window, searching for Matthew. He'd already called Curtis to let him know he had his luggage and would be standing outside, but so far they didn't see him.

"What door did he say he'd be coming out of?" Charlotte asked.

"He didn't. But I know he flew in on American."

They drove a little slower, and Charlotte hoped they saw Matthew soon, because these curbside police were no joke. No parking in the passenger pickup lane had been O'Hare's policy for a good while now, but sometimes even if you slowed and crept along for too long, one of the officers barked at you like a criminal. And it wasn't just the men who did it, because some of the women could bring a person to tears, too. This had all become commonplace ever since 9/11, though, so Charlotte understood the reason they had to be so strict about it.

"There he is!" Curtina yelled with sheer joy from the backseat. "There's Matt!"

Curtis rolled to a complete stop and got out.

"I wanna get out, too," Curtina said, already unbuckling her seat belt.

Charlotte turned all the way around. "No, sweetie. Your dad is only getting out so he can help Matt put his bags in the back. Then we'll be on our way."

"Okaaaayy," she sang.

Charlotte watched Matthew hug his father for a bit longer than usual, and she knew he was glad to be back in Illinois. He was thrilled about heading to the hospital to see his son. It would take about an hour for them to drive back home, and she could tell from the excitement on his face that he couldn't wait.

Matthew opened the door and got in, and Curtis walked around to the driver's side.

"Hey, Matt," Curtina said, smiling and reaching out to hug her brother.

"Hey, little girl."

"Can I see my baby nephew? Mommy and Daddy won't take me to see him."

"That's because you're too young to go up to the baby floor. But you'll get to see him when he comes home."

Charlotte listened to her children and wondered when Matthew was going to speak to her. It was true that Curtina had started right in with her questions, but she had a feeling Matthew didn't have much to say to her, anyway.

"Is the baby going to come live with us?" Curtina wanted to know.

"No, he's going to live with Racquel and her parents."

At this point, Charlotte wanted to scream at the top of her lungs. Just hearing the idea of little MJ being around Vanessa every day made her cringe.

Curtis finally eased his way into traffic, then looked in his rearview mirror. "Son, I'm not sure if you spoke to Racquel when you landed, but this afternoon the doctor said little MJ is making so much progress, he might go home by the end of the week."

"Yep, I called her while I was waiting for my luggage. She'll be going home tomorrow herself."

"That's great," Curtis said.

"It really is," Charlotte added. "Actually, I'm surprised they haven't released her before now since she didn't have a C-section."

"She didn't wanna leave until she knew MJ was okay," Matt said. "So her dad made arrangements for her to stay as long as she wanted."

Charlotte had known all along that Neil's position at the hospital carried a lot of weight, and it was for that reason that she was going to stay in close contact with him until the baby went home.

"I sure hope Vanessa won't try to stop me from seeing little MJ when they discharge him," Charlotte said out loud but hadn't meant to. If she could take it back she would, because there was no telling how Matthew was going to react. As it was, she was still sort of shocked that he'd just answered her question about Racquel.

But it wasn't Matthew who spoke up at all, it was Curtina.

"Mommy, why would Miss Vanessa do something like that?"

Charlotte hated having to answer her but responded quickly. "No reason, honey. Mommy was just saying that just in case."

"Just in case what?"

Matthew playfully punched his sister in her shoulder, and Charlotte knew it was because he didn't want to hear any more about Vanessa.

"Stop it, Matt," Curtina said, cracking up and hitting him back.

Matthew punched her again. "So did you really miss me, little girl, or were you just faking?"

"I really, really missed you for real, Matt, and I wish you never had to go back to that Harvard place. I wish you could stay home."

"I wish I could, too, especially now that little MJ is here."

"It'll be fine," Charlotte couldn't help saying. "The semester will be over before you know it."

"Maybe, but I'm seriously thinking about taking it off."

Charlotte swallowed her words. She wanted so badly to talk some sense into him, though, and to remind him of how important getting a college education truly was. But she knew Matthew would never receive her advice in a positive manner. He'd already proven his disregard of her opinion when she'd spoken to him this morning. She'd encouraged him to stay at school so he wouldn't miss any of his classes this week, but here he was. He'd come home, and now he was contemplating taking a break from the second half of his freshman year? She totally understood that he was worried about his son and was dying to see him, but Charlotte also wanted him to think and be logical. She wanted him to consider the consequences of his leaving school to be a hands-on dad. Not to mention, she knew it wouldn't be long before Racquel tried to make things permanent between them. She hadn't heard Matthew mention anything about marriage, but Charlotte knew it was only a matter of time before Racquel started pressuring him. Actually, the more Charlotte thought things through, the more she wished Matthew had never gotten hooked up with Racquel. All of his high school years, Charlotte had worried day and night about the possibility of some desperate girl getting too close and then trapping him with a baby. And while Curtis didn't see Racquel as being that kind of girl and neither did Matthew, for Charlotte the jury was still out. For her, she still didn't trust Racquel, and she dealt with her accordingly.

Charlotte rode along in silence, listening to Matt, Curtina, and Curtis conversing about one thing after another. She did this because while they were chatting, she was thinking—and plotting her next move. In a perfect world, Vanessa would lose that nasty, uppity, condescending attitude of hers, stay out of Charlotte's way, and accept that Charlotte should have just as much say-so about MJ as she did. She would also welcome Charlotte to spend time with her grandson as often as she wanted and even allow her to become MJ's primary caregiver when Racquel left for college; especially since Vanessa ran a consulting business from home and didn't have the kind of free time Charlotte had to raise a baby. But again, this kind of thing could only happen in a perfect world and not in Charlotte and Vanessa's, so Charlotte didn't have a choice but to plot, plan, and do whatever she had to in order to protect her rights as a grandmother. She would hope for the best, but if that hussy, Vanessa, didn't back down soon, Charlotte would be ready. Worse, Vanessa would be very sorry she'd ever crossed her.

Chapter 10

Charlotte, Curtis, Matthew, and Curtina walked toward the elevator, and as soon as Matthew pressed the button, Curtina started in again.

"Why can't I see little MJ, Matt?"

"I already told you. You're not old enough. You have to be twelve or be a sibling."

"What's that?" she asked, clearly not happy.

"It means a brother or a sister."

Curtis shook his head. "You guys go ahead, and I'll stay down here in the main waiting area with Curtina."

"You ready?" Charlotte asked Matthew.

"Actually, Mom, I'd really like to have some time alone with Racquel. Then see the baby with just her."

Charlotte's feelings were hurt, because if she knew Vanessa, she was still here visiting with Racquel and likely seeing the baby as much as she wanted. "I understand that, Matt, but can I at least just go say hi to her and peek in on the baby? Then I'll leave."

"Fine, Mom."

When Charlotte and Matthew stepped off the elevator, they strolled down the hallway and saw Neil. He was walking out of Racquel's room.

He smiled, shook Matthew's hand, and hugged him. "I'm glad you made it, son, and I'm very proud of you."

"Thanks for everything, Dr. Anderson."

"Well, I won't hold you up because that daughter of mine can't wait to see you. And by the way, 'Neil' or 'Dad' will do just fine."

Matthew chuckled. "I'll remember that."

"Take care," he said. "You, too, Charlotte."

As Matthew and Charlotte walked inside Racquel's room, Racquel smiled wider than Charlotte had seen her smile since the baby was born. She was sitting in the recliner and was about to get up, but Matthew couldn't wait for that. He leaned down, squeezed her tightly, and kissed her on her forehead. Then he kissed her on the lips. "It's so good to see you, baby, and thank you."

"It's great to see you, too, but why are you thanking me?" she asked.

"For going through all of this without me. For not complaining."

"Please. We agreed that it was important for you to go to school, and you know I support that. Plus, you're here now."

Matthew hugged her again. "I love you so much."

"I love you, too, sweetie."

A chill ripped through Charlotte's heart. She wasn't sure why, but she couldn't control the way she felt. She'd heard Matthew and Racquel share their feelings for each other out loud before, but this time, it seemed different. It sounded more intense and...well...like they really meant it. Hopefully, this I-love-you phase was merely a result of high emotions relating to the baby, and it would quickly pass.

Charlotte glanced around the room at all the greeting cards and floral arrangements. Then, to her great disappointment, Vanessa walked in. Charlotte had been relieved that she wasn't there.

"Oh my goodness, Matt!" she said with open arms. "I was so glad to hear you were coming home."

"Hey, Mom. It's good to be here."

Mom???? Charlotte must have been hearing things, and if for some reason she wasn't, why on earth was Matthew calling her that? *She* was his mother, not that witch, Vanessa!

"Just wait until you see that little one of yours!" Vanessa said, beaming. "Talk about the most handsome baby ever."

Racquel shook her head and laughed at her mother. "She acts as though there are no other babies in the country. But, Matt...he really is perfect. He's everything you and I could have hoped for."

"He certainly is," Vanessa said. "And what are you waiting for? Racquel and I were planning to go down to the nursery, but now the two of you can go together."

Matthew helped Racquel up. "Do you want your wheelchair?"

"No, I'm fine. I need to walk as much as I can."

"Okay," Matthew said to Charlotte and Vanessa. "We'll be back."

"Have a good time," Vanessa said, but as soon as they left the room, she walked past Charlotte and started gathering all of Racquel's cards. Charlotte guessed she was helping Racquel pack up to go home tomorrow.

As usual, the atmosphere was awkward and icy and Charlotte felt out of place, so she sat down. Vanessa kept her back to her and continued pulling down cards. Charlotte picked up the television selector, flipped through a few channels, but she couldn't take all this silence. It was maddening, to say the least, and given the way Matthew had looked at Racquel and the warm connection between him and Vanessa, she wondered if maybe she should swallow her pride and try reaching out to Vanessa. It was the last thing she wanted to do, but she also couldn't chance losing her son to this woman.

"Vanessa, can I talk to you?"

Vanessa never turned around but said, "About what?"

"Our grandson, and the fact that you and I are going to have to see each other pretty regularly... whether we like it or not."

Vanessa never even grunted.

"Maybe you didn't hear me."

"Of course I did."

This woman was already trying Charlotte's patience. "Well, since you didn't respond, I figured maybe you hadn't."

Now Vanessa faced her. "Look, Charlotte. To be honest, I really don't have anything to say. We do share a grandchild, but I think we both know that we'll never be friends."

"Nonetheless, we need to treat each other with

respect and stay peaceful for little MJ."

"As long as you stay in your lane and I stay in mine, we'll be fine. Little MJ is going to be living with us, and your time with him will be left up to Matthew and Racquel."

"And what does that mean?"

"That whenever you want to see little MJ, you'll need to clear it with them. That way once my daughter and grandson leave the hospital, I won't ever have to deal with you. As a matter of fact, I think it'll be best if you never come to our home again."

Charlotte's mouth dropped open. "Wow. So you hate me that much?"

"I don't hate anybody, but it's a little late for first impressions. You've already shown me who you are, and I'm done."

"Who exactly am I, Vanessa?"

"You're a controlling, narcissistic, underhanded snake."

Charlotte stood up. "Come again?"

"My words were very clear. I figured out who you were a long time ago. You're afraid of losing your son to my daughter, you'll sleep with any man who will have you, and you'll betray anyone, including your own family, if it means getting what you want."

Charlotte laughed out loud. "Honey, you just *think* you know me. And the real reason you don't like me is because of who I am and the kind of life I'm able to live."

Vanessa turned her back to Charlotte again. "Go ahead and believe that if it makes you feel better."

"You're pathetic, Vanessa, and that's why Neil—"

Vanessa whipped her head back around. "That's why my husband what?"

Charlotte smirked at her.

"Get out of here, Charlotte! Now!"

There was a knock at the door. A nurse slowly opened it and stuck her head inside. "Excuse me for interrupting, but is everything okay?"

"We're fine, but thanks for checking," Vanessa said.

Charlotte could tell the sixty-something woman wasn't convinced, but she closed the door and went on her way.

Now Vanessa spoke through gritted teeth. "I know you heard me. Get out of here, Charlotte!"

Charlotte eyed one of the large flower vases and had a mind to thrash Vanessa across her head with it. This woman needed to be put in her place, and Charlotte was the best person to do it. But she took a deep breath and tried calming down. There were better ways to handle women like Vanessa, so Charlotte threw her handbag across her shoulder, gazed at Vanessa, and quietly strutted out of the room.

This whole scenario with Vanessa was worse than Charlotte had thought, and now she was done kissing that witch's behind. She'd tried to call a truce, as much of one as she'd thought the two of them could muster, but now Charlotte was finished. From this point on, she would treat Vanessa like the ruthless enemy she was and focus primarily on her grandson. Vanessa seemed to believe she had the upper hand, given the fact that little MJ would be living with her, but Charlotte had news for her: not everything turned out the way people wanted them to, and if folks weren't careful certain things were sometimes snatched away from them without warning. Sometimes people underestimated their adversaries, and this was what Vanessa was doing with Charlotte. She just didn't know it.

Chapter 11

It was a new day, but Charlotte still didn't feel any better about things. She tried to focus on something other than Vanessa and Racquel and even the baby, but she couldn't. Now, she'd dropped by the church to see Curtis. He'd wanted to get an early start working on this coming Sunday's sermon, so he'd left home earlier than usual.

"You look sad," Curtis said, closing the door to his study and caressing the side of her face.

"Maybe because I am."

Curtis sat down on the leather sofa, and Charlotte sat next to him.

"Baby, I know you're upset about your argument with Vanessa yesterday, but you have to let it go. Maybe you should just step back altogether."

"Why should I have to step away from anything?"

"Because things are getting worse instead of better. Sometimes it's best to let things cool down. Then figure out another way to tackle the problem. Matt's going to be here through the weekend and will be spending all his time with Racquel and the baby, anyway."

"What does that have to do with me?" she asked.

"Everything," Curtis said, resting his arm across the back of the sofa. "If you let them have their time together, then you can focus on something else for a few days. I'm really worried about you, baby."

Charlotte was livid. "If I allow too many days to pass without seeing little MJ, not only will he not know me when he sees me again, but Vanessa will think this is the way things are going to be. Matt will go back to school on Sunday, and she'll think they can keep the baby away from us until he's home again."

"Maybe you, Vanessa, Neil, and I need to sit down and have a talk. Just the four of us."

"Well, I'm not sure what good that'll do, since Vanessa has already made her feelings very clear: she doesn't want me at her house under any circumstances."

"Something's gotta give. This whole mess is

uncalled for, and it's unfair to Matt and Racquel."

"Well, I'm going on record right now," she said, crossing her legs. "I won't be treated this way and not do anything about it."

"That kind of talk isn't going to help anything. What you need to do is pray. Let go and let God."

Hmmph. Charlotte wished it were that easy, and the reason she'd never been good about letting go and letting God the way Curtis did was because sometimes God took a little too long to fix things. Sometimes she saw no other choice except to handle situations herself.

Curtis's office phone rang, so he got up to answer it. "Yes."

Charlotte could tell it was Lana, and she hoped he didn't have to end their visit because she really needed him right now.

"Oh, that's right," he said. My time got away from me. I'll leave now."

Curtis laid the phone on its base. "Baby, I'm really sorry, but we're gonna have to cut this short. I have a lunch meeting with Elder Jamison and Elder Dixon, and then I have to rush back here to do a counseling session. I didn't realize how late it was."

Charlotte stood up, already heading toward the door. "I guess I'll see you at home, then."

"Baby, wait," he said, coming after her. "What's wrong?"

"Everything. And now you've gotta run off to some meeting."

"But you know I can't help that. Elder Jamison and Elder Dixon do a lot for me and for the church, and a month ago I asked Lana to schedule lunch with them. I wanted to take them out. I told you about it yesterday."

"Like I said, I'll see you at home."

"No kiss good-bye or anything?"

Charlotte wasn't in the mood, but she turned and kissed Curtis anyway.

"I'll call you this afternoon," he said, grabbing his blazer and walking out with her.

When they made it to the parking lot, Charlotte got in her car, pulled out her cell phone, and called Matthew. She'd debated whether or not she should, but since Matthew had spent the night in Racquel's room and she was going home today, Charlotte wanted to see how the baby was doing.

"Hey, Mom."

"Hey, son, how are you?"

"Good."

"And little MJ?"

"Great. He's going home tomorrow or Friday."

"That's wonderful, Matt. I'm so thankful and glad to hear that. Can I come see him?"

"That's fine, but I wanna make sure Racquel's mom isn't here when you do. So, I'll call you back to let you know what time."

Charlotte was outraged all over again, but all she said was, "Okay, I'll just wait to hear from you." When she hung up, she immediately dialed Curtis.

"Hey, baby. Everything okay?"

"Do you wanna know what your son just said to me?"

"What?"

"That he'll have to call me back to let me know when it's okay for me to come to the hospital. He wants to make sure Vanessa isn't there."

"Well, as much as I know you don't wanna hear it, this is probably a good thing."

Charlotte hit the steering wheel with her fist. "A good thing for who?"

"Everyone involved. You know what happened when you went there yesterday, so why even take a chance on running into Vanessa?"

"You know what this is really about, don't you?" she said.

"What?"

"Vanessa and how she probably told Matt all kinds of lies about what happened when he and Racquel went down to the nursery. She's trying to turn my own son against me, and if you don't watch out, she'll turn him against you, too."

"Baby, you're not serious?"

"Why wouldn't I be? This woman is evil, Curtis."

"You know what?" he said. "I'm staying out of this, because I already asked you to take a step back."

"I'm not about to go four whole days without seeing my grandson. Today is only Wednesday, Matt isn't leaving until Sunday, and then who knows when I'll get to see MJ after that?"

"I don't know what else to tell you."

"Say you have my back and that you're gonna demand that I be allowed to see our grandson whenever I want."

"I'm not doing that, Charlotte. We shouldn't have to demand anything; we should all be getting along like adults. And I'll tell you something else: if you don't stop this, you're going to push Matt farther and farther away from you, and I know you don't want that."

"But what about me, Curtis? What about my rights as a grandmother? And why isn't Matt standing up for me and setting Vanessa straight?" Tears streamed down Charlotte's face. She could barely breathe.

"Look, baby. For months now, I haven't wanted to say anything because I knew you wouldn't receive it well, but you caused all of this."

"What do you mean?"

"From the time you found out Racquel was pregnant, you started calling her every day. Making sure she was reading the right books, and asking her for the dates and times of all her doctor appointments. Then, you started going to those appointments uninvited."

"And what was wrong with that?"

"A lot," he said. "Baby, Racquel has a mother who loves her, and if Racquel wanted you hanging around all the time or going to all her doctor visits, she would have asked you."

"But I was only trying to let her know that I'm here for her."

"Even when you ordered baby furniture and never asked her what kind she wanted? And let's not forget the way you started driving over to their home unannounced."

"I only did that when Matt left for school. I wanted to make sure she was okay, and that she didn't need anything."

"Why would she? Her father is a neurosurgeon. But you wanna know the worst part of all?"

"I'm sure you can't wait to tell me," she said.

"The day you started talking down to Vanessa."

"When have I ever spoken to that woman like that?"

"You did it all the time. I remember once when they invited all of us over for dinner, and Vanessa was saying how she and Neil were going to start a college fund for the baby. But then you quickly rattled off something like, 'Actually, Curtis and I will be able to pay for everything. You guys won't have to worry about a thing. And if you want, the baby can even live with us when Racquel leaves for college because we're having a huge nursery designed. It'll be finished in a month or so.'"

Charlotte was flabbergasted. Curtis was officially blaming her for everything, and it would be hard to forgive him for this.

"I'm sorry I had to say these things to you, but it was time."

"I'll talk to you later," she said.

"Baby, I know you're angry, but I hope you think about what I've said. Bragging and boasting can turn people off."

"I'll see you later," she said and hung up.

How dare Curtis make her out to be the villain? He was her husband, for God's sake, yet he had the nerve to defend Vanessa? It was bad enough that Matthew was doing the same thing, but this was a bit much.

Charlotte took a deep breath, started up her Mercedes, and pulled out her sunglasses. It was clear that just about everyone had made up their minds about her and sided against her, but it was like she'd been saying all along: she would do what she had to when it came to being with her grandson. She didn't want to resort to drastic measures, but now even Curtis was forcing her hand. Once Matthew went back to school, Charlotte would see how things played out, but if Vanessa and Racquel stopped her from seeing little MJ, she would get the help she needed. She would turn to Neil in a heartbeat.

Chapter 12

Curtis drove out of the restaurant parking lot. As always, he'd had a great time socializing with his two favorite elders, but he also couldn't help thinking about Charlotte and the conversation they'd had. At first, he'd thought telling her the truth was a good idea, but now he sort of regretted his decision. Not because he didn't think she needed to know that her problems with Vanessa were her fault, but because one never knew what Charlotte might do when things didn't go her way. She loved Curtis, he loved her, and for the first time in years, their marriage was healthy and stable. But she was so caught up with this whole MJ situation that there was no guessing how she might respond. He could tell by her voice how hurt she was to hear all that he was saying, but he also knew that Charlotte's pain almost always turned to rage. Then, it wasn't long before she set out on a mis-

97

sion of revenge. Normally, he never saw it coming and hoped for the best, but this time he had a bad feeling about it. She acted as though she hated Vanessa, and what worried him most was that she was obsessing over little MJ like he was hers—as if she'd carried him since conception and had now given birth to him. It was no secret that many times, Charlotte had talked about her desire to have another baby, but what Curtis had noticed over the last few months was that she didn't mention it very much at all anymore; not since Racquel had gotten pregnant.

Curtis drove through the intersection, but looked down at his phone when it rang. Whoever was calling had blocked their number, but he answered it anyway.

"This is Curtis."

There was no response.

"Hello?"

Still nothing.

"Hello?"

Curtis held the phone to his ear a few more seconds until the call ended. He couldn't help thinking about the anonymous letter he'd received yesterday, and he wondered if the same person was calling now. But how would they have gotten his phone number? It was one thing for them to have the church's number, but there were only a few select people who knew the number to his cell. Regardless, he wished this vengeful person would leave him alone and go back to whatever they were doing before contacting him. He was the first to admit that his past wasn't pretty and that he'd committed a list of wrongdoings, but when would he ever stop paying the consequences? When would he finally be able to live his life without worrying about the next blackmailer, or, in this case, worrying about a person who didn't want money or anything else from him, but just simply wanted to ruin him—ruin his life, his family's lives, and his ministry.

As a pastor, he knew as much as anyone that every human being reaped what he or she sowed, but he was starting to feel as if he would never catch up. Maybe he'd done so much wrong that he would never live in peace. Maybe this was his fate, and it was time he accepted it.

Curtis slowed his vehicle when he saw the light turning red, and his phone rang again. He almost hated to look at it, but he was relieved when he saw that it was Alicia.

"Hey, sweetheart."

"Hey, Daddy. What's up?"

"Heading back to the church. Just came from

having lunch with Elder Jamison and Elder Dixon."

"Wow, I can only imagine how fun that was. Elder Dixon cracks me up."

Curtis chuckled. "You can't imagine half the stuff he said. We had a great time, though. Don't know what I would do without them."

"They've been very loyal to you, and it must feel good having two longtime staff members you can trust."

"It does. My assistant pastors are great, too. Minister Simmons and Minister Morgan carry a lot of weight when I have to travel, and no one ever complains about them. They both know the Word extremely well, and they deliver their messages in a very straightforward format."

"I like them both, too, and you know what else would be great?"

"What's that?"

"If Phillip were there again."

"Well, you know how much I love my son-in-law, and the offer has always been on the table for him. One of the saddest days for me was when he resigned."

"I've always felt bad about that, Daddy."

"The past is the past, though, and all is well."

"I know, but if I hadn't gone out and had an affair, we would still be married and he'd still be one of your pastors."

"Maybe, but we all make mistakes, baby girl."

"I still love him so much, though, Daddy. I love him more now than when I first married him. Isn't that crazy?"

"No, not at all. That happens all the time."

"To be honest, I'd really thought we'd be married again by now. It's been three years since I divorced that awful JT."

"Yeah, but it's like I've been telling you for a while. You really hurt Phillip, and he's afraid. There's no doubt that he still loves you, but some people have a hard time getting past certain situations."

"I know, but I just wish he knew that I would never, ever hurt him again. Even if I wanted to I wouldn't, because I know how good he is for me."

"Just hang in there. I know Phillip is taking a while to come around, but it'll happen."

"I hope. I don't know why it's taking him so long, though, when we spend just about all our time together."

"Spending time and living in separate households is a lot different than being married. But if you really love him and want to be with him again, there's nothing wrong with waiting. You owe him that."

"You're right, Daddy. And hey, before I forget—I just talked to Matt, and boy, is he happy. I've never heard him so excited before."

"Yeah, he's definitely a proud father. We all wish he and Racquel could have waited until they'd graduated college and gotten married, but we love little MJ already."

"Matt told me the baby will be home by this weekend, so Phillip and I are driving over to see him. Oh, and he sent a photo to my phone. What a gorgeous little thing he is."

"Wait until you see him in person."

"I can imagine. Matt also told me about Charlotte. He said things between her and Vanessa have been horrible."

"That's an understatement."

"Why is she acting this way?"

"She's obsessed. The baby is all she talks about, and she thinks Vanessa is trying to keep her away from him."

"That's crazy."

"She'll never admit it, but Charlotte hasn't liked Vanessa since the beginning. And once she decides something, that's just the way it is. No one can change her mind about anything."

"That's really too bad, and I can tell Matt feels like he and Racquel are in the middle of all this."

"It's unfortunate, but I'm not sure what else to do," he said. "I just talked to her earlier about it, but she was pretty upset when she hung up."

"Well, you know Charlotte and I still aren't on the best of terms, so I'm not saying anything to her."

"Hopefully, this'll pass."

"I hope so, too. Especially for Matt's sake."

"Well, I'm almost at the church, so I'd better go. But it's good hearing from you, baby girl," he said.

"I'll see you this weekend."

"Sounds good. Love you."

"Love you, Daddy."

Chapter 13

*C*urtis jotted down a few notes relating to the sermon he was writing but glanced over at his phone when it rang. It was another blocked phone call. There was no doubt that it was the same person who'd called earlier, and these calls were beginning to unnerve him. Still he answered.

"Hello?"

No response.

"Hello...who is this?"

There were still no words from the other party.

"I really wish you'd stop calling me."

Finally, Curtis heard a click, and he laid his phone down.

This was only the second call, but it worried him. So much so that he unlocked the right drawer of his desk and pulled out that threatening letter he'd received. He read it again, still not wanting to believe anyone would dredge up such old news.

Yes, he'd been wrong—dead wrong—about the way he'd handled a couple of situations in the past, but he had repented and was now a good man. He was a faithful man of God, he was faithful to his wife, and he was dedicated to his children and the members of his church. So why wasn't that enough for everyone? God had certainly forgiven him, so why couldn't folks worry about themselves and just leave him and his family alone? Curtis blew a sigh of frustration, folded the letter back up, and slipped it inside the envelope. If only he'd thought twice about doing what he'd done so many years ago, he wouldn't have to worry about anyone finding out about it now. But it was too late for regrets, because the deed had been done and someone was planning to use it against him. Well, actually, there were multiple deeds, but the one outlined in that letter would become the news of the century if this mystery person followed through on his or her promise to go public. He would likely lose his ministry over this one, and there would be nothing he could do about it.

Curtis placed the envelope back in the drawer and locked it. He wasn't sure what to think or how he was going to sleep at night, but for now, he would pray and try his best to keep his faith strong. He would ask God to soften this person's heart before they told things that Curtis wanted no one to know about. Obviously, those who'd been involved knew the full story, but Curtis hadn't heard from them.

Curtis leaned back in his chair and closed his eyes, but then his phone rang. This time it was his office line, and he knew it was Lana.

"Yes."

"Pastor, your two o'clock appointment is here."

"Give me five minutes."

"Of course."

Curtis tidied up his desk a bit, said a prayer, asking God to clear his mind of his own problems so he could focus on the couple he was about to meet with. When he finished, Lana knocked on his door.

"Come in."

"Hello, Pastor," the caramel-skinned, muscular man said. "I'm Dillon Tate, and this is my fiancée, Melissa Warren." Melissa was nearly the same height as Dillon, who was about six feet tall, and she'd been blessed with the looks of a supermodel. They each looked to be no more than in their mid- to late twenties, though.

Curtis shook their hands. "It's very nice to see you both. I remember meeting you a few months ago after service, and I'm glad you decided to come in for counseling."

"Thank you for seeing us," Melissa said.

Curtis walked around to the other side of his desk. "Please have a seat."

They both sat down, and Melissa set her handbag at her side in the chair. She was just that small. Not too small, but it was obvious that she watched what she ate and worked out pretty regularly.

"So," Curtis said, leaning back and clasping his hands together. "Lana tells me that you're wedding is scheduled for August?"

"Yes," Dillon said.

"That's seven months from now, so I'm glad you came in early."

Melissa crossed her legs. "We really wanted to get started with our sessions before we continue on with the rest of the planning."

"Understandable. Well, what I normally like to do is give you an opportunity to lay out any concerns or crucial questions you might have."

Melissa looked at Dillon. "Are you sure you're okay with this?"

"Go ahead," he said.

"This is kind of embarrassing to bring up, Pastor," she said, "but it's really bothering me, and

I'm afraid of what it will do to our marriage if it doesn't stop."

"Okay," Curtis said.

Melissa paused and then said, "Dillon is addicted to porn. He watches it all the time."

Curtis knew that tons of people struggled with this kind of addiction, but this was the first time anyone had brought it up during premarital counseling. "So, Dillon, when did this start?"

"About a year and a half ago."

"Had you and Melissa already begun dating?"

"I met her shortly afterward."

"Is there a reason you started?"

"Not really...well, actually it was because I'd gone through a very bad breakup. Back then, I was looking for anything to take my mind off that."

"I see," Curtis said, then he looked at Melissa. "And when did you find out he was watching this kind of thing?"

"A few months ago. I was visiting him one evening and when he ran down to the store, I signed on to his computer. All I was planning to do was browse a couple of bridal sites, but I ended up checking his browser history. I saw all the sites he'd marked as favorites. That's when I realized every one of them was porn."

"But it's not like any of that takes away from the love I have for Melissa," Dillon said. "I don't even think about those women once I turn off my computer. I watch those videos strictly for entertainment."

"Nonetheless," Melissa said, "I don't like it, and to me it feels like you're cheating."

"But baby, you know I'm not. I don't even know those women."

"Still. I don't like it, and I really doubt that watching porn is the Christian thing to be doing."

Dillon didn't say anything else, and neither did Melissa.

"Do you feel as though you can't stop?" Curtis asked.

Dillon sighed loudly. "I tried."

"And what happened?"

"I thought about it all the time...not the women...but the sexual activity. It even kept me up at night, and then I started thinking about it all day at work."

"And how long did you abstain?"

"One week."

"Did you pray about it? Because sometimes the only way to rid yourself of a bad habit is to literally get down on your knees and ask God to remove it."

Dillon shook his head. "No."

Melissa looked at Curtis. "He didn't pray because he didn't really wanna stop."

"Is that true, Dillon?" Curtis asked.

Dillon hunched his shoulders.

"I know talking about this is uncomfortable, but it really is a good thing. Getting this out in the open and admitting that you have a problem is the first step."

"I believe that," he said. "But Pastor, I'll be honest. I love porn. And maybe if Melissa wasn't putting me off, I could let it go."

She cast her eyes at him. "But you knew how I felt about sex before marriage when we first started dating. And you said you were fine with it."

"Well, I'm not," he said matter-of-factly. "I thought I was, but baby, I'm a twenty-seven-year-old man who's been having sex most of my life, so this abstinence thing is a bit much."

Melissa narrowed her eyes. "Wow. Well, that's news to me."

"I'm sorry, but you need to know how I feel."

"And you couldn't tell me that before today? You had to wait until we were sitting in front of Pastor Black?"

Dillon looked away from her.

Curtis knew it was time he intervened. "This

is the reason premarital counseling is so important. Sometimes, couples aren't able to express themselves openly until they have a third party present."

"I understand that, but I'm a little shocked that he hasn't told me this before now."

"I knew you wouldn't be happy about it," he said, "so that's why I never said anything. I really do love you, though, Melissa, but I'm also not without problems. I'm not perfect."

"I don't expect you to be. But I do expect you to be honest."

Curtis leaned forward. "Are you willing to get help for this, Dillon?"

"Yes, but how?"

"I really want you to pray about this. First thing in the morning and then again before bedtime. Even in the middle of the day, if the desire hits you. I also want you to read Matthew 5:27–28 every day, which says, 'Ye have heard that it was said by them of old time, thou shalt not commit adultery. But I say unto you, that whosoever looked on a woman to lust after her hath committed adultery with her already in his heart.'"

"Can you write that down?" Dillon asked.

"Yes," Curtis said, picking up his pen. "I'll give you a few other scriptures to meditate on as well.

The other thing you need to know is that you're not alone. As men, some of us struggle with our sexual nature. Even I have in the past, but I also know right from wrong and that sexual sin begins in the mind."

"We really appreciate this, Pastor," Melissa said.

"I'm glad to help in any way I can."

"Yes, thank you, Pastor," Dillon said.

"I'd also like you to start going to Sex Addicts Anonymous meetings. Prayer and scripture are a huge part of the process, but a 12-step program can also make a difference."

Dillon's nervous stare indicated that he wasn't too happy about Curtis's latest suggestion.

"It might not be easy having to share your personal feelings with a group of strangers, but these kinds of programs can do wonders for a person. Most people want to believe that sex, porn, shopping, and food addiction aren't the same as alcoholism and excessive drug use, but they are all very similar in the way they affect addicts and their loved ones."

"I'll give it a try," Dillon said.

Melissa grabbed his hand. "Thank you for being so willing to get help."

He smiled at her. "I know this is hurting you,

and as much as I love it, I know it's wrong. I wanna stop."

"And you can," Curtis said. "It'll take a lot of prayer and hard work, but you can do it."

"I'm so glad we came to meet with you, Pastor," Melissa said.

Curtis smiled. "I am, too. These are the kinds of things I'm here for," he said. But then for some reason, he thought about those two phone calls and that scathing letter he'd received, and his smile vanished. Maybe because it wouldn't be long before he would need help himself—a lot more help than Dillon needed—and that terrified him.

Chapter 14

Matthew had finally *authorized* Charlotte's visit, and she was now sitting in the parking lot of the hospital. She still had the car and heat running, though, since it was a little on the nippy side today, but she wanted to call her mother before going inside.

"Hi sweetie," Noreen said.

"Hey, Mom. How are you?"

"I think I'm coming down with some sort of stomach flu, but other than that I'm fine. Your dad's doing well, too. But how are you doing and how's that new grandbaby?"

"If only you knew."

"Why, what's wrong?"

Charlotte leaned her head against the backrest. "I've been through hell and back ever since MJ was born."

"Why haven't you said anything? We've talked every day."

"I know, but I didn't want to bother you with this craziness. Especially since it shouldn't be happening."

"What?"

"That Vanessa woman. She's doing everything she can to keep me from seeing MJ, and now she's trying to turn Matt against me."

"You've got to be kidding."

"No, and the only reason I just got to the hospital now is because I had to wait for Matt to tell me when to come."

"Why couldn't you go whenever you wanted?"

"He asked me to wait until Vanessa had already visited."

"Excuse me?"

"It's a total mess, Mom."

"I had no idea we needed to make an appointment to see our own grandson, and the only reason Joe and I haven't been down there yet is because you'd told us they weren't allowing a lot of visitors in to see MJ. But I didn't think that included you."

"Well, it does, and Vanessa has been nasty to me the whole time."

"I know one thing: when little MJ comes home, you and I are gonna set Miss Thing straight. We'll handle this once and for all."

"I really appreciate that, Mom, because Curtis and Matthew are blaming me for everything. They're acting like I'm the one who's wrong. They think I'm the one who should work harder at trying to get along with that woman."

"You don't have to work hard to get along with anybody! You're MJ's grandmother, I'm his great-grandmother, and Vanessa is going to recognize that one way or another. You shouldn't have to tiptoe around her or anyone else when it comes to having a relationship with your own grandchild. That's just crazy, and I'm behind you a hundred percent."

"I love you, Mom, and I can't wait for you and Daddy to drive over here. This is so painful."

"Of course it is, and you should have told me about it from the beginning."

"I know, but I was hoping things would get better. Especially once Matt got here, but if anything, they're worse."

"What is Racquel saying about all this?"

"Not a lot, but you know how it is with most mothers and daughters. They're going to stick together no matter what."

"Well, you just hang in there. This'll all work out."

"I hope so. I'm getting ready to go inside, though, so I'll talk to you later."

"I love you."

"I love you, too, Mom."

Charlotte left the parking lot, strolled through the main lobby, and pressed the elevator button. It didn't take long before the door opened, and to her surprise, Neil was standing inside of it.

"Hey," he said.

"Hey yourself. You getting off?"

"Not now," he said, practically undressing her with his eyes.

Charlotte stepped on, and if she'd said she wasn't flattered, she'd have been lying. She'd had a rough day thus far, and she needed this kind of attention.

"So, I guess you heard," he said, as they waited for the door to close. "Little MJ has made a lot of progress. He's definitely going home tomorrow."

"Yes, Matt told us when we picked him up from the airport that it would be tomorrow or Friday."

"That's what Dr. Koster had thought, but this morning he was doing so well they removed him from his incubator. They ran all sorts of tests and said he was good to go. They still wanted one more day to monitor him, though, so Racquel has decided to stay on until tomorrow, too."

Charlotte's eyes watered. "Such great news. I'm so glad he's healthy now."

"Are you crying?"

"No."

"Are you okay?"

"I'm fine. Really," she said, and the elevator opened again.

"Let's go down here," he said, heading toward the small room she and he had privately spoken in on Sunday. When they walked inside, he closed the door. "Tell me what's wrong."

Charlotte burst into tears just like she had the other day when she'd been talking to him, but this time she wasn't faking. This time, she was hurt to the core.

"I feel so left out, Neil. Things aren't going well between Vanessa and me, so Matt is starting to distance himself. I spoke to him twice today, and not once did he tell me little MJ was going home tomorrow or that he'd been removed from the incubator. All he said was that he would call to let me know when I could visit."

"Why?"

"He didn't want Vanessa and me here at the same time."

"I hate things have turned out like this, but I'm sure they'll get better."

Tears flowed down Charlotte's face. "I'm so hurt."

Neil pulled her into his arms. "It'll be fine. I promise."

Charlotte held on to him, sniffling, and she felt safe. She could tell he meant what he said, and that he was on her side more than he was his wife's. He genuinely wanted her to have a relationship with their grandson.

Neil held on to her but lifted her chin with his hand. "It really will be okay."

Charlotte gazed into his eyes and then quickly pulled away from him. This was a tad too close for comfort. Earlier, she'd been thinking how she would in fact turn to Neil if she had to—use him to get what she wanted—but now she wasn't so sure that was a good idea. Not with her stomach churning the way it was, or with the way his gentle touch had shot tantalizing chills through her body. She loved her husband with all her heart, and she wouldn't betray him. She wouldn't allow her problems with Vanessa and the baby to get her into trouble. She wouldn't make the same kinds of mistakes she'd made in the past with other men. She would never give Curtis another reason to consider divorcing her. But, oh, how electrifying this man's touch and gaze were. On Sunday when

he'd held her in his arms, she hadn't noticed anything special because she'd been totally focused
on her plan to gain his sympathy. She'd geared
all of her attention toward the fake crying she'd
had to muster. She'd also had to make sure she'd
said all the right words so he'd feel even sorrier
for her. Today was a different story, though. Today she was vulnerable, and these sensual feelings
he'd drawn out of her were scary.

"Did I do something wrong?" he asked.

"No, but I'd better go."

"That's fine, but at some point we're going to
have to stop pretending we don't want each
other."

"I don't know what you mean."

"I think you do. You've known ever since we
first laid eyes on each other, and to be honest, I'm
tired of ignoring it."

Charlotte turned around, opened the door, and
hurried down the hallway as fast as she could.
*Dear God, no. Please don't let this be happening
again.*

She strode a few more steps and into Racquel's
room. Matthew was holding his son.

"Oh my," she said. "Isn't this a Kodak moment?"

Racquel and Matthew laughed, and Charlotte

walked closer. "He's so precious, Matt. Simply flawless."

"I'm sure you said the same thing about me when I was born."

"I did. But now little MJ has taken your spot."

They all laughed again.

"I mean he's literally the spitting image of you, sweetie," Charlotte said, and then looked at Racquel. "Can I hold him?"

"Of course," she said, smiling.

Matthew carefully laid MJ in her arms, and Charlotte thought her legs might give away. When Matthew had come into the world, she hadn't thought she could love anyone more, and then when Marissa had been born, she'd felt the same way about her. But this special moment with MJ was different. She wasn't sure why, but if she could walk out of there with MJ right now and keep him forever, she would. She was utterly mesmerized by her new grandson and loved him more with every second. She could barely take her eyes off him, and she guessed she'd been so consumed with MJ that she'd lost time, because she now heard Matthew practically singing her name over and over.

"Moooomm. Hellooo? Earth to Mom."

"Honey, I'm sorry. Did you say something?"

"Only a few different times."

"I guess I was somewhere else, but I can't help it. Little MJ is an absolute angel. He's everything a family could hope for."

Racquel smiled. "My mom was saying the same thing this morning when they took him out of the incubator."

Charlotte swallowed hard. "Oh, so she'd already gotten here by then?"

"No, when the doctors told us they were going to do it around ten o'clock, I called to tell her. So she hopped in her car and drove over."

Charlotte could barely breathe. She didn't want to think the worst of her son or anyone else, but it had been around nine-thirty when she'd spoken to him, and he hadn't said a word. She was already bothered by the fact that he hadn't told her the great news about MJ when he'd called her back this afternoon, but she'd had no idea that he'd already known before she'd called him the first time. It was clear that he'd purposely not told her, and she wanted to cry again.

But she didn't. Instead, she held things together, smiled through her pain, and admired her little grandson. She spent as much time as she could with MJ while he was still there in the hospital, because she now knew she was going to have a huge fight on her hands once he went home with the Andersons. Matthew would be gone in a few days, and she'd have to resort to begging to see her own flesh and blood. She wished this wasn't going to be the case, but her gut told her something different. Her intuition screamed trouble and loads of drama, and she knew the road ahead would be tough; for this reason, she had no choice but to shield herself with the best artillery. She had to be ready. It was unfortunate, to say the least, but there was no getting around it.

Chapter 15

I'm not sure why I even called Curtis...well, the first time I called, it was just to make sure my friend had given me the right cell number. She works for the same mobile company Curtis has his account with. But for some reason, after I hung up, I couldn't get his voice out of my head. All he'd done was say hello a couple of times, but even then his tone had infuriated me. He sounded so confident and full of himself and as if life couldn't be better. So, I called him back just to mess with him, and sure enough, this time, his feathers sounded a little ruffled. He sounded as though he'd hated to answer his phone and like he was frustrated. I could tell, too, that he's been racking his brain trying to figure out who sent him that letter. But the joke is on him, because he would never guess in a million years. He would never suspect it was me, but how could he? How could he begin to make any legitimate guesses, when he'd hurt so many? I'm also wondering how his son, Matthew, will deal with the news about his father. Matthew and Alicia, Curtis's firstborn, have certainly witnessed their fair share of family scandal. But now Matthew has a brand new baby boy, and I can't imagine he'll be happy about his father's upcoming news bulletin. Then, there's his wife, Charlotte, and his bastard child, Curtina... well, actually, Matthew is his bastard child, too, because Curtis definitely wasn't married to his wife back then. He was *married, but not to Charlotte. Anyway, I can't help wondering what this news will mean for Charlotte and Curtina, either, but if I were to be truthful with myself I'd have to admit that I couldn't care less about any of them. There was a time when I was a lot more caring and sympathetic toward people, and even as I began planning my revenge on Curtis many years ago, there were times when I would hesitate and change my mind because of his children. I didn't think any child deserved to be humiliated because of the stupid mistakes their parents made, but eventually I got over it. As time continued, I began focusing on myself and my own satisfaction, and I also realized something else: Curtis's children are not my responsibility. Not my worry. It will be interesting, though, to see the look on his face when this all comes to a head. I've even dreamed about it. I literally can't wait.*

Chapter 16

Charlotte listened to the choir, but she wasn't happy. The situation with little MJ had turned out exactly the way she'd expected. Vanessa, Matthew, and Racquel had taken the baby home on Thursday, and now here it was Sunday, yet Charlotte and Curtis still hadn't seen him. Actually, the only time they'd seen Matthew was when he'd come home yesterday to get more clothes and to pick up Curtina. He'd taken his little sister to see the baby for the first time, but then when he'd brought her back, he'd hung around for all of twenty minutes and was out the door again. Charlotte had wanted to ask him if it was okay for them to come visit MJ, especially since Curtina had told her she'd seen Alicia and Phillip at the Andersons. But Curtis had told Charlotte she should give Matthew and Racquel some time alone. Give them space, he'd said. Let them get the baby settled, he'd continued. Curtis had even advised her to ask her parents to wait a few more days before driving over, too, but she knew that was only because Curtis knew his mother-in-law well. It would be nothing for Noreen to handle Vanessa in a noticeable way if she stepped out of line.

But not only was Charlotte sad about not seeing her grandson, she was also sad about not being able to spend time with Matthew, particularly since he was flying back to Boston this evening. It was as if Matthew had completely forgotten about his own family—his own mother—and had found a new family to love and be a part of.

The choir sang "How Great Is Our God" as beautifully as always, but Charlotte found herself questioning God the same as she had in the past. It seemed that there was always one thing or another to deal with. Just last year, they'd been faced with the likes of that Sharon woman who'd become obsessed with Curtis; and the year before, Charlotte had gotten herself mixed up in a couple of affairs. Now, this year, things still weren't going her way. She knew that not every day could be happy and perfect, but this not-seeing-her-grandson-whenever-she-wanted-to thing was difficult to tolerate. It was pushing her over the edge, and she couldn't find peace with it. For the last few days, ever since holding little MJ for the first time in the hospital, Charlotte hadn't thought about much else. She daydreamed about the little smile she'd seen on his face while he'd been sleeping and also about all the places she wanted to take him when he was older. She would even settle for just having him for one overnight stay, but she had a feeling this was out of the question, too.

The choir sang another song, and then Minister Simmons walked into the pulpit.

"Let's give our wonderful choir another round of applause."

The clapping of hands and verbal amens could be heard throughout the entire sanctuary. Deliverance Outreach truly did have a most talented music director and brilliant choir, and Charlotte looked forward to hearing them each Sunday.

Minister Simmons looked across the congregation. "As our great pastor would say, 'This is the day the Lord hath made, so let us rejoice and be glad in it.'"

Curtis sat next to Charlotte and smiled. Lately, Curtis had been allowing Minister Simmons to say a few words before their tithe and offering period, and he seemed to love speaking before so many people. Charlotte knew she might be wrong about him, but sometimes she thought Minister

Simmons enjoyed being in the pulpit just a little too much. He was only in his early thirties and was very knowledgeable when it came to the Bible, but he sometimes seemed drunk with ambition. He talked a lot about having his own megachurch one day and how he couldn't wait to be the kind of minister Curtis was, and Charlotte wasn't sure he could be trusted. Last year, she'd shared her feelings about it with Curtis, but Curtis had told her Minister Simmons was simply young and hungry for the Word. However, Charlotte would never forget one of the other assistant pastors they'd had, Reverend Tolson, and how he'd tried to take the ministry right from under Curtis. He'd been drunk with power, too, and he had betrayed Curtis in the worst way.

Maybe she was being paranoid, but after all she and Curtis had been through, it was hard for her to trust everyone. Most of their staff members were good, honest, loyal individuals, but within every organization, there were always a few who wanted to take over, and Charlotte couldn't ignore that. Curtis never ignored it, either, but he still tended to give most of his people the benefit of the doubt. He believed in them until they gave him a reason not to.

"As always, it's a blessing just to be alive,"

Minister Simmons commented, and the members nodded and said "Amen." I also want to thank Pastor Black for allowing me to serve at this great church. It is by far the highlight of my life. This ministry means everything to me. The other thing I wanted to say is how happy I am that our pastor and first lady's grandson is finally home and in good health."

This time there was more applause than before.

Curtis and Charlotte smiled with joy.

"God is good," Minister Simmons said. "And I guess that brings us to our next phase of service. The giving of tithes and offerings."

Some members took envelopes from their purses or suit jackets with checks or cash sealed away in them, and others hurried to write out their checks or pull cash from their wallets. For whatever reason, most of the members at Deliverance never had to be told how important it was for them to tithe from all of their earnings. They didn't do it because Curtis or one of the ministers asked them, but because they believed in the Word and understood that 10 percent of everything that God had blessed them with was to be returned back to Him. Then, there were those who were having a hard time economically who gave only what they could, and Curtis and the rest of the staff were grateful. They never tried to force anyone to do any more than what they were able to, and their members appreciated that.

After the ushers went through the aisles, passing the buckets down each row, they formed a single line and left the sanctuary. Each Sunday, they took all that had been given into a room where hired staff members waited. The gifts were then counted, totaled, bagged up, and taken to their bank's night depository. Finally, on Tuesday, a different set of employees would enter the amounts given into the system with each person's assigned contribution number, so that tax statements could be mailed at a later date.

Just as Curtis stood and walked over to the stairs of the pulpit, Charlotte saw Matthew and Racquel walk in through the side door. She was a little surprised, because Matthew hadn't mentioned anything about them coming. He waved at his church family, and they applauded. They were happy to see their pastor's son, and they were all very proud of his educational accomplishments.

When Curtis walked over to the podium, Matthew pointed toward the cordless microphone, silently asking if he could address everyone. Curtis motioned for him to join him, and Matthew walked into the pulpit and hugged his father. Racquel took a seat one section over from Charlotte on the front row.

"Good morning," Matthew said.

"Good morning," everyone responded.

"Well, as all of you know, I became a father last Saturday. Our baby was born a little early, but by the grace of God he's doing fine and he's now home with us."

There were lots of happy chattering and more applauding, and many thanked God out loud.

"I also wanna thank all of you for standing by my family and for praying the way you did... and for not judging me. I know you didn't expect me to have a child so young or without being married, and I just want to apologize for that. I apologized months ago, but I wanted to say I'm sorry again. I made a mistake, but as my father has always told me, 'It's not about the mistakes you make, it's about whether you learn from them and whether you go on to become a better person,' and that's exactly what I plan to do, starting today."

Charlotte looked over at Racquel but all she did was look straight ahead, and that made Charlotte nervous. What did Matthew mean when he'd said, 'starting today'?" She hoped it wasn't for the reason she was thinking, but before she could barely finish her thought, she heard her son say,

"So while not even my parents know this yet, I've asked Racquel to marry me."

The congregation went wild. Charlotte had never seen them more excited, and Curtis hugged Matthew again. But all Charlotte did was wonder if Matthew had lost his mind. Was he that caught up with the idea of being a new father that he thought he had to marry the mother? Or had Racquel begged and pleaded and worn him down? He'd been staying at their home for three days, so she'd had plenty of time to work her magic, sweet-talk him and make him see that getting married was the right thing to do. And there was no doubt that her mother, the wicked witch of Mitchell, had encouraged every bit of this misfortune. It was bad enough that Charlotte had tolerated Racquel for all these months. But now, as she looked over at her, she wondered how long Racquel had been planning this scheme of hers. Charlotte had always said she was a gold digger, and that she'd only gotten pregnant as a way to trap Matthew, and now her suspicions had been realized. This impromptu announcement was all the proof Charlotte needed, but if she had anything to do with it, this shady engagement of theirs would be the longest engagement in history. Racquel was the mother of Matthew's child, but she just wasn't right for him, and Charlotte would rather die than accept her as a daughter-in-law. This girl was ruining everything, right along with her obnoxious mother, and something had to be done about it. Someone also needed to talk to Matthew before he made some other rash decision, like dropping out of college. What a disaster that would be. What a nightmare this whole fiasco had turned into. What a total and complete mess this was—period.

Chapter 17

As soon as Matt walked into the kitchen, Charlotte started right in on him. "Why are you doing this, Matt?"

"Because I love her, Mom."

"You love *her* or you love your son?"

"Both."

"You do know that just because you have a baby with someone, it doesn't mean you have to marry them."

Matt looked away from her. "See, this is why I didn't tell you. I asked Racquel to marry me before the baby was even born."

Charlotte had known the conversation between her and Matthew wouldn't go well, so before they'd left church, she'd asked Aunt Emma if Curtina could go home with her. Aunt Emma loved her great-niece, so keeping her for a few hours or even overnight was never a problem.

"You're making a huge mistake," Charlotte said.

"Why, Mom? Because you didn't choose her for me? Because she and her mom won't let you run everything?"

Charlotte looked at Curtis, who sat quietly at the island with his arms crossed. "Aren't you going to say anything?" she asked him.

"Matt already knows what I think. Yes, he and Racquel are too young to be getting married, but at the same time, he's grown. It's his decision."

"And it's the wrong decision, too."

Matthew packed a couple of apples inside his duffel bag. In a few hours, it would be time to take him to the airport. At least for now, he was still planning to stay in school, and Charlotte was somewhat relieved.

"Mom, you've disliked Racquel since the first time you saw her, and for no reason. You never even gave her a chance."

"Because I always knew what she was up to. I told you to be careful with these little fast-tail girls, but you wouldn't listen. I knew one of them was going to trap you with a baby and then trick you into marrying her."

"Trick? Mom, I'm not some child who can be fooled into doing something I don't wanna do.

I'm almost nineteen years old. I'm not saying it'll be easy, but things will be fine. We'll get our degrees, and we'll be good."

"So who's going to take care of MJ?"

"Racquel's not leaving for school until fall."

"And after that?"

"He'll stay with her parents."

"And what about us, Matt? What about your father and me?"

"You'll be able to see him all the time."

"Yeah, right!" Charlotte said, shoving one of the chairs out of her way and storming over to the sink.

"Mom, why do you always have to be so difficult? Why can't you just be happy for me and support my decision?"

"Because I want something better for you."

"But what about what *I* want?"

"You're only eighteen, so you don't know what you want. You're just doing what you think is right, even though it isn't."

Matthew shook his head. "Dad, can you please talk to her?"

Curtis blew a sigh of frustration. "Baby, Matt has already made up his mind, and it's not like they're getting married right now, anyway."

"Fine, then let's talk about the baby," she said.

Matt packed a couple of other items from the cupboard and zipped his bag. "What about him?"

"When can we see him again? And when can Mom and Dad come down for a visit? It is their great-grandchild, you know."

"All you have to do is call Racquel. I already talked to her about it. We realize now that you and her mom are never going to like each other, so Racquel is going to bring the baby over whenever you want."

"What if I want to babysit him or keep him overnight?"

"I'm sure that'll be fine, too."

"Yeah, well, I won't hold my breath," she said.

"For one thing, Mom, you have got to change your attitude toward Racquel. If you keep acting this way, it's only gonna make things worse. That's the reason her mom stopped wanting you around."

Charlotte ignored his last comment and walked back over to the island and sat down. "You really should have told us what you were planning to do at church this morning."

"I wanted to. But I knew you would try to talk me out of it. I also wanted to apologize to our congregation, and that's the only way I could think to do it. When I got Racquel pregnant, I know I em-

barrassed both of you. I set a bad example for all
the other young men in the church, too, and I've
always felt bad about that."

"You did the right thing, son," Curtis said.
"You're a good kid, and we'll always be here for
you and little MJ."

Curtis and Matthew bumped fists, and Charlotte wondered why Curtis couldn't see what she
saw. He couldn't have been that naïve when it
came to Racquel, or any young girl for that matter. Had he forgotten that he was *the* Reverend
Curtis Black? And with the kind of popularity
and fortune he'd amassed over the years, what
girl wouldn't want to be the mother of Curtis's
grandchild? What better grandfather could Racquel have chosen for her son? What better man
could she have chosen to trap than the son of a
wealthy pastor? It all made perfect sense to Charlotte, but for some reason, Curtis and Matthew
had their heads in the clouds. They saw only the
good in Racquel and refused to consider her real
motives.

Matthew's phone rang, and he answered it.
"Hey baby," he said. "How's the little one?"

As Matthew walked out of the kitchen, chatting
with Racquel, Charlotte watched his body lan-
guage and saw the grin plastered on his face. Boy,

did that girl have his little nose stretched wide open.

Curtis reached over and grabbed Charlotte's hand. "You have to get over this, baby. You have to let Matt make his own decisions."

"But you know he's too young for all this."

"Doesn't matter. We're no longer in a position to tell him what to do. He's an adult, and he has a child of his own now."

Matthew strolled back into the kitchen, still chatting with Racquel. "I was gonna drive back over, but I'll just ask my parents to bring me on the way to the airport. That way they can see the baby."

Charlotte was pleasantly surprised. She wasn't looking forward to seeing Vanessa or Racquel— or Neil, either, since she didn't want Curtis picking up on their chemistry—but she was thrilled about seeing her grandson. For now, she'd forget about this engagement drama and would enjoy her time with both her babies—MJ and Matthew—before Matthew left for Boston.

Chapter 18

The Tuxson was still the best restaurant in Mitchell, and even though it was Valentine's Day, much of the lunch crowd had cleared out. Late this morning, Charlotte and Janine had gone to their favorite spa to receive massages and facial treatments, and for the first time in a while, Charlotte felt refreshed. Ever since little MJ had been born, she'd been through more than she wanted to emotionally, so this outing with her best friend was the therapy she needed.

The distinguished-looking maître d' seated them in their usual section, near the window overlooking the scenic river, and placed lunch menus in front of them.

"Dino will be with you shortly, Mrs. Black."

"Thank you, Thomas."

Janine set her purse on the chair next to her. "This place never changes. Always so relaxing."

"That it is," Charlotte said, scanning the restaurant and seeing the cutest little boy, sitting in a high chair. "Gosh, I so look forward to the day when MJ is that age."

Janine looked in the same direction. "I can imagine."

"Although, if Racquel doesn't start bringing him around a lot more and letting us keep him overnight, he won't even know us."

"I thought you said you saw him this past weekend."

"We did, but he and Racquel only stayed for a couple of hours, and we've only seen him six times since Matthew went back to school. My parents were here the second time she brought him over, but seeing my grandson only a few times in three weeks is ridiculous."

Janine looked at her strangely. "And you don't think a couple of times a week is a lot?"

"Not for grandparents. As a matter of fact, I called Racquel first thing this morning, hoping she'd bring him by, but she wouldn't answer her phone."

"Well, you and I both know how it is with newborns. They keep you up all night, and you sort of have to sleep whenever they do. And didn't you tell me he's a little whiny?"

"He cries a quite a bit, but only because Racquel doesn't know how to hold him. She's just a kid, so what does she know about being a mother? What experience does an eighteen-year-old have with anything?"

Dino walked over to the table. "How're you ladies today?"

"We're great, and you?" Charlotte said.

"Wonderful. Before I take your drink orders, let me tell you our specials. We have a great chicken salad with walnuts, mandarin oranges, and a very tasty vinaigrette dressing; broiled sea bass with spinach and potatoes; and finally our house rib eye."

"Actually," Charlotte said, "I'll have a glass of red wine and the sea bass."

"I'll have water and the chicken salad," Janine said.

"Still or sparkling?"

"Still is fine."

"Sounds good, ladies. I'll bring out a basket of warm rolls with your drinks."

When Dino walked away, Janine wasted no time. "When did you start drinking again?"

"I'm not really drinking. At least not in the sense you're talking about. I just felt like a glass of wine."

"I really wish you wouldn't."

Charlotte pursed her lips. "I'm only having one drink, J. You worry too much."

"And for good reason."

"This is the first drink I've had since last year, and it's not like I'm gonna make a habit of it."

"But you know what happened before, Charlotte. You were completely out of control."

"Only because of the problems Curtis and I were having. But this is different."

"Well, you're not the happiest now."

"No, but I would be if Matthew would break off that silly engagement."

"I can't believe you're still upset about that. I mean, I know you want him to wait, but at the same time, he's an adult."

"Yeah, an adult who's making the biggest mistake of his life."

"Things have a way of working out for the best. And even if for some reason they do get married and it doesn't work out, you have to let Matt live his life."

Dino set their drinks and bread onto the table and left again.

Charlotte took a sip of her wine. "I can see where this is going to be one of our agree-to-disagree moments."

"I guess so," Janine said, setting her glass of water back on the table. "And anyway, I've got my own issues to worry about."

"Like what?"

"My marriage."

Charlotte was a little surprised at this, because Carl had always been a wonderful husband. He worked hard, he loved his wife and daughter more than anything, and he had such a kind and caring personality. "What's wrong?"

"I don't know, maybe it's me. But I'm not happy, and I feel like something is missing."

"But you and Carl have always been so great together."

"We used to be. But now, all he wants to do is go to work and spend the rest of his time at home. The only reason we went away four weekends ago was because I made reservations and told him we were going. It didn't matter, though, because all he did was watch basketball while Bethany and I ventured out."

"I'm really sorry, J. Do you think he's depressed about something?"

"I don't think so. He seems fine as long as we're at home doing nothing. But he doesn't even want to go to the movies anymore, and I can't remember the last time we got a sitter so we could go out to dinner. As far as I know, we don't even have anything planned for tonight, and it's Valentine's Day."

"Have you talked to him about it?"

"Too many times, and that's why I'm really getting tired of it."

"I pray things get back to normal for you guys. I'm sure this is just a rough patch. We all go through them," she said, but then she almost dropped the knife she'd picked up to slice one of the rolls. Vanessa, Racquel, and little MJ had just walked in. Vanessa looked dead at Charlotte, but she never told Racquel, who hadn't seen her.

"That witch," Charlotte said. "This is never going to get any better."

"What?"

"Look," she said, pointing.

Janine turned around and then back to Charlotte. "You're not going over there, are you?"

"What do you think?" she said, already out of her seat and heading to the other side of the restaurant. When she walked in front of Racquel and Vanessa's booth, she smiled and said, "Well, hello."

Racquel seemed nervous. "Hi, Mrs. Black."

"And how are you, Vanessa?" Charlotte said.

But Vanessa turned to the baby, who was lying next to her, nestled away in his carrier, and opened up his blanket.

Heifer. "So did you get my message?" Charlotte asked Racquel.

"Uh ... yes. I tried to call you back."

"Hmmm. I didn't see any missed calls from you."

"I called your home number. I even left a message."

"I was probably already gone, so why didn't you call my cell?"

"I saw your home number and didn't think to try it. I'm really sorry."

"Can I hold him?" Charlotte asked.

Racquel looked at her mother. Vanessa blew a sigh of disgust but picked little MJ up and passed him over to Charlotte.

"Hi, sweetie," Charlotte said in a babylike voice. "How's Nana's handsome little man doing? Nana and Grandpa love you so, so much."

Charlotte admired the baby and played with him, but she couldn't get him to smile. "So when can Curtis and I keep him overnight? We're just dying to spend a whole weekend with him."

"When he's a little older," Racquel said.

Charlotte swallowed her anger. So at barely a

month old, there was nothing wrong with exposing MJ to germs in a restaurant, yet he was way
too young to spend time with her and Curtis?
You'd think Neil, being the doctor he was, would
have stopped them from dragging MJ out like
this, anyway, but maybe he didn't know what
they were up to.

Instead of lashing out like a madwoman,
though, Charlotte mentally calmed herself and
forced a perfect smile. "If it's okay, I'd like to
take little MJ over to see Janine."

"That's fine," Racquel said, looking at her
mother. Charlotte guessed she was waiting for
approval, but Charlotte walked away before
Vanessa could say anything.

"Look who I have," Charlotte said, when she arrived back at her and Janine's table.

"Awwww," Janine said. "What a cutie you are,
little MJ."

"Say thank you, Auntie Janine."

"He looks like Matt already."

"I told you," Charlotte said, moving her chair
back and sitting down.

Janine leaned forward. "What are you doing?"

"Enjoying my grandson. Racquel wouldn't answer her phone this morning, so I'm spending
time with him now."

Janine looked on in silence, but her face was flustered.

Charlotte started her baby talk again. "Nana is so happy to see you, sweetie. Yes she is. And she loves, loves, loves you so, so much," she said. MJ whined a little, so she rocked him and kept talking to him, but now he cried.

Janine turned around and then said, "Racquel and Vanessa seem worried about him. I think they want you to bring him back."

"Oh yeah? Well, I've been wanting to see my grandson for three days, so Racquel and her mother can just wait." She rocked the baby more. "Shhhhhh," she whispered, but MJ cried louder. "Honey, what's wrong? Aren't they treating you right over there?"

"Charlotte, people are starting to stare," Janine told her. "He's probably hungry."

"He'll be fine," she said, still rocking and quietly shushing him. "He just doesn't see me enough, is all."

"But you said he cries a lot with Racquel, too."

"Yeah, but it's like I told you. He only does that with her because she doesn't know how to take care of him. Babies know when another child is holding them."

Janine leaned back in her chair but looked up when Vanessa strutted over to the table.

"He's hungry, Charlotte, so I'll just take him now."

Charlotte slowly glanced up at her. "If he's hungry, then why didn't you bring his bottle over here? I can feed him just as well as you can."

"Please don't do this, Charlotte," Janine said.

Now little MJ screamed with more tears, and Charlotte finally surrendered. "Fine. Take him."

Vanessa cradled him in her arms and walked away.

Janine stared at Charlotte, clearly not happy.

Charlotte drank more of her wine. "What?"

Janine shook her head, seemingly confused and disappointed.

Charlotte took more sips of her wine as if nothing had happened.

Chapter 19

*D*ad, you won't believe this! Racquel just called me all upset and saying she saw Mom at the Tuxson." Matthew was talking a mile a minute, and he was outraged.

"What happened?"

"I guess she and Aunt Janine were having lunch, but when Racquel and her mom came in, Mom went over to them. She questioned Racquel about not calling her back this morning, and then she wanted to take MJ to her own table."

"Why?"

"To see Aunt Janine, but when MJ started crying, she wouldn't take him back. Racquel said he cried louder and louder until her mom couldn't take it anymore."

"Lordy. Son, I just don't know what to say."

"And then she keeps badgering Racquel about MJ spending the night. Racquel keeps telling her it'll be fine when he's older, but she won't listen.

I told her the same thing when she asked me a few days ago, but she's not hearing it."

"I'm really sorry, son. Your mom was completely out of line this afternoon, and I'll have a talk with her."

"Dad, this really does have to stop, because Racquel is afraid of Mom. She's getting to the point where she hates being around her, and I don't blame her. I mean, how often does she think she should see the baby, anyway? Every day?"

"Actually she does, and this obsession she has is starting to concern me."

"I'm worried, too, because who keeps a baby while he's crying like that and doesn't take him back to his mother?"

Curtis was speechless. He'd known things weren't getting better for Charlotte when it came to the way she felt about little MJ, but now she was causing scenes out in public.

"Dad, this is crazy, and all this drama is affecting my study time. I have a huge biology test tomorrow."

"Try not to worry. I know that's easier said than done, but eventually this will pass. I'll call your mom as soon as we hang up. Hopefully, I'll be able to reason with her."

"I really need to withdraw and just start back up in the fall."

"No, son. I know you're upset, but don't do it."

"It'll only be for the rest of this semester."

"Yeah, but one semester can turn into two."

"I just feel like I need to be there for Racquel and MJ...to protect them from my own mother."

"I understand, but son, you have to hang in there. You need your education, especially if you want to take care of a family."

Matthew paused, sniffling. "I know you're right, Dad...but this is so hard. I'm miles and miles away from Racquel and MJ, and now Mom keeps acting like something's wrong with her."

Matthew's tears broke Curtis's heart, and it was all he could do not to weep himself.

"I mean, why does Mom do this kind of stuff? Last year, she started drinking out of control; the year before that, she messed around with two different men; and the year before that, she walked around for months hating Curtina. Why is Mom so cruel to people?"

"I don't know. Your mom gets caught up in her own feelings, and she doesn't think. It doesn't dawn on her that her actions will hurt other people."

"Well, I wish she would stop. I wish she would

just be a normal, kind, respectable mother. That's all I want."

"I'm gonna call her now, but you get back to your studies, okay?"

"I'll try to—and Dad?"

"Yeah?"

"Thanks, and I'm sorry about all the crying."

"Don't you ever apologize for that. Letting things out is the best thing you can do."

"I love you, Dad."

"You take care, son. Love you, too."

Curtis never set his phone down and dialed Charlotte immediately. Her phone rang and rang until her voice mail answered. She'd told him that she and Janine were going to the spa and that they were then going to have lunch right after, so maybe they'd gone to the mall or something. He wasn't sure why she would, though, since the two of them had already exchanged Valentine's Day gifts this morning. But knowing Charlotte, she'd found a reason to do more shopping.

He thought about trying her again, but his phone rang. He figured it was her until he saw Private on his screen. "Not again," he said. This time he refused to answer it.

He reviewed his upcoming speaking engagement schedule for the summer, but it wasn't long before his phone rang again. It was the anonymous caller. He didn't want to answer it, but he also didn't want his phone to keep ringing or to have to place it on Silent.

"Hello?"

"Hello yourself," the computerized voice said.

Curtis creased the middle of his forehead. "Who is this?"

"That's really not important. What you *should* be worried about, though, is that letter I sent you."

"I'm not sure why you're playing these games, but I wish you'd stop harassing me. And how did you get this number?"

The voice was technologically disguised, so Curtis couldn't tell whether the caller was a man or a woman. Whomever it was, though, seemed tickled out of this world. The sound was strange, but the person was definitely laughing at him.

"What is it you want from me?" he asked.

"Nothing. You've already dished out enough to last a lifetime, but the buck stops here. You're finally going to get what's coming to you."

"I'm not listening to this, and please don't call my number anymore."

"Don't worry. This is my last call...I promise."

Curtis's heart rate sped up a few notches as the caller hung up. He didn't like what this person had just said, because it sounded like the next time he'd hear from them was when they exposed his secret. *Dear God, I'm begging you. Please make this person go away. I know I did a terrible thing, but I was a different man back then. I saw no limits when it came to getting what I wanted, and I'm sorry. Lord, please forgive me.*

Curtis wasn't sure why he kept asking God to forgive him, because deep down he knew God already had. It was this mystery person who still had it in for him. And it was driving him insane. He'd tried his best to forget about that letter and the annoying phone calls, but lately he'd been burdened with sleepless nights, guilt, and regret. What was Charlotte going to say once she found out? What about his children and his congregation? What would they think and how would they react to the news? And what about everyone else who'd come to know, love, and trust the good man he was today?

If he had one chance to change anything, it would certainly be that particular time in his life, but the past couldn't be corrected. That was always the problem when it came to making the wrong choices; once the deed had been done, there was no taking it back. A person could move on from the sins they'd committed, but they could never erase them. And apparently the person who was calling couldn't forget or forgive and had decided to do something about it.

Curtis's office phone rang, and it startled him.

"This is Curtis."

"Pastor, Dillon and Melissa are here to see you," Lana said.

"Please send them in."

He looked at his watch and saw that they were a little early, but he was ready for them. When they entered, he shook their hands, and they each took a seat.

Curtis leaned forward and rested his hands on his desk. "So, how are things going?"

"Not too well," Dillon said.

Melissa crossed her legs. "Not well at all, is more like it."

"Did you read the scriptures I gave you, and have you been praying?"

"Sort of."

Curtis chuckled. "Well, either you have or you haven't."

"I did at first," he said, "but it wasn't working."

"Did you attend any meetings?"

"One."

"Why didn't you go to more?"

"I don't know. I guess because the more I read

157

scripture and prayed, the more I wanted to watch porn. So to me it was pointless to go back to those meetings."

"You do know that when we try to do the right thing, the enemy doesn't like it, and he works even harder to bring you down. The devil is a powerful individual, but you have to stay strong. You have to keep your faith strong."

"Why don't you tell him what else you did?" Melissa said. She seemed a lot less supportive of Dillon than before and very irritated.

Dillon looked at her and then toward the other side of the room.

"Tell him," she said.

"What is it, Dillon?" Curtis asked.

"I went to a strip club."

Melissa crossed her arms. "And not just once, either. He's been going every single night."

"Have you ever gone before?" Curtis asked.

"Not really. I mean, I went back when I was in college but not since then."

"Well, what made you start now?"

"I don't know. I had the urge to go, so I went."

"And you told Melissa about it?"

"No, he never told me anything," she interrupted. "But two weeks ago, it seemed like he was hurrying me off the phone. So, I waited until about midnight and called his house number, but he never answered. Then, when I asked him about it the next day, he said he must have been asleep."

"I only said that because I knew you would go ballistic if I told you the truth."

"Well, after calling you three nights in row, I'd had enough," she said, then looked at Curtis. "And that's when I rented a car, waited outside, and followed him."

"I'm sorry this has happened," Curtis said.

"I'm sorry, too," Dillon added. "I know I have a problem, but I can't help what I'm doing. I like sex, and since I'm not getting any of my own, porn and strip clubs satisfy me."

Melissa jerked her head toward him. "So what are you saying? That until we're able to have sex, you're not gonna stop this madness?"

"I'm not saying anything. I'm just telling you and Pastor Black how I feel. And at least I'm not going out sleeping with other women."

"And that makes it okay?" she said loudly.

Dillon looked at her. "Baby, I'm not saying that, either."

Melissa uncrossed and recrossed her legs. "Well, I don't think this is going to work."

"So you're just gonna give up on me?"

Melissa didn't respond.

Dillon looked at Curtis. "Pastor, I really do want to stop this, so can I schedule some time with you on my own?"

"Why would you need to do that?" Melissa asked.

"There's nothing wrong with that at all," Curtis said. "Sometimes talking man to man is a good thing. There are times when a man can't say certain things in front of a woman because of pride."

"I don't get any of this," she said.

"Dillon, why don't we schedule an appointment for just the two of us for tomorrow or Thursday. Will either of those days work for you?"

"Yeah, sounds good."

"Lana will take a look at my calendar, and you can confirm the time on your way out."

"I really appreciate this, Pastor," he said.

Melissa still wouldn't say anything, so Curtis finally said, "At least he's trying. He's willing to work on this problem he has, and he loves you."

"I love him, too, but this porn-strip-club thing has got to stop."

"And it will, baby," Dillon said. "I promise."

Curtis looked at both of them and hoped Dillon could in fact stop what he was doing, because he could tell Melissa wasn't having it. She wasn't the kind of woman who would put up with this kind of thing, and it was only a matter of time before she called off the wedding. It wouldn't be long before she dropped him completely.

Chapter 20

*I*t was just before five. Curtis was on his way home but still hadn't heard back from Charlotte. He'd called her again about five minutes ago, his fourth time since talking to Matthew, but she hadn't answered. Two years ago, when she hadn't answered her phone, she'd been out drinking and sleeping with another man. Then, last year, she'd taken to the bottle again and had ignored a good number of his phone calls, too. But outside of those sort of isolated incidents, this kind of thing was totally unlike her, and he was starting to worry; especially since she knew they had dinner reservations for six. It was the reason he'd showered and changed in his private bathroom and dressing area at the church, so they could leave as soon as he got home.

Curtis headed down the street and dialed their

home number. Maybe Charlotte's cell wasn't working.

"Hi, Mr. Curtis," Agnes said.

"Hey, is Charlotte around?"

"No. I picked up Curtina a couple of hours ago, but I haven't seen Miss Charlotte since this morning. She met Miss Janine."

"Yeah, she told me, but I've been calling her all afternoon."

"That's strange," she said.

"I thought so, too. I think I'll call Janine to see if they're still together."

"Oh, and right after Miss Charlotte left, Racquel called. I was at the grocery store, but I saw her number on the caller ID when I got back. So, if you talk to her, please tell her."

"I will."

Curtis ended the call and searched for Janine's number in his contact list. She answered right away.

"Hey, Curtis."

"How's it going?"

"Fine. Happy Valentine's Day."

"Same to you. But hey, do you know where Charlotte is?"

"No. We left the Tuxson around three, and we were only there for an hour and a half because of a little run-in she had with Vanessa."

"Matthew told me, and that's why I was trying to call her."

"It was very sad, Curtis. Then after Vanessa took the baby back to her table, we ate our lunch, and Charlotte said she was ready to go. Said she couldn't sit there any longer watching her grandson lying in the arms of that 'witch.'"

"I just wish she would stop this."

"I do, too. I tried to tell her that seeing the baby a couple of times a week is a lot, but she wouldn't hear it. Anyway, when we left the restaurant, we got in our cars, and I haven't heard from her."

"Okay, well, I'm sorry to bother you with this."

"No problem. Let me know if she doesn't turn up soon."

"I will. Say hello to Carl, and take care."

Curtis pressed the End button. Where in the world was she? There was always something going on with Charlotte. She was never satisfied for more than a few months, and though he was trying his best to be understanding, his patience was wearing thin. It had only been eight months since they'd reconciled and gotten their marriage back on track, yet now a whole other problem was brewing because of little MJ. Of course, Curtis didn't even want to think about his own mess that might soon be discovered because he wasn't sure his marriage, ministry, or anything else could survive it. This thing he'd done was just that bad, and he needed to prepare for the worst.

Curtis turned down the street leading to their home, and his phone rang. Finally.

"Baby, where have you been?" he asked.

"Driving around."

"Where?"

"I had a bad day, and I needed to think."

"What about our dinner reservation?"

"I'm sorry, but I can't."

"What are you talking about?"

"I can't go to dinner. I have a lot on my mind, and I need to be alone. I need to clear my head."

"Why? Because of what happened at the restaurant?"

"That's exactly why. I'm tired of Vanessa and her daughter and these games they keep playing. I'm sick of it."

"Well, Matt's sick of it, too. He called me earlier all upset. He was so worked up, he talked about withdrawing from school."

"I'll talk to him," she said.

"He has an important test tomorrow, so I really wish you wouldn't."

"I don't want him quitting school, Curtis. Especially for that tramp."

"Why are you calling her that? What has that girl ever done to you?"

"She's keeping my grandson from me. At first I blamed Vanessa, but today I realized the two of them are in this together. Neither of them want me to see MJ."

"That's ridiculous. And even if they do ignore your phone calls or act like they don't want to have anything to do with you, it's because of the way you treated them from the start. I told you that a few weeks ago."

"And I'm telling *you* that I'm not backing down when it comes to my own son."

"You mean 'grandson,' don't you?"

"That's what I said."

"No, you said, 'son.'"

"You know what I meant, Curtis."

He pulled into the beginning of their driveway, opened his window, pressed the button to the iron gate, and waited for it to open. "Look, when are you coming home?"

"I told you I need to be alone."

"So I guess it doesn't matter to you that it's Valentine's Day?"

"It does, but I can't help how I feel. I can't

help the way Racquel and Vanessa are treating me."

"You never cease to amaze me," he said, driving up the long winding path. He parked in the circle between the sprawling brick mansion and the fountain.

"I'll be home tomorrow," she said.

"Tomorrow?"

"I'm sorry, but I need this time away, Curtis. I know you don't understand, but I promise things will be different when I get home. I'll have a whole new attitude."

Curtis got out of the SUV. Her spending the night somewhere else was killing him, but he would never let her know how hurt he was. "I know one thing. If I find out you're having another affair, you might as well start packing."

"I would never do that."

"You have before."

"But I won't again. I just need some time to think and relax my mind. That's all."

"Good-bye, Charlotte," he said, and went into the house.

Chapter 21

S he'd already made up her mind, but after speaking to Curtis, Charlotte knew there was no other way except to follow through on her decision. Because of rush-hour traffic, her drive from Mitchell to downtown Chicago had taken her nearly two hours, so she'd had a lot of time to think. She'd debated her options back and forth, but then she'd finally come up with the perfect plan, the perfect solution—and the only logical thing that had to be done if she were to ever have a true relationship with her grandson.

Still, it hadn't been until she'd heard the disgust in Curtis's voice a few minutes ago that she'd known he would never side with her, and that he would never fully understand her position. Even as she'd checked into this fabulous hotel, she'd been hoping her husband would wake up. She'd prayed for him to see what she saw. They were losing their one and only grandchild, but unfortunately, Curtis was clueless.

Charlotte sat in the armchair across from the king-size bed, with her legs resting on the ottoman, and eyed the minibar. Ever since checking into her suite, she'd been trying not to take another drink the way she had at the Tuxson, but she needed something to relax her nerves, something to prepare her for the days ahead. To a certain extent, she was also a little depressed, but mostly she felt abandoned. Over the last two weeks, she'd thought maybe Racquel would warm up to her and would bring MJ over more often, but after seeing him only twice last week and twice the week before, it had been clear that this was the best it was ever going to be.

Charlotte just wished everyone understood where she was coming from. Even Curtis had gone as far as saying she was obsessed and overbearing, and her own son believed she was self-centered and controlling. He'd actually told her that while they were speaking on the phone, and she hadn't forgotten it. Then, there was that witch, Vanessa, and her gold-digging daughter who thought Charlotte was Satan's sister, and even Janine had acted as though she disagreed with Charlotte's desire to see her grandson as much as possible. Charlotte didn't know what kind of best friend that was. The only reason she wouldn't hold it against Janine, though, was because she knew she and Carl were having problems. Nonetheless, Charlotte felt forsaken and blackballed by everyone, all except her mother, and that saddened her.

Charlotte stared at the minibar again but fought the urge to open it. Instead, she decided it was time she called Matthew, because there was no telling what that Racquel had told him. Vanessa had likely tossed in her two cents, too, and Charlotte could only imagine what Matthew was thinking.

She dialed his number, and he answered on the third ring.

"Hello?"

"Hey, son, how are you?"

"Fine." His tone was as dry as two dead leaves, so she knew this wouldn't go well. Still, she had to try to talk to him.

"Is this a bad time?"

"I'm studying."

"I really need to talk to you."

"About what? Racquel already told me what happened, so I hope you're not calling me about that."

"All I want is to see my grandson, Matt. You

said I could see him whenever I wanted, but Racquel hardly brings him over. And I still don't see what's so wrong with us keeping him for the weekend. I've had two children, so I certainly know how to take care of a newborn—which is more than I can say for Racquel and her mother."

"And what is that supposed to mean?"

"That if they knew any better, they never would have brought MJ to that restaurant in the first place."

"I'm sure MJ is just fine. But let me ask you this, Mom. Would you have turned *me* over to someone else for the weekend right after I was born?"

"Your grandparents kept you all the time."

"Mom, that's only because you lived with them. Just like Racquel lives with her parents. But it's not like you would have dropped me off somewhere else. But regardless, I really don't have time for this," he said.

"Okay, just a few more minutes."

"Now what?"

"She won't even return my phone calls. I called her this morning, and I never heard from her."

"Racquel told me she left you a message."

"Matt, if she was really trying to get in touch with me, she would have called my cell."

"Whatever, but the bottom line is this: there's

no way you should expect to see MJ every single day and then keep him an entire weekend."

Charlotte swung her legs off of the ottoman and scooted closer to the edge of the chair. "So what are you saying?"

"That Racquel will continue to bring the baby over one time during the week and once on the weekend. She doesn't need to bring him out seven days straight, and had you not started all that trouble with her mom, you'd be able to visit him over there."

"I still don't know why I can't."

"You know exactly why."

"So is that how it's gonna be, Matt? You're gonna keep defending that witch over your own mother?"

"It's not like that, Mom, but you're gonna have to accept the fact that you're not MJ's mother."

Charlotte eyed the minibar again. "What?"

"It's true, Mom. You're his grandmother, and grandmothers don't usually get to see their grandchildren every day."

"Well, Vanessa certainly does, now doesn't she? That heifer gets to see and hold my grandson every waking moment."

"Only because he and Racquel live with her. We just talked about that."

"Why can't MJ spend a week with them and a week with us? He's your child, too, Matt, so we should see him just as much as his other grandparents."

"Why are you so obsessed with him?"

There was that nasty word again—*obsessed*—and Charlotte was tired of hearing it. To her, it was starting to sound as though Curtis and Matthew were calling her crazy.

"Mom, I have to go," he said.

"But, Matt, I'm begging you. Just call Racquel. Ask her to let us keep MJ this weekend. Just this one time."

"I can't do this with you, Mom."

Charlotte didn't say anything, just walked over to the minibar and opened it.

"You know what, Matt? I'll talk to you later."

She heard Matthew saying, "Mom, please just—," but she pressed the button on her phone. She'd tried to reason with Racquel and even get her own husband, son, and best friend to support her right to see little MJ. But being nice and cordial wasn't working. Actually, it rarely did when you were dealing with a ton of resistance from folks—but this tiny bottle of Jack Daniel's would make her feel a lot better. It would give her all the love, understanding, and help she needed, and there would be no hard feelings from Jack or his close friends...Mr. Hennessy or Mr. Bacardi. She'd never drunk whiskey, cognac, and rum all in one sitting, but she would tonight. She would enjoy herself one last time before going home and gearing up for the task at hand. Just thinking about the near future gave her peace.

Chapter 22

Charlotte stretched her arms, her body twisting from side to side. Her head was killing her. She was severely hungover, but after drinking until the wee hours of the morning, what had she expected? She'd known what the outcome would be if she kept downing one libation after another, but she hadn't been able to stop herself—hadn't wanted to stop herself, and even though her head ached to no end, she didn't regret it. She'd wanted to feel numb and lifeless, because it meant she didn't have to hurt. She hadn't wanted to shed any more tears, and she hadn't.

She pried her eyes open and squinted at the clock. It was almost noon. She was surprised housekeeping hadn't banged on her door and tried to open it, but as she gathered her thoughts, she sort of remembered hanging that little do-not-disturb sign out on her doorknob. She'd also turned off her phone, right after swallowing her first drink of the night, so no one would bother her. She could only imagine how many times Curtis had called and the number of messages he'd left, but she didn't want to talk to him. All she wanted was to recover from this hangover so she could go home and prepare to be the best grandmother alive. She would show MJ that it wasn't just Vanessa who loved him, and that he had another grandmother who loved him more; not to mention, Charlotte and Curtis had so much more to offer him. They had both the financial means and the kind of prestige that would afford him the best life possible, and this was the reason she'd settled on what she had to do. Before calling Matthew last night, she had thought maybe there was a chance he would finally listen to her, because if he had, she wouldn't have to take matters into her own hands. But only minutes into their conversation, he'd quickly proven that contacting him had been a waste of time. Charlotte understood that, though, because she'd finally had to accept something: like Racquel, he was only eighteen and didn't know any better. He barely knew what was best for himself, let alone what was best for a baby, and he would never stand up to Vanessa the way he needed to. So, again, Charlotte had to take matters into her own hands. It was time for her to do all that was necessary to protect little MJ's interests, and when MJ was older, he would thank his nana for making such important sacrifices for him. Matthew would thank her, too, sometime down the road, and so would Curtis.

They couldn't see it now, of course, but little MJ belonged with them. He had since the day he was born, and there was only one way to make that happen. She'd thought about it long and hard, making sure there were no alternatives—and there weren't. This was absolutely the only way she could protect him now and in the future. It was a shame that the relationship between the two families hadn't turned out better, but it was what it was, and Charlotte was fine with it. Sometimes life wasn't meant to be easy, and you had to fight for what you wanted. Sometimes you had to fight for what you believed was right—you had to risk everything to safeguard your loved ones, and Charlotte had no problem doing that for her grandson.

Charlotte pushed the comforter and Egyptian sheet away from her, took a deep breath, and slowly raised herself up. Her head was heavy, and she couldn't wait for this feeling to pass. This was definitely her last time drinking, or at least to this extent—no, it truly was her last time, because from here on out she had to focus on taking care of MJ. She had to make sure he grew up with the best role models and the most respectable kind of family life. She had to make him proud. It was true that he was only a tiny baby, but in no time, he'd be entering kindergarten, then junior high, then high school, and then a top university.

She finally touched her feet to the floor, got up, and dragged into the bathroom. There was no point looking in the mirror, so she didn't. She knew it wouldn't be a pretty sight, so she pulled one of the white towels from the rack, ran it through cold water, and wiped her face with it. The cold towel hadn't made a huge amount of difference, but she did feel somewhat better.

When she went back into the room, she strolled over to the bed, sat down, and turned on her phone. Just as she'd thought, there were six messages. If she had to guess, at least three of them were from Curtis, asking her when she was coming home and then eventually telling her he was through with her.

She dialed into her voice mail, and sure enough, Curtis had left three messages. The others were from her mom, Aunt Emma, and Janine. Charlotte was sure Curtis had told all three of them that she was "missing," so she would make sure to call and let them know she was fine. She called Curtis now, though, because it was time to put her plan into action. She waited for him to answer, but she got his voice mail instead.

"Hi, this is Pastor Black. I'm unavailable right now, but if you'll leave a message, I'll get back to you at my earliest convenience. Thanks and God bless."

Charlotte waited for the tone. "Hi, baby, it's me. I really don't know where to begin except to say I am so sorry for the way I acted yesterday. I'm sorry for ruining Valentine's Day for us, and I'm sorry for...well...everything. I took a long look at myself last night and then again this morning, and I finally realized you were right. I definitely could have handled things with Vanessa and Racquel a lot differently. I was wrong, but I'm going to make things up to them. Anyway, baby, I'll see you at home, okay? I love you."

Charlotte ended the call, thought about little MJ, and smiled. Her head still hurt, but she was happy out of her mind. Things were finally looking up. They were about to change forever.

Chapter 23

*C*urtis and Curtina sat at the island, her reading a book and him watching a political segment on MSNBC. He'd just heard the garage door opening, so he knew Charlotte was home. She'd left him a message earlier in the day, but he hadn't bothered calling her back. A part of him had wanted to, mostly to see where she'd spent the night and when she was coming home, but he had been too angry to dial her number. Then, about an hour ago, she'd called him again, but he'd hit Ignore as soon as her name had displayed. He loved his wife, there was no mistaking that, but sometimes he despised some of the things she did. Her actions were irrational, and there were days when he wanted to shake her and tell her to grow up. It was one thing when spoiled little children didn't get what they wanted and threw tantrums, but it was something different when you were talking about a woman in her thirties. It was uncalled for and annoying, and Curtis wished she would check herself. What he wanted was for her to realize that in the real world, people rarely got everything they demanded, but they still did what they needed to do to get along with others. They pushed forward and recognized that there was no such thing as a perfect life. Having a good life was possible, even a very blessed one, but flawlessness simply wasn't attainable.

Charlotte walked inside the kitchen, and Curtina jumped down from her chair and ran over to her.

"Mommy!"

Charlotte squeezed her tightly. "Hi, sweetie. How was school today?"

"Good, but I missed you. Where were you? And why didn't you call me?"

"Mommy had a really rough day yesterday, and she needed some time away. I'm fine now, though."

"Were you sad about something?"

"No."

"Were you upset about little MJ?"

Charlotte looked over at Curtis, but he shook his head and looked back to the television. He could tell she didn't know how to answer Curtina, who had obviously picked up on her rants about the baby over the last three weeks.

"No, honey," she lied. I just needed some time to myself. Sometimes mommies need that."

"Well, I missed you, and I wish you would take me with you next time. Maybe we can have a mommy-and-daughter sleepover."

Charlotte laughed quietly. "That's a good idea. We'll have to see about planning something like that. But more importantly, what kind of home-work do you have for this evening?"

"A lot. Our teacher has been giving us a bunch of work to do, and that doesn't leave a lot of time for me to watch my shows."

Curtis still didn't have a whole lot to say to Charlotte, but he couldn't stop himself from laughing at Curtina.

"What's so funny, Daddy?"

"You."

"What did I do?"

"Nothing," he said, "but I think you'd better go up to your room and get started." He didn't have the heart to tell her that thirty minutes of preschool homework was hardly "a bunch of work."

"Okaaaayy," she groaned. "But can I watch TV when I finish?"

"If you get done with everything before eight o'clock."

"Brianna gets to stay up until nine, so why can't I?" Brianna was one of Curtina's schoolmates.

"Because your bedtime is at eight," he said.

"I know, but why?"

"We've already been over this, little girl," Curtis said. "And the longer you stay down here asking questions you already know the answer to, the less time you'll have to watch your programs."

Curtina left the kitchen and went upstairs in a hurry.

Charlotte walked around the island, pulled out the chair next to him, and sat down. "Can I talk to you?"

Curtis didn't look at her but said, "What about?"

"Yesterday. I'm really sorry for the way I acted. I was completely out of line, and I was wrong for driving over to Chicago and not telling you until after the fact."

Curtis flipped the channel on the television.

"Baby, I know you're angry, but I promise this won't happen again. I'm even going to call Racquel first thing in the morning to see if I can go talk to her and Vanessa."

Now Curtis turned his head toward her. "So when did you decide that?"

"Today. I'm going to make peace with them and then do what you're always telling everyone else to do: let go and let God. And Curtis, what I mostly want you to know is how much I love you."

It was all he could do not to grab her into his arms, but he couldn't let her off that easy, so he turned toward the TV again.

Charlotte touched the bottom of his chin with her hand and turned his face back toward her. "Baby, I'm serious. No matter what I say or do, it never changes the way I feel about you. I love you with all my heart, and I feel awful about ruining our dinner plans. Especially on Valentine's Day. But I promise to make it up to you tonight," she said, caressing his cheek.

"How?" he said, smiling slightly.

"I think you know."

"Maybe, but why don't you explain it to me?"

"Why don't you just wait and see?"

"Actually, I'm still mad at you, so I think I'll pass."

"Come on, baby. Please forgive me. Pretty please," she begged in a playful tone.

Curtis looked at her again. "You really get under my skin sometimes, and I'll be honest. You had me so worked up last night that if I were a cursing man, I would have rattled off every word I could think of. I was just that outraged."

"I know, but I really needed that time to think and reflect, and it was worth it."

"I hope that's true."

"I'm serious. I spent the entire night at my favorite hotel all by myself."

"And there was no drinking?" Curtis hadn't wanted to think about that, but he also hadn't been able to stop worrying about the possibility.

"Of course not," she said. "I learned my lesson from that last year."

Curtis didn't know if he believed her or not, but he took her word for it for the sake of his sanity. As it was, he had other issues to concern himself with.

"Can I have a kiss?" she asked.

"You're only being this way because you know you were wrong."

"Okay, fine," she said, getting up.

But Curtis grabbed her arm and pulled her back to him. "I love you, too," he said, and kissed her.

Charlotte was a handful, to say the least, but there was no denying how much he loved her, and he didn't like arguing with her. He never liked when they weren't speaking and things weren't good between them.

They kissed for a while, until Charlotte said, "Can't you get someone else to cover Bible study tonight?"

"I was thinking the same thing," he said, still holding on to her. "I'm sure Minister Simmons will be glad to do it."

"Ha! I'm sure he will be, too. He never says no to you about anything. He'll be thrilled to death."

"You're funny. Let me call him now."

Curtis lifted his phone from the island, dialed, and waited.

"Hey, Pastor," Minister Simmons said.

"How's it going? I hate calling at the last minute, but I need a favor."

"What's that?"

"Can you teach Bible study tonight?"

"Of course," he said. Curtis wanted to laugh, because Charlotte had been right about how excited he'd be. Minister Simmons sounded as though someone had offered him a million dollars.

"I really appreciate this," Curtis said.

"I already studied ahead, anyway, so it's no problem at all."

"Really? I'm impressed."

"You mentioned the topic last week, and you know what the Bible says: 'Therefore be ye also ready,' and that's what I try to do with everything."

"That's great to hear."

"Also, Pastor, since I have you on the phone, I wanted to ask if you've thought more about my suggestion. About my starting a separate Bible study class for teens."

"I have, but I think our challenge will be getting them to attend. Many of their parents attend Bible study on Wednesdays, so I'm not sure they'll want to bring their children out on a separate evening."

"Well, what if we offered it on the same night? I could just teach it in the main seminar room."

"That's a possibility. Why don't we discuss it more at the next staff meeting?"

"Sounds good. I just want to help however I can. I know I've said this many times, but Deliverance Outreach is my life, and you can always call on me."

"I believe that, and I'm grateful for it."

"I'm serious. Even if you wanna take a long vacation, I'll be glad to speak on Sundays for as many weeks as you want."

Curtis was a little shocked by his last comment.

"That's good to know, and thanks again for leading the study session."

"I'm glad to do it. You have a good night, Pastor."

"You, too."

Curtis ended the call but wondered whether Charlotte was somewhat right about Minister Simmons and how determined he was. The whole time he'd been working there, Curtis had decided he was simply a young man with honest and innocent aspirations. Curtis had been highly motivated when he'd started out as a young minister, too, so he understood the desire to grow and move ahead quickly. Nonetheless, right now, Minister Simmons gave him pause. Or maybe it wasn't Minister Simmons at all—maybe it was Curtis's newfound paranoia in regard to who was out to get him. Because he'd learned a long time ago that even the most unsuspecting and seemingly loyal person would stab you in the back if you weren't careful. There was just no telling, and now Curtis couldn't help wondering about Minister Simmons and a slew of other folks he could think of. He didn't want to, but given the calls and the letter he'd received, he had to.

Chapter 24

C harlotte turned her car off, gathered her thoughts, mentally practiced the way she would smile, along with the words she would say, and took a deep breath. Then, she stepped out onto the pavement. A couple of hours ago, she'd called Racquel, asking if it was okay to come talk to her and her mom. Racquel had seemed shocked, of course, but the more Charlotte had promised her that it would make things better between them, the more open to it she seemed. Then, when Charlotte had asked her to check with Vanessa, interestingly enough, she'd agreed. Charlotte wasn't sure if Vanessa had said yes because she was tired of all the battling or if it was because Charlotte had asked Racquel to tell Vanessa how sorry she was and that everything was all her fault. If Charlotte had to guess, she knew it was the latter, because Vanessa believed Charlotte was to blame, anyway, and she was likely happy that Charlotte was finally admitting it. If only she knew, though, that there was a good reason Charlotte was backing down and preparing to apologize in such a genius fashion.

Charlotte walked up the brick-patterned driveway, looking across the property and then at the brick-and-stucco structure. It was a nice enough house, but Charlotte wanted something better for MJ. Neil earned a good living as a surgeon, and overall he and Vanessa did well by most people's standards, but six figures were a lot less than seven, and it showed. Curtis had worked hard to get where he was, not just with the ministry—since he took only a minimal salary from the church—but also with his speaking and writing accomplishments. His talent and charisma had earned him a lot of money, and Charlotte wanted MJ to benefit from it. She wanted her grandson to have all that he was entitled to.

She walked up to the cement porch and rang the doorbell. She heard footsteps, and the door opened. Racquel smiled.

"Hi, Mrs. Black."

"How are you, Racquel?" Charlotte said, hugging her.

"Come in."

Racquel closed the door, walked down a long

wooden hallway, and went into the family room. Charlotte followed her and thought about the baby shower that had taken place there. What a time that had been.

"Can I get you something to drink?" Racquel asked.

"No, thanks."

"Mom's on a conference call right now, so would you like to look in on little MJ? I just put him down about twenty minutes ago, but you can still take a peek if you want."

Charlotte was thrilled about seeing him, but she didn't want to seem too eager. She had to appear to be a changed woman. It was also the reason she pushed Vanessa's conference call out of her mind, because it was just another reminder of why MJ truly did belong with her and Curtis. Vanessa was simply too busy for her grandson. "I would love to, but only if you're okay with it."

"Follow me," she said, and they walked back down the hallway and went up the stairs.

As they entered the nursery, Charlotte scanned the yellow-and-lime wallpaper. This was a result of Racquel's big bright idea of not wanting to know the sex of the baby—meaning it was the reason she hadn't been able to choose any pattern with too much blue or pink. Charlotte hadn't been able to choose those colors, either, but now, Charlotte would have the nursery in their home completely redone so that it portrayed the perfect atmosphere for a boy. Worse, this nursery was way too small for little MJ. He deserved something much bigger and classier, and soon he would have it.

Charlotte moved closer to the bassinet. Her precious little grandbaby slept peacefully, and she couldn't imagine a more beautiful sight. She wanted to pick him up and cuddle him so badly, she could hardly contain herself. But she kept her cool and acted as though little MJ was no big deal; that he wasn't any more special than any other child she knew.

After a few minutes, they went back down to the family room. Vanessa was already sitting on one of the plush red chairs, and Charlotte smiled. Actually, Charlotte's smile felt so convincing she was sure Vanessa believed it was genuine, too. Charlotte was proud to be such a talented actor.

Charlotte took a seat across from her on the sofa. "Thank you for agreeing to see me. Both of you."

Racquel sat in the chair adjacent to her mother, but neither of them commented.

"Wow," Charlotte said, taking a deep breath.

"This is a little embarrassing, but I guess the first thing I want to say is that I'm sorry. I was wrong on so many levels, and when I left the restaurant yesterday, I did a lot of thinking. I thought about how unhappy both of you seem with me, and how Matthew and Curtis also blame me for what's been happening. And that's when I remembered something my grandmother used to say: 'When you can't seem to get along with anyone, it's time to ask, "Lord, is it me?"' So, that's exactly what I did. I went all the way back to the first day I met you, Racquel, and also when I finally met you, too, Vanessa, and I had to admit that I could have been a lot nicer to you both."

Racquel's face softened, but Vanessa sat with a blank stare. The wicked witch of Mitchell was going to be a lot harder to break, but Charlotte wasn't leaving there until she'd succeeded.

"I even asked myself why I felt the way I did, and it finally dawned on me, Vanessa, that I was jealous of you."

Now Vanessa raised her eyebrows and seemed more interested.

"It's true. All I could see was that the baby was going to be living with you and that you'd have a much closer relationship with him. I told myself that eventually he would love only you and Neil, and he would never want to be around Curtis and me. I know that sounds crazy, but I'm just being honest."

"But you know that would never happen, Mrs. Black," Racquel said. "Matt is little MJ's father, and you and Pastor Black are his grandparents. You're his blood relatives, and he'll always love you."

"I realize that now, but I let my fears get the best of me. And then, Racquel, even before you got pregnant, I was worried that you were trying to trap Matt. But now I know that you truly love him, and that you don't care about our money."

"I do love him."

"I know, sweetie," Charlotte said, and the tone of her voice proved again how great her acting abilities were. "That's why I also want to officially congratulate you on your engagement. I'm sorry for not acknowledging it before now. I never even asked to see your ring."

Charlotte had noticed the ring that evening they'd stopped by the Andersons' so Matthew could see them before heading to the airport. She'd seen it each time Racquel had brought the baby over, too, but she hadn't said anything. She couldn't wait to compliment her new piece of jewelry now, though.

Racquel walked over and held out her hand.

"It's absolutely beautiful," Charlotte said.

"Thank you," she beamed. "I'm so glad you like it."

It wasn't the largest ring she'd seen, but it was still pretty costly for an eighteen-year-old. Matthew didn't know it, but his credit card statement had arrived yesterday, and Charlotte had opened it this morning. He'd spent a little over three thousand dollars for it, and there was no question that she and Curtis would be the ones paying for it. Actually, since Curtis never liked having any revolving debt on their credit histories, she knew the whole thing would be paid in a matter of days. That was fine, though, because when the engagement was broken off, at least Racquel wouldn't walk away empty-handed. At least she'd have a ring to pawn if she wanted to.

Charlotte looked at Vanessa, who still seemed leery of her sincerity, so Charlotte pulled out the big guns. "There's something else I wanted to mention. Not that I'm using this as an excuse, but I'm not sure the two of you know that I lost a little girl. She fell to her death, and ever since then I've been extremely protective of Matthew, and I found myself starting to feel the same way about little MJ. I realize neither of you knows the pain of losing a child, but it's devastating. It changed me forever, but I still had no business treating either of you so badly, just because of my own insecurities and issues."

Vanessa's face softened with sympathy. "No, I had no idea. Did you know, Racquel?"

"Yes. Matt mentioned it to me, but he doesn't talk about it much."

"I'm very sorry," Vanessa said. "And as a matter of fact, I *do* know how you feel. I didn't lose a little girl, but before Racquel was born we had a son who died at birth. That's why when Racquel went into early labor I knew she could lose MJ, and I blamed you. All I could think about was my own son and that because of you, Neil and I might lose another child we loved."

Bingo. Charlotte hadn't counted on her and Vanessa relating to any of the same things, but she was glad she'd brought up the loss of Marissa. She hated using her daughter's death and memory to get what she wanted, but right now little MJ's needs were more important.

They chitchatted a while longer, but then MJ screamed out crying.

"Uh-oh, there he goes," Racquel said. "I'll be right back."

When she left, Charlotte hesitated but then said, "So he still cries a lot, doesn't he?"

"Yeah, but the doctor says he's fine. Mostly he does it because Racquel holds him all the time, and he's gotten used to it. He's spoiled rotten already, and he loves to eat. He drinks one bottle after another but never seems to get enough," she said, laughing.

Charlotte laughed with her for the sake of keeping her award-winning performance intact, but deep down she couldn't wait to leave there. She'd won Vanessa and Racquel over as much as she needed to, and it was time to move on to the next phase of things. Her conversation with Curtis last night and her visit with Racquel and Vanessa today had worked smoothly and according to plan, so now all she had to do was make another phone call to the person who was going to be a lifesaver. She'd called this kind individual yesterday afternoon during her drive home from Chicago, explaining the kind of help she needed. But now she wished she'd made the call two weeks ago when Matthew had returned to Harvard. If she had, she would already have everything she wanted. As the saying went, though, "better late than never," so all would be fine before she knew it.

Chapter 25

*C*urtis wondered when this was going to stop. He'd allowed himself to believe that when this mystery person had claimed they wouldn't be calling him again, that this also meant they wouldn't be sending any more letters. But here he was holding another envelope with the word *urgent* written across the top of it. He didn't want this awful person to expose his secret, but because the anticipation had turned dreadful, he was getting to the point where he almost wished they'd do what they were threatening to do and get it over with—almost. But then, he knew that wasn't true, because in reality he wanted no one to ever learn about that unfortunate time in his life. This morning, he'd thought about maybe telling Charlotte the whole truth and nothing but the truth, but they'd enjoyed each other in such a wonderfully passionate way last night, he hadn't been able to find the words. He also hadn't wanted to ruin her new attitude toward Racquel and Vanessa, because this was a revelation in itself.

He slowly pulled out the letter and unfolded it.

Curtis,

I'm going to keep this short, but I just had to write you one last time before your big secret goes viral. I figured the best place to start would be on the Internet, then with every major media outlet, including national newspapers and magazines. I've spent a lot of time preparing for this day, so I don't want a single soul to miss it. Not that anyone would want to miss the news of the century, anyway. This is going to be huge, but by now, you have to know that. It might not be news if maybe if you were like me, a simple nobody, but because you fought, struggled, schemed, cheated, and walked over decent people to make a name for yourself, you've reached top celebrity status; meaning that people everywhere care about everything you do, especially all your ungodly sins. Both the ones you committed in the past, like the one I know about, and also those sins people are hoping you'll commit in the future. They're hoping they'll have something to laugh and talk about. In this age of Facebook and Twitter, your story will be re-

shared and retweeted millions of times, and there will be no explaining it. You won't be able to talk your way out of this one, Curtis. You'll have to man up and deal with the situation. You'll be forced to do right by the people you've hurt. Most of all, though, I can't wait to see the terrified look on your face, probably the same look you have on your face right now while reading this letter. You must be wondering day and night when the ball is going to drop, but guess what? That's for me to know and, well...for me to know!!!! I'll bet you thought I was going to say "and for you to find out," didn't you? At least that's what me and my little friends used to say when we were kids. But not today, Mister. You see, you're not going to find out anything until the moment it happens because I want you to suffer. I'm going to go now, but in the words of Victor Newman, "You have a nice day." You have watched The Young and the Restless before, haven't you?

Curtis dropped the letter onto his desk, grabbed his face with the palms of his hands, and stroked his hair from front to back. He tried not to let this thing fluster him, but he was failing miserably, mainly because he was frantically trying to figure out a way to stop this from happening. It just wasn't possible, though, because how could he stop anything when he had no idea who was behind all this? How could he stop people from gossiping online or calling up TV and radio producers with the kind of news story that not even *Good Morning America*, CNN, or Oprah would turn down? This was even the kind of thing his favorite nighttime comedian, David Letterman, would joke about. The sad thing, though, was that to Curtis and so many others, this awful secret of his wouldn't be funny. To him it would be life-altering and catastrophic. He had a mind to call D.C., his trusted street warrior, but while D.C. had been known to handle anyone who was causing trouble, he couldn't see where D.C. would be able to do a thing about a person Curtis didn't even have a name for. He couldn't even offer him clues that might help. Last year, D.C. had saved the day when that Sharon woman had gone too far with her fatal-attraction tricks and had also started threatening him and his family, but this was different—so different that Curtis felt like crying. He was a grown man, but he wanted to weep louder than little MJ had the last time he'd seen him. The only reason he didn't was because he knew tears weren't going to help anything. They wouldn't prevent what was bound to happen, and the only thing he could do was what he'd been doing all along, and that was to keep praying.

Curtis snapped out of his misery when someone knocked at the door. "Yes?"

"Pastor, do you have a few minutes?" Minister Simmons asked.

Curtis hurried to set a stack of documents on top of the letter and envelope he'd received. "Sure. Come on in."

He opened the door, strolled in, and took a seat in front of Curtis's desk.

"So I hear Bible study went very well last night," Curtis said.

Minister Simmons nodded with excitement. "If I must say so myself, I had the Word on fire."

Curtis laughed. "Good for you."

"Actually, that's why I wanted to chat with you."

"Oh?" Curtis couldn't imagine he was going to bring up his Bible study idea again, not when they'd just discussed it by phone last night.

"Well, I was sort of wondering if you might consider letting me do the early service on Sundays."

"When you say, 'do the early service,' I'm not sure I know what you mean."

"Deliver the message."

"Oh. That would likely be fine, except the congregation expects me to give all sermons, regardless of which service they attend."

Minister Simmons seemed disappointed. "I guess I'm just trying to figure out ways I can grow as a minister."

"You will, but it takes time. The good news, too, though, is that you're definitely on the right track."

"Maybe, but I do a lot more than Minister Morgan does, yet he earns more."

Now Curtis understood better what this conversation was about. Curtis also no longer thought Minister Simmons was out to betray him the way Charlotte had sort of believed and that his ambition was all about making more money.

"I understand what you're saying," Curtis said, "but Minister Morgan has a lot more experience than you do as a minister. He was also hired a year before you."

"But everyone talks about the fact that I'm a lot more knowledgeable than he is and a better speaker. I don't mean any disrespect toward him, but I'm just sayin'."

Curtis wanted to ask him who "everyone" was, but he didn't want to sound combative. "We all have gifts, abilities, and talents in various areas, so it's hard to compare apples to oranges."

Minister Simmons clasped his hands together on his lap. "But even you say I'm a dynamic speaker."

"Because it's true, but that still doesn't take away from Minister Morgan. He's twenty-five years older than you, and he's extremely wise. I know this may be hard for you to understand, but sometimes wisdom supersedes book knowledge."

Minister Simmons showed a look of defeat. He seemed sad even. "I'm not sure what to do then."

"The same thing you've been doing. Reading and studying the Word daily, fulfilling all the responsibilities you have here at Deliverance, and giving sermons when the opportunity presents itself. I have a lot of travel dates coming up this fall, so you'll be giving a number of messages then. You and Minister Morgan."

"I don't mean to sound ungrateful," he said, "but I just wanna keep climbing. I don't wanna become stagnant, and I want you to be proud of me."

"I'm very proud of you. And it's like I told you, moving higher in the ministry takes time. It did for me and every other minister I know. Having your own congregation doesn't happen overnight.

But this is also why you see so many congregations with less than thirty members. Not all of them, but most of them were started because an assistant pastor wanted to be in control and wanted to lead his own church."

"I really appreciate you talking to me and listening," he said.

"Come see me anytime, and I hope you'll hang in there."

He scooted his chair back and laughed slightly. "Where else am I gonna go?"

"There are always other options, but I'm hoping you'll stay here. I think this is a good fit for you, and down the road you'll have your own church. At some point, we'll likely start a satellite location, and since Minister Morgan has made it clear that he's happy being an assistant until he retires, you'd certainly be a top candidate."

Minister Simmons's face brightened. "That's encouraging, and thanks for believing in me as much as you do, Pastor."

"You're quite welcome. Sometimes it helps just talking about it."

Chapter 26

*I*t was hard to believe two weeks had passed, but Charlotte had accomplished everything on her to-do list, including revamping little MJ's nursery. She stood inside the doorway with her arms folded, admiring all the changes, and just thinking about how perfect these new colors were for her little grandson gave her a warm feeling. After sitting and consulting with her decorator, she'd decided to go with baby blue, mint green, and white. Even the blankets, the sheets, the stuffed animals, the washcloths, the new clothing, and the plush pad on the seat of the rocking chair all contained hues of this particular color scheme. Some items were solid in pattern and some not, but everything down to the wallpaper, blinds, and carpet was coordinated appropriately.

She couldn't wait to introduce little MJ to his new surroundings. Surprisingly, he'd just visited three days ago, but the final touches of the new design hadn't been completed until yesterday. Charlotte hadn't seen it coming, but without warning Racquel had called her to see if she wanted to keep MJ for a few hours, and Charlotte had been thrilled. She'd known it was a result of that visit she'd paid to Racquel and Vanessa, though. Still, it had been the first time she'd gotten to spend time alone with him, and it had felt like heaven. They'd bonded in such a touching way, and after a couple of hours had passed, he hadn't seemed to cry as much. She'd held him a lot, though, even when he'd fallen asleep, so she was sure this had given him comfort. Vanessa had claimed that little MJ was spoiled, and that this was the reason he whined as much as he did, but as far as Charlotte was concerned, there was no such thing as spoiling a baby you loved. You simply held them and gave them whatever they needed, because you cared and wanted the best for them.

Charlotte thought she heard her cell phone ringing, so she hurried down the long hallway and into the master bedroom. Sure enough, it was Matthew calling.

"Hey sweetie," she said, smiling.

"Hey Mom. What's goin' on?"

"Well, actually, I was just checking out your son's nursery. I made a few changes to it."

"You crack me up."

Charlotte was glad she and Matthew were finally on good terms again. "I know you think I'm fussing over him too much, but I can't help it. Plus, now that he gets to spend some time over here, I want his room to be comfortable for him."

"I'm really proud of you for doing what you did, Mom. I've wanted to tell you that ever since you went over to visit Racquel and her mom, but I didn't know how to bring it up."

"I was wrong, Matt, and it was time I owned up to it and made amends. You and your dad had been right all along. All the drama between Vanessa and me was my fault."

"Racquel is so much happier now and so relieved. She's a good person, Mom, and she's always wanted to have a relationship with you. From the very beginning."

Charlotte almost felt guilty about the storm that was coming, but she had to remember that everything she'd done had been for her grandson. There would certainly be a few people hurt in the process, but eventually everything would settle and all would understand.

"I'm glad we were able to work things out."

"So am I," he said, "because the whole thing was really stressing me out. It took a toll on my studies—and I might as well tell you now, I got a B on my biology test and a B on the calculus."

Charlotte remembered the day he'd been trying to study—the day she and Janine had gone to the Tuxson for lunch and had run into Racquel, Vanessa, and MJ. The afternoon had gone horribly, and, of course, Racquel had called Matthew with an exaggerated story.

"Honey, I'm really sorry I caused you so many problems that week. There was no excuse for it."

"It's in the past, but I just wanted to let you know because I know how you feel about Bs."

"I know you're doing the best you can, and you can still get As for your final grades."

"We'll see. Harvard is no joke. I think I can handle it, but it takes a lot of study time. Now I'm glad I passed on playing football."

"You'll be fine. These four years will be over before you know it."

"I guess I'd better get going. Just wanted to check in and to thank you for making things right with Racquel and her mom. That was really important to me, Mom."

"I know, honey. You have a good day, okay?"

"You, too, Mom. Love you."

Charlotte ended the call and sat down on the side of the bed. She felt bad about ruining Matthew's study time and causing him to not do as well on his tests as he could have. Maybe if Racquel hadn't called him whining and complaining the way she had, things might've turned out differently. But there was no sense backtracking and trying to figure things out, because what was done was done and there was no changing it. The goal and plan now was to move ahead and on to better days. It was true that life in the Black household was about to shift pretty drastically, but Charlotte believed that when you did things for the right reasons, even if others didn't understand it, it all worked out in the end. So, again, she reminded herself that she was doing this necessary deed for little MJ.

Charlotte closed her bedroom door, just in case Agnes came upstairs to do some cleaning. Then she called her mother. "Hey, Mom."

"Hey, sweetie. Any news yet?"

"Not so far, but I'm sure we'll hear something soon."

"You sound a little hesitant," Noreen said.

"More nervous than anything," Charlotte admitted.

"I can imagine, but it's not like you had any

other options. Racquel and her mother made it pretty clear that you really didn't count when it came to MJ. I know they're treating you a little better now, but you're still doing the right thing."

"I agree, but I'll just be glad when all this passes."

"So will I, and I'm here for you if you need me."

"I'm so glad you have my back with this, Mom, because there's no one else I can share this with."

"This will always be our little secret."

Charlotte thanked God for her mother, because only a mother could love and stand by her daughter the way Noreen was doing. Not even Charlotte's father would be okay with what was about to happen, and Curtis would likely divorce her. Actually, he wouldn't *likely* do anything—he would *definitely* end their marriage. It was the reason he could never find out the truth; the reason no one except her mother and the parties who were carrying out her plan could know that Charlotte was behind everything. She'd plotted the initial idea, made the right call to the right person, and then allowed that person to take it from there. That person was Meredith Connolly Christiansen, the same trusted friend who'd paid a DNA technician to fudge the test results for Curtis and Marissa. Because of the affair she'd been having with Curtis's best friend, Aaron, Charlotte had known that there was a chance Marissa might not be Curtis's daughter, but she hadn't wanted to take a chance on losing Curtis and had called Meredith for help. Now Meredith, a woman in her early eighties and who was still the wealthiest woman in Mitchell, had come to her rescue again, and Charlotte couldn't be more grateful. The only difference this time was that Charlotte had her own money and was able to pay for services rendered. She hadn't paid the four individuals who were directly involved, but she'd gone to the bank, gotten a cashier's check, and given it to Meredith. Meredith had deposited it into her account and then taken care of the final payments.

Now Charlotte waited. Meredith had told her that because this was such a delicate situation, they had to think things through, take their time, and be extra careful. Falsifying DNA results was one thing, but the task Charlotte needed handled now was in a different category. If something went even slightly wrong, people could lose their jobs and get jail time, and Meredith didn't want that. So again, Charlotte waited to hear from her and tried to go on with business as usual. She went about her daily routine with no one suspecting anything, and she planned to keep it that way. When the grand finale commenced, Charlotte would seem more shocked than anyone. She would act as though she was in the dark about everything.

Chapter 27

Curtis scanned the upcoming itinerary that Lana had just given him. "I knew I had a lot of travel coming in the fall, but it looks like I said yes to a lot more speaking engagements than I realized."

Lana chuckled. "That you did, but what else is new?"

"It never feels like I'm taking on too much when things are booked months ahead, but this is going to be a grueling schedule. I'll have to take a vacation after this."

"That's a good idea, anyway, because you and Charlotte haven't been anywhere for a while."

"Not since our trip to the Caribbean last Thanksgiving. And it's not like I don't have someone dying to fill in for me while I'm gone."

"Who?"

"Minister Simmons. I've been meaning to tell you about the conversation we had. He wants more responsibilities, and he asked if he could take over our first service on Sundays."

"Really?"

"I explained to him that the members expect me to deliver both messages, but that he'll get lots of opportunity while I'm traveling. Then, he mentioned that Minister Morgan earns more money."

"Well, of course, he does. He's been in the ministry for years, long before he came to us."

"That's what I told him, but I'm not sure he thought it was fair."

Lana shook her head. "Minister Simmons is a nice young man who has a lot of potential, so I hope he doesn't jump ship. It wasn't long ago that he asked about starting a teen Bible study. But he needs to take things slowly and get more experience."

"I told him that, too, so we'll see. Charlotte has always thought he was a bit too motivated."

Lana crossed her legs. "I think he means well, and I'm a pretty good judge of character."

Curtis wasn't sure why the thought had just hit him, but suddenly he wished he could tell Lana about those letters he'd received. It was hard walking around with this kind of information and not being able to share it with anyone, but maybe it was best to keep it to himself. He'd done so thus far, and actually, over the last two weeks he hadn't heard a thing. He wasn't sure what to think, but he hoped this was a good sign and that maybe God had answered his prayers.

"Oh and by the way," Lana said, "we now have a date for the meeting with the architects."

"When?"

"Next Thursday."

Lana leaned forward and passed him his mini calendar, the one she updated for him every few days.

Curtis read through the document. "That gives our staff a week to pull together any questions. We need to have a brainstorming session."

"I was thinking we could do it at our normal meeting on Tuesday, but we may have to re-schedule it for Wednesday. Elder Jamison, Elder Dixon, and some of the others will just be returning from a leadership conference."

"That's right, so, yes, go ahead and make the change. But let everyone know that the meeting is mandatory and that our entire focus will be on the expansion project."

Curtis and Lana discussed a few other items until his phone rang.

Lana moved to the edge of her seat. "I'll bet that's Shelia. I asked her to call you when Dillon arrived. At least I hope so, because he's called and changed his appointment three times."

"Pastor Black," Curtis said.

"Hi, Pastor. Dillon is here to see you."

"Thanks. I'll be with him shortly."

Lana got up. "I have a few more updates for your schedule, but that's pretty much it. Is there anything else you need this afternoon?"

"No, and if I can, I'm gonna head out of here early so Charlotte, Curtina, and I can go out for pizza. Normally, we try to do it on Friday, but Curtina begged us to go tonight."

"It sounds like she loves pizza as much as Matt always did."

"Matt still loves it now. Probably eating it every chance he can get out in Boston."

"Make sure you tell him I said hello."

"I will. I'm sure he'll be home again in a couple of weeks."

"He must be thrilled about Charlotte and Racquel becoming closer."

"We're all glad about that. There's been so much peace in the house lately."

"Okay, I'm outta here," she said. "I'll send Dillon in."

Curtis sipped some of his bottled water and moved his travel itinerary to the side of his desk.

"Hey, Pastor," Dillon said, walking in.

Curtis stood and shook his hand. "Well, it's about time."

"I know, and I apologize," he said, sitting down. "I wanted to meet with you, but I just couldn't seem to pull it together."

"How have things been going?"

"Worse than ever."

"Have you been going to meetings?"

"I tried it again the day after Melissa and I met with you, but I just don't see myself doing that on a regular basis. Felt too outta place."

"What about the scriptures I gave you?"

"Sometimes I read them, and sometimes I don't. Even when I pray, that doesn't seem to help, either."

"I'm sorry to hear that."

"I'm totally at a loss, and now Melissa wants to call off the wedding"

"That's what I was afraid of. She wasn't too happy the last time she was here, but you have to understand her point."

"I do, but I also can't get a handle on this thing. My urges and desires are getting worse."

"How so?"

"The other night I almost took a stripper home with me."

"That's the worst thing you can do."

"I know, but I could barely control myself."

Curtis hated hearing this. Dillon's addiction was in full force, and unless he truly wanted to quit, he was doomed. He also needed to attend those Sex Addicts Anonymous meetings.

"If you don't mind," Curtis said, realizing there was only one thing he could do for him, "I'd like to pray for you."

"Now?"

"Yes."

Curtis got up, walked around his desk, and rested his hand on the top of Dillon's head. Then he closed his eyes. "Father God, we come right now, asking You to remove all lustful desires from Dillon's spirit. We ask that you give him the kind of peace he needs and to fill whatever void he is struggling with. Lord, we ask that You would give him the will and determination to do whatever necessary to beat the enemy and to eliminate all association with porn videos, strip clubs, and the women who are connected to them. Father God, we ask that You bless and protect Dillon from all harm and danger and that You would guide his every thought and footstep, and all decisions. Be with him, Father, at all times, during every waking moment and even when he is sleeping. Lord, we lay every ounce of this problem before You and ask that You would remove it from Dillon's life completely. Then, Lord, we ask that You would give Melissa the strength and understanding she needs at this time. Please comfort her and guide her decisions as well. Father God, we ask these and all other blessings in your precious son Jesus' name. Amen...amen...praise God...amen."

Curtis placed his hand on Dillon's shoulder. "You're going to be fine. You just have to trust and believe in God. Keep your faith strong and completely give your life over to Him. You're dealing with a serious demon, and it's going to take a lot of work and attention."

"Thank you, Pastor, for taking so much time with me."

"I'm glad to do it. There is maybe something else you can try, though, if things don't get better."

"Like?"

"Going to a residential rehab facility. There are many in-treatment locations for drug and alcohol use, but there are definitely places designed for the problem you're having, too."

Dillon sat there emotionless. Curtis could tell he wasn't all that open to his suggestion.

"I'm gonna try this on my own for a little while longer," he finally said. "Then, I'll go from there."

"Just let me know."

"I do have one request, though, Pastor. If it won't be too much of a burden."

"Of course, what is it?"

"If I find myself caught up again and planning to take some woman home with me, can I call you?"

"Definitely. I'll give you my cell number."

"I really appreciate that. If I'd had your number the other night, I would have called you then. I fought the urge to sleep with that woman on my own, but I'm not sure what'll happen if I go to that strip club again."

"Maybe you should call me *before* you go there. I'm hoping you won't, but if you can't stop yourself, I'd rather talk to you then."

"That's a good idea."

Curtis felt bad for Dillon, because he remembered what life had been like for him a long time ago and even in recent years. He'd loved sex and women more than anything else, and he'd struggled daily, trying to overcome it. If he was honest, he'd have to admit that it was because of carnal desires that he'd done that awful thing so many years ago. Sex wasn't the only part of it, but it had played a major role.

But Curtis didn't want to think about that now, not when he needed to keep his focus on Dillon and helping him. So that was what he did: focus on Dillon. That way he could pretend his own skeletons didn't exist.

"I really appreciate everything you're trying to do, Pastor," Dillon said.

"You're welcome. We'll keep working on this."

"I'm really gonna try harder, but I hope it's not too late. I hope Melissa doesn't leave me for good."

Curtis hoped the same thing, but if Dillon didn't get it together soon his relationship with Melissa would be history. It was practically inevitable.

Chapter 28

O h my God, Mom!" Matthew said. "You have to get over to Racquel's!"

"Why, honey, what's wrong?"

"Children and Family Services is trying to take MJ!"

"What? Take him where?"

"They're trying to take him away from Racquel!"

"What are you talking about, Matt? Are you sure?"

"Yes, so Mom, please go get him. Go get him now before they give him to some foster home."

"Oh God, no. Okay, honey, let me grab my purse and I'll call you when I get there."

Charlotte hung up the phone and tried to calm her nerves. This was the call she'd been waiting for, but she hadn't thought it was going to be today. She also hadn't considered that Racquel or Vanessa would call Matthew first. She hated this for her son, because she could hear how distraught he was, but thankfully, all would be back to normal very soon.

Charlotte rushed down the staircase, quickly explained to Agnes what was going on, and told her she was headed over to the Andersons'.

"Oh dear Lord," Agnes said. "This is crazy. There must be some sort of mistake."

"Has to be," Charlotte said, "but I'll keep you posted."

Charlotte went into the garage, got in her car, backed out, and sped down the driveway. As soon as the iron gate opened, she checked both ways for traffic and stepped on the accelerator. She hurried, because that was what everyone would expect her to do after hearing such upsetting news, but she knew little MJ was going to be fine. No one would be taking him anywhere, because she'd paid a lot of money to make sure they didn't. She did wonder, though, why Meredith hadn't called to warn her ahead of time, but maybe her contact hadn't gotten in touch with her.

She slammed on her brakes, almost running a red light, and realized she'd better call Curtis. He would certainly want to know and would jump in his SUV and be on his way to the Andersons' ASAP. But when she dialed his number, the call went straight to voice mail without ringing. At first, she wondered why, but then she realized Matthew had probably contacted him. Again, she hated this for her son, because no matter how much she knew she was doing the right thing for all of them, she didn't want to hurt him. She didn't want Matthew to worry about his son any more than he needed to, but once he knew MJ was safe he would feel a lot better. He would be a lot calmer as the evening and the next few days went on.

When the light changed, Charlotte took off and then her phone rang. It was Curtis, so she prepared to be just as upset and flustered as Matthew was.

"Oh my God, baby, I just tried to call you," she said, sounding as though she were crying, though no tears fell.

"I just hung up with Matt. But what happened?"

"I don't know. He didn't tell me any details. All he said was that he wanted me to go over there."

"This doesn't make any sense," Curtis said. "Why would DCFS be making any accusations at all about little MJ?"

"It's crazy, Curtis. They must have the wrong baby."

"They have to, because there's no way Racquel

would ever hurt MJ," he said. "And neither would her parents."

"Are you meeting me over there?" she asked, almost hoping he wasn't so she could deal with this on her own.

"I'm only a few miles away. I was in my truck before I hung up with Matthew."

"Racquel must be scared to death," Charlotte said. "Poor, poor thing."

"I'm sure she is. Anyone would be if DCFS showed up out of nowhere to take their baby."

Charlotte stopped at another red light, pulled down her visor, flipped open the lighted mirror, and checked her makeup. "We'll get this straightened out in no time. This has to be a mix-up."

"Of course it is, but I still hate it's happening. Racquel and Matthew don't deserve this, and neither do Neil and Vanessa."

Charlotte retouched her lipstick. "I'm so disturbed by this, I can barely drive. I'm a nervous wreck."

"You be careful," he said. "We definitely don't need you having an accident."

"I'm almost at their subdivision."

"Then I'll be right behind you."

"I'll just wait outside in the car for you."

"See you soon."

Charlotte drove into the subdivision, then curved around the first street and down the one the Andersons lived on. There was a police car parked out front, and some white midsize vehicle parked in the driveway. She guessed that this one belonged to the caseworker.

She drove closer, slowed down when she passed the driveway, and parked on the opposite side of the street. She had a mind to call her mother, but if someone looked outside and saw her on her phone they might wonder what she was doing. Thankfully, Curtis drove past and parked in front of her, so she got out. Curtis grabbed her hand and they walked onto the sidewalk, up the drive, and onto the front stoop. As soon as Curtis rang the doorbell, Vanessa opened the door in tears. She even reached out and hugged Charlotte.

"Vanessa, what happened?" Charlotte said, caressing her back. "What's going on?"

"Someone called and said that MJ wasn't being handled properly. They said he was being hurt, and now there's a chance we'll be charged with child endangerment."

"What does that mean?"

"DCFS got a call from someone who said they heard MJ crying and that when they looked outside, they saw me yelling at him to stop. They said I dropped his carrier onto the pavement so hard, they thought he was going to tip over onto his face."

"That's ridiculous," Charlotte said, knowing she was the one who'd suggested that the "eye-witnesses" use crying as part of their made-up accusations. Crying babies could prove to be very irritating for new mothers and for anyone else who lived in the house with them, so Charlotte had thought this particular allegation would be perfect—especially since MJ did in fact cry a lot.

"I would never do that," Vanessa continued. "My car was already out in the driveway, and all I did was put his carrier inside and secure the seat belt. And on top of that, he was asleep."

"Did they say who reported this?" Curtis asked.

"Just that it was one of our neighbors, but they won't tell us who."

"Where's Racquel?" Curtis asked.

"She's upstairs with the caseworker, packing MJ's clothing."

"But if the accusation is against you," Charlotte asked, "why did Matt say they were trying to take MJ away?" Charlotte already knew the answer, but she had to play along. She had to make Vanessa, Curtis, and the officer believe she was desperately concerned about the situation.

"Because the call about me wasn't the only one," Vanessa said sadly. "Another witness called a couple of hours later, saying that yesterday they saw a young girl walking down the aisle at the pharmacy yelling at her baby and telling him that she wished he'd never been born. They said she told him if he didn't stop crying, she was going to throw him in a garbage dumpster. Then, supposedly, the person waited until Racquel went outside, and when they saw her toss MJ's carrier into the car, they wrote down her license plate number."

Curtis frowned, and Charlotte could tell he wanted to punch something. "That's the silliest thing I've ever heard, and how can words be considered child endangerment?" he asked.

Vanessa's eye makeup streaked down her cheeks. "They're taking the baby because there were two complaints in two days about two different adults in the same home. When this happens, they can't take any chances—they have to do an investigation."

"Did Racquel take the baby to the pharmacy?"

"Yes, but all she did was purchase some baby oil, and then she was out of there. She said MJ was a little whiny just like he always is, but she never yelled or said those awful things to him."

"Does Neil know?" Curtis asked.

"He's in surgery."

Charlotte almost felt sorry for Vanessa—almost—and although it was sad to say, given the fact that Racquel definitely must have needed her father right now, Charlotte was glad Neil wasn't there, and she hoped that she and Curtis were out of there before he got home. With the exception of the night she and Curtis had brought Matthew by there on the way to the airport, she hadn't seen Neil since the time he'd held her in that hospital conference room. She had purposely and successfully avoided him, and she wanted to keep it that way. "So what's going to happen now? I mean, it's not like they can take MJ away just because of hearsay."

Vanessa wiped her face with her hands. "They can, and they are."

"Can we go and talk to this *caseworker*?" Curtis asked the male officer.

The man stepped forward, and he acted as though he would physically stop Curtis if he tried to go upstairs. "Unfortunately, no," the officer said. "They'll be down very soon, and you can speak to her then."

"We've already tried to reason with her," Vanessa added, "but the decision has already been made."

"Oh my God," Charlotte exclaimed. "What's going to happen to MJ?"

"Well...we were hoping the two of you would take him. The caseworker has already spoken to Matthew, and she says it won't be a problem."

Charlotte wanted to burst with excitement. Her plan was working perfectly, and not even Curtis or Vanessa suspected she had anything to do with this. "Of course we will."

Curtis sighed. "We wouldn't have it any other way, but I just hate that you and Racquel have been accused of something you didn't do. These accusations are outrageous."

"This is such a nightmare," Vanessa said, clasping her hands together and pressing them under her chin. She looked as though she hadn't slept in weeks. Poor, pitiful thing.

"This will all be straightened out in no time," Curtis said.

"This is true, Vanessa, so try not to worry," Charlotte said, but she also thought about how she was going to do everything she could to keep MJ permanently. She would convince Matthew to break off that silly engagement to Racquel, file for full custody of his son, and then encourage him to finish all four years at Harvard the way he'd planned.

Charlotte, Curtis, and Vanessa looked toward the top of the stairs when they saw the slender, fifty-something caseworker carrying little MJ. Thankfully, he was sleeping. Next came a short and stocky female officer, followed by Racquel, who slowly toted MJ's suitcase and baby bag. Tears flooded her face, and soon she stopped for a few seconds, trying to keep her balance.

"Are you Pastor and Mrs. Black?" the caseworker asked.

"Yes," Curtis answered.

"I'm Linda Jacobs. I spoke to your son, and he and Racquel have decided they want the two of you to care for their son. Are you agreeable with that?"

"Yes," Curtis said.

"Mrs. Black?" she said.

Charlotte nodded. "Yes."

"We'll have to run a quick background check, which will only take a few minutes, but after that you can take him with you."

The woman passed him over to Charlotte, and though MJ nestled into his blanket and stretched his little arms, he never woke up.

But Racquel dropped the bags and fell onto the stairs, weeping loudly. "Why are you taking my baby from me? MJ is my whole world, and my mom and I would never hurt him! We would never do what those people said!"

"I'm very sorry," Linda said, "but we have no choice."

"Oh God, I'm just begging you," Racquel pleaded with massive tears soaking her face, screaming. "Please…don't…take…my…baby. What am I gonna do without MJ…" Her voice trailed off, and her chest heaved up and down. She was becoming hysterical, and Vanessa rushed up the stairs, sat next to her, and held her.

Linda looked on with sadness but stepped into the living room to make a call. Charlotte assumed she was doing the mini background check she'd mentioned, the one Meredith had already briefed her about days ago. It was standard procedure, but of course she and Curtis would be approved instantly.

Charlotte wished there had been another way. She found no joy in taking any child from a parent, but as she gazed down at little MJ, one thing hadn't changed: she knew she was doing the right thing. She wasn't MJ's mother but she was the next best thing, and he was going to be so much better off living with her and Curtis. Life would be good for their little grandson from now on.

Chapter 29

*C*harlotte drove into the garage and was glad to be home. When the caseworker had authorized them to take little MJ, Racquel had lost it even more. She'd rushed out the door behind them, yelling and screaming, and Vanessa had held her back as much as possible. At one point, when Curtis had turned to look at her, he'd broken into tears himself. It had been too much for him to bear, and now as he pulled in next to her and got out of his SUV, Charlotte could tell he still wasn't happy.

She stepped out of her car, too, opened the back door, unfastened the seat belt, and slid MJ out of his carrier. He'd been fast asleep, but now he was wide awake, rustling around in her arms and looking at her.

Curtis walked around his vehicle, unlocked the door leading to the kitchen, and disarmed the security system. "I'll bring his bags in."

"Thanks," she said.

Charlotte repositioned her shoulder bag and walked inside. As soon as she did, however, MJ started to fret.

"Ohhh, what's the matter?" she said, rocking him. But it did no good, as MJ whined louder. "Are you hungry, sweetie? Is that what the problem is?"

Curtis came in, set the little suitcase down on the floor and MJ's baby bag on the island.

"Here," Charlotte said. "Hold him while I fix his bottle."

Curtis took his grandson and sat down in one of the chairs. "It's okay," he told the baby, trying to calm him. "Papa's baby is going to be just fine."

Charlotte pulled one of his bottles from the bag, turned on the faucet, and waited for the water to warm up. When it did, she held the bottle under it for a bit, squirted a few drops on the top of her hand, and went back over to where Curtis was sitting. Now MJ cried real tears.

"Okay, okay, okay," she said, taking him back and cradling him in her arm. "Here you go, sweetie."

MJ acted as though he hadn't eaten in weeks, and before long he'd sucked the formula so intensely, he had to stop every now and then to catch his breath.

Curtis raised his eyebrows and smiled. "Our grandson's a greedy little baby, isn't he?"

Charlotte thought about the comment Vanessa had made about that very thing. "I guess so."

She sat in the kitchen until MJ finished eating, then she tossed a soft cloth across her shoulder, held him upright, and gently patted his back. When he'd given one last burp, she got up and saw that he was sound asleep.

"I'm going to go put him down," she said to Curtis, who seemed sad again.

"That's a good idea. I'll call Matt. I spoke to him on the way home, and he was in tears, baby."

"Once I get MJ situated, I'll call him, too. This whole thing was totally unexpected, so I'm sure he's pretty upset."

Charlotte went up the stairs and while she'd been planning to lay MJ down in his bassinet, she couldn't help sitting down with him in the wooden rocker. "You're finally home where you belong," she whispered to him. "And no one loves you more than I do."

She rocked back and forth and closed her eyes. It had taken a lot of maneuvering and plotting, but she'd finally gotten what she wanted. MJ was there with them for good, and she no longer had to worry about visitation. She didn't have to ask Racquel or anyone else when she could see him or when he would be able to sleep over.

Charlotte rocked in the chair for what seemed like a whole hour, but when she heard someone knocking, she opened her eyes. Curtina and Agnes eased the door open and strolled in. Agnes had picked Curtina up from school, so they'd probably just gotten home.

Charlotte pressed her forefinger against her lips, letting Curtina know that right now even her inside voice would be too loud, and that she needed to whisper.

"Hi, Mommy," she said softly. "Can I hold little MJ?"

"No, sweetie you'll wake him, and he's also too small. You can hold him when he's older."

Interestingly enough, Curtina didn't ask any more questions, but she couldn't stop admiring her baby nephew.

"So how was school?"

"Good," she said, a little louder than a few seconds ago.

Charlotte pressed her finger against her lips again.

"Sorry, Mommy," Curtina whispered.

"He's such a fine-looking little man," Agnes said.

Charlotte smiled and stood up. Since MJ was still asleep, she figured it was best to lay him down while she could. She'd purchased two bassinets, the one there in the nursery, and the one downstairs in the family room, and she was glad she'd remembered everything.

She pulled the blanket over the lower half of his body, lifted the baby monitor from the dresser, and she, Agnes, and Curtina tiptoed out. When she closed the door, leaving it slightly cracked, Curtina said, "Is MJ spending the night with us?"

"Actually, sweetie, he's going to be staying for a while."

"Yayyy! Is Matt coming home, too?"

"Maybe this weekend."

"I can't wait to see him."

"Honey, I have to make a couple of phone calls, so why don't you go downstairs with your dad? I'll be there as soon as I can."

"Okay." Curtina turned and headed down the hallway.

"I'm really sorry that this happened, Miss Charlotte. I know you and Mr. Curtis don't mind keeping little MJ, but poor Racquel must be devastated."

Right after Charlotte and MJ had left the Andersons, Charlotte had called Agnes and updated her.

"She really took it hard, and I totally understand," Charlotte said. "People are so dirty and cruel nowadays, so there's no telling why someone has lied on her and Vanessa."

"The truth will prevail, though," Agnes assured her. "God will see to it."

Charlotte forced a smile onto her face, but Agnes's words troubled her. This wasn't the kind of comment she wanted to hear, so she quickly pushed it from her mind. "I'm sure it will."

"Well, I'm going to warm up dinner and head home," Agnes said. "But let me know if you need anything before I go."

"Thanks for everything. I think we'll be fine, so I'll just see you tomorrow."

Charlotte went into her bedroom and closed the door. She pulled out her phone to call Matthew, but first she took deep breaths to settle her nerves. She knew she had to sound the way he expected her to sound or this conversation wouldn't go well. She needed to show as much sympathy and compassion toward Racquel as possible.

The phone rang two times before Matthew answered. "Hey, Mom."

"Hey, son...how are you?"

"Not good, and I don't know if Racquel can take this. After you and Dad took MJ, her mom said she laid around like a zombie. She wouldn't even talk to me."

"She was having a very tough time while we were there, and I was heartbroken. She doesn't deserve this and neither does Vanessa. But you know they're innocent, Matt."

"I may have to come home."

"Honey, I know you want to and I understand why, but you really can't afford to miss more days. And you know we'll take very good care of MJ."

"I know that, but Racquel needs me."

"Well, you should at least go to class tomorrow."

"Tomorrow is already Friday, so I'd only be missing one day."

Charlotte wanted to say more, but she could tell how adamant he was about flying home and she didn't want to anger him.

"I need to check on Racquel again," he said, almost as if he couldn't think about anything else. "I'll call you back, Mom."

"Okay, honey."

Charlotte ended the call and wanted to call Meredith to thank her for all she'd done. But since

Curtis might walk into the room at any time, she decided it was best to wait until he left for the church in the morning. She had called her mom during the drive from Racquel's, right after she'd called Agnes, and of course Noreen couldn't have been happier.

But then it dawned on her. She still hadn't called Janine. She hurried to dial her number because had Charlotte not planned this DCFS episode and hadn't seen it coming, Janine would have been one of the first people she would have contacted. If she didn't tell her until tomorrow or another day, Janine might get suspicious.

"Hey, girl," Janine said.

"J, you'll never believe what happened this afternoon."

"What?"

"DCFS took MJ from Racquel."

"What? Why?"

"It's a long story, but apparently two accusations were made. One by a neighbor about Vanessa and one by someone in a store about Racquel. They were accused of child endangerment."

"No!"

"Yes. Racquel called Matt, and he called us. So, we had to go get MJ."

"He's in your custody?"

"Yes, but only until the investigation is complete."

"I don't get this," she said.

"Neither do we. It doesn't make any sense."

"So, they accused both Vanessa and Racquel?"

"Yes, and when that happens, DCFS can remove the child."

"Gosh, I really don't know what to say. And poor Racquel. She must be crazy out of her mind. I know I would be."

Charlotte sat on the side of the bed. "She's pretty upset and so is Matt."

"Is he coming home?"

"He wants to, but I'm trying to get him to stay."

"This is so unfair to both of them. Yes, they made a mistake, but they're good kids and they don't deserve this."

"I know. I'm just sick over this whole thing, and I'll be glad when Racquel and her mom are cleared."

"Well, at least they have you and Curtis. And if you need me to babysit or do anything else, just call."

"I really appreciate that, J, and please keep us in your prayers."

"Of course. I'm going to pray daily that Racquel

is reunited with MJ, and that the people who did this are found and arrested."

It wasn't until now that Charlotte thought about something. Why hadn't anyone considered that maybe the accusations might hold some relevance? Why hadn't anyone realized that even the most innocent-looking people could be guilty as charged? Instead, Curtis, Matthew, Agnes, and Janine were mad at the world because of the *lies* someone had told on Racquel and Vanessa, and they wanted justice. To them, Racquel and Vanessa simply weren't capable of abusing little MJ, and Charlotte just wished people weren't so trusting. This was the very reason so many children truly were abused and nothing was ever done about it.

"Well, I just wanted to fill you in, but I'd better go," she said to Janine.

"I'll check on you guys tomorrow."

"Thanks, J."

Charlotte ended the call and was sort of glad it was over. She loved Janine, but she could tell she was planning to do exactly what she'd said: pray every single day until MJ was returned to his mother—and until the "people" who were behind these accusations got what was coming to them. Janine didn't know it, but she was praying for bad things to happen to her own best friend. It was the reason Charlotte would have to limit her conversations with her. At least until she figured out a way to keep MJ for good and everyone accepted it.

Chapter 30

Charlotte smoothed baby lotion across MJ's arms and chest, and he happily kicked his legs. She'd just finished giving him a bath, and this was one thing he seemed to like. Charlotte was glad, because last night he'd cried on and off for hours until she'd finally had to get up for good, go into his nursery, and hold him. She'd rocked him for so long that she'd eventually dropped off to sleep herself, and it hadn't been until Curtis had come in around six a.m. that she'd woken up. Before then, Curtis hadn't even noticed she was missing from their bed, but this morning he'd told her that if this continued she should just wake him. He wanted to help take care of MJ as much as he could, and Charlotte appreciated that, especially since it had been years since they'd had to get up with a baby in the middle of the night.

Charlotte dressed MJ in a baby-blue-and-white

onesie and rubbed a tiny bit of baby oil between her hands. She delicately massaged it across his hair and then skimmed over it with his tiny little brush. He didn't seem to mind that, either, so maybe he was just the kind of baby who enjoyed feeling clean and refreshed. Charlotte also knew that once he got used to being with her versus living with Racquel and Vanessa, he'd soon be sleeping through the night and wouldn't need someone to hold him all the time. He just needed to become familiar with his new environment and the people around him.

Charlotte cradled him in her arms. "So does that feel better, sweetie?" She smiled at him, and the joy stirring in her heart was unexplainable. She wondered if all grandmothers felt this way about their first grandchild, because she'd never experienced anything comparable. Curtis certainly loved his grandson, too—she could tell by the way he gazed at him and the way he cuddled him—but she didn't believe Curtis or anyone else could love MJ as much as she did. She was sure Matthew and Racquel loved him a great deal, but her feelings for MJ were on a whole other level. MJ would know she was his grandmother, but when he was older he'd tell others how his nana had been more like a mother to him.

Charlotte fed MJ, rocked him to sleep, then laid him in his bassinet. Curtis had already left for the church, Curtina was at school, and Agnes was at a doctor's appointment, so Charlotte was finally free to call Meredith. She answered on the second ring.

"It's good to hear from you," she said. "I've been wondering how things were going."

"Everything's great, and thank you, Meredith. I couldn't have done this without you."

"You were very kind to me right after my husband passed away, and I've never forgotten that."

When Curtis and Charlotte had first founded Deliverance Outreach, she'd worked as a paralegal for Schaefer, Williamson, and Goldberg, one of the top law firms in Mitchell, and this was how she and Meredith had met. Meredith's husband had owned a number of companies, but after he passed, she'd fired the current legal team and hired Charlotte's bosses. As time had gone on, when it had become necessary for Meredith to come in to sign numerous documents, Charlotte had been the person to meet with her. They'd hit it off from the very beginning, and Meredith had become her mentor. She'd even advised Charlotte on her personal life and had given her many words of wisdom.

Then, as their relationship had progressed, she'd told Charlotte that if there was ever anything she could do for her, all Charlotte had to do was ask. This, of course, was the second time she'd had to do so, and she couldn't be more grateful to her friend.

"I wanted to tell you, too," Meredith said, "that the reason I didn't call you right before DCFS showed up was because I thought it would be better if you were naturally surprised. That way your reaction wouldn't seem orchestrated."

"I wondered why I hadn't heard from you, but I'm glad you didn't call, because it worked. I was totally caught off guard, and I responded to Matt and everyone else accordingly."

"So how is Matthew taking the news?"

"Not well. He's already called twice this morning, and he's flying home tonight or tomorrow."

"Did the caseworker say how long the investigation will take? That was the one thing my contact never told me."

"No, but I looked online and read that it could be thirty to ninety days. It just depends."

"Have you thought about what you're going to do if the mother and grandmother are cleared?"

"By then, I'll have gotten Matthew to call off his engagement and file for custody."

"Do you think he'll really do that?"

"If I'm persuasive enough. I just need to get him to see how wrong Racquel is for him."

Meredith didn't respond.

"Is there something wrong?" Charlotte asked, not understanding why the conversation had turned awkward.

"Well, I guess I'm not sure how well this is going to end. I'd told you long ago that if I could ever do anything for you I would, but I have to tell you…I never felt good about taking someone's baby. I just feel so sorry for that poor mother. I also think you need to make sure you've covered all your tracks, because if this backfires I'm not sure your son will ever forgive you. I've covered everything on my end, but all I'm saying is that you should be careful."

Charlotte heard her, but she didn't see where she had anything to worry about. She'd done right by her grandson, and God was going to honor that. "Matt has been upset with me many times before, but he's always gotten over it."

"This is different, though. You've hurt the young woman he loves, and you've taken their son away."

"It'll all work out. You'll see."

"I hope so, but just be sure about what you're

doing. The deed is done, but once the baby's mother is cleared you could easily give your grandson back and pretend this never happened. You could do the right thing."

Charlotte hadn't come this far for nothing. "MJ will be so much better off with Curtis and me. We'll be fine."

"It's your choice, of course, but because my part in this is really troubling me, I thought I should tell you: I've been having a lot of come-to-Jesus moments, and my conscience has been getting the best of me."

"Why?" Charlotte asked.

"Let's just say I've been a little under the weather, and at my age you never know when you're last day is coming. I've done a lot of things in my life that I'm very sorry for, and if I could take this one back, I would. I'm starting to lose sleep over it."

Charlotte wondered where all these morals and regrets were coming from. "I appreciate everything you've done for me, and taking MJ really was necessary. Not everyone is meant to be a mother, and unfortunately, Racquel wasn't ready. She's too young, and now that she doesn't have a baby to take care of, she'll be able to go to college with no worries or responsibilities. She may not see it now, but someday she'll be thankful things happened the way they did."

"I hear everything you're saying, but I'm also trying to get you to see that you can correct this. You don't have to continue with this scheme."

Charlotte could appreciate these come-to-Jesus moments Meredith had mentioned, but she hoped Meredith would get over them soon—at least until Matthew was able to take MJ from Racquel for good. Charlotte had always been able to trust Meredith, and she prayed her friend wouldn't disappoint her. There was also no room for anything or anyone who could end up ruining things.

It was the reason Charlotte chatted with Meredith for another five minutes but then ended the call. As soon as she did, though, her phone rang, and Racquel's name and number displayed. Charlotte held the phone in her hand, listening to it ring and watching the screen, but she never answered it. Maybe she would have, had it not been for all the times she'd tried calling Racquel and Racquel had ignored her. When the ringing stopped, she heard MJ crying through the baby monitor, so she went to the nursery and picked him up. He hadn't slept even thirty minutes this time, so Charlotte took him with her to the family room. She knew he couldn't be hungry. Thankfully, before long, he settled down and just looked at her. He seemed content, and now Charlotte knew everyone was right about his wanting to be held all the time. He loved it, but she would have to find a means to break him from that. Matthew hadn't acted this way, nor had Marissa, so this was something very new for Charlotte. Although, maybe it was like she'd been thinking earlier—MJ just needed to get used to them.

Charlotte flipped on the television, but her phone rang again. She shook her head when she saw that it was Racquel. It had only been ten minutes since her first call, and Charlotte wasn't planning to answer this time, either. Then, when her cell stopped ringing, the house phone rang, and Charlotte got up and walked over to it. It was Racquel again. Charlotte wasn't in the mood for hearing all the crying she knew Racquel would do, but maybe she would call her back later. Maybe once Matthew got home, he could deal with her, and Charlotte wouldn't have to talk to her at all.

She waited a few minutes and then called her mother.

"Hey, honey," Noreen said.

"Hey."

"So how's my great-grandson?"

"He's good. Just laying here in my arms."

"Did he sleep well last night?"

"Not at all, and he likes to be held a lot."

Noreen laughed. "Like you."

Charlotte hadn't thought about that and laughed, too. "I guess you're right. I was just thinking about Matt and Marissa and how they rarely cried about anything, but maybe he got this from me."

"I'm sure he did, because you were awful. You only slept if you were in my arms, your father's, or someone else's. You really didn't care who held you, just as long as you didn't have to lie in your crib."

"Well, I hope this gets better."

"It will, but I can't say when."

"Oh well. But hey, are you and Daddy still driving over this afternoon?"

"Yes, we were planning to leave by noon, but your dad had a few things to do this morning. We'll be in the car by one, though."

"Sounds good," Charlotte said, looking to see who was beeping her phone. "Mom, this is Curtis, so I'll call you back, okay?"

Noreen told her they would just see her in a few hours, and Charlotte pressed the button.

"Hey," she said.

"Hey. Look, I have a conference call in a few minutes, but did Racquel try to call you? She says she tried you twice but didn't get an answer."

Charlotte rolled her eyes toward the ceiling. "I haven't checked my phone. MJ just woke up, so I had to feed him again," she lied. "I also just got off the phone with Mom. Maybe she called and left a message."

"She says she called the house phone, too."

"If she did, I didn't hear it."

"Well, baby, please call her back. She wants to know how MJ is doing."

"I will."

"I'll call you later," he said. "Oh, and one more thing. Matt's taking an eleven o'clock flight, so he's already at the airport in Boston. He just called me."

"That's great," she said. She'd been hoping Matthew wouldn't arrive until late tonight or sometime tomorrow, though, because that way he'd have very little time to spend with Racquel. He'd have to return to school on Sunday evening, so if he hadn't come home until tomorrow, they'd have only one day together.

"Okay, I have to go," Curtis said. "Love you."

MJ had only been away from the Andersons for one day, actually not even twenty-four hours yet,

so Racquel needed to get a grip. She was starting to annoy Charlotte. But Charlotte knew if she
didn't call her back, the next thing Racquel would
do was complain to Matthew. So she forced herself to dial the number.

"Hello?" Racquel answered in panic mode.

"I'm sorry I missed your call," Charlotte told
her.

"Is MJ okay?"

"He's fine."

"Did he sleep well?"

"Yes."

"Has he been crying a lot?"

"Not at all."

"Is he eating all right?"

"Yes."

"Mrs. Black, I miss him so much. Can you believe this is happening?" she said. Charlotte heard
tears in her voice.

"No, I can't, but this is only temporary. We all
know you and your mom are innocent, so you've
got to hang in there, sweetie. You have to be patient."

"But I'm his mother, and he needs me. I need
him."

Charlotte looked down at MJ, who was still lying in her arms, wide awake. "I think he's about

to go to sleep, so I'd better go. I can call you back if you want, though."

"Do you mind putting the phone up to his ear? I just wanna tell him how much I love him."

What a waste of time, Charlotte thought, but she placed the phone up to MJ's ear, anyway. She only did it as a way to get rid of Racquel, but she hoped this wouldn't be a daily request. She wanted Racquel to stop calling her, period.

Chapter 31

*M*atthew hadn't had a lot to say during the drive from O'Hare, but mostly it was because he'd been on the phone with Racquel for most of the way. Now he and Curtis walked into the kitchen, and Curtina rushed toward him.

"Hey, Matt!"

"Hey, little girl." He leaned down and hugged her. Then he pulled her ponytails. There was no mistaking that Matthew was six foot two, but for some reason he seemed to tower over his sister more than usual. Maybe Curtis was noticing how tall he was, because though Matt was eighteen and attending college, he was still a child at heart. He was mature in many ways, responsible even, but he was still very young to have his own son.

Matthew hugged his mother and grandparents, who had driven over from Chicago.

"It's so good to see you, honey," Noreen said.

"Glad you made it safely," Joe added.

"Thanks, Grandpa," Matthew said, already on his way over to the bassinet. He carefully picked up MJ, but he seemed nervous. Curtis knew it was because he wasn't used to holding newborns on a regular basis.

Everyone looked on, not saying anything, but then Matthew turned around. His eyes watered, and Curtis was sad for his son. He'd been through a lot lately. First, getting his girlfriend pregnant during their senior year in high school, then having a premature baby while miles away at college, then dealing with the drama his mother had caused with Racquel and Vanessa, then having a hard time focusing on his exams, and now dealing with this DCFS disaster.

MJ was sound asleep, but Matt looked at him and said, "I'm taking MJ out for a while."

Curtis saw how he wasn't able to make eye contact with any of them and knew what he was up to. His real plan was to take the baby to see Racquel. He hadn't told Curtis anything, but Curtis had wondered if he might do something like this; mainly because of how cryptic his phone conversation had sounded with Racquel while in the SUV. Curtis knew this idea of Matthew's went against DCFS regulations, but he understood how his son felt. It was the reason Curtis didn't comment.

Of course, Charlotte spoke up. "Where, Matt?"

"To see Racquel's dad."

"I don't think that's a good idea."

"Why? Dr. Anderson hasn't been barred from seeing MJ."

"Well, why can't he come here?"

"Because I told him I'd bring him there."

"To his home?"

"Yes."

Charlotte sighed with frustration. "But Matt, you know MJ can't be around Racquel and Vanessa."

Matthew turned away from her. "They won't be there."

"I don't believe that," she said.

"Doesn't matter. I'm still taking him."

"I'm sorry, but we can't let you do that." Charlotte spoke matter-of-factly.

Now Matt turned around and faced her. "Mom, this is *my* little boy. Not yours. And if I want to leave with him I can."

Charlotte looked at Curtis and then at her mom for help.

"Sweetie," Noreen said, "why don't you think about what you're doing? I know you don't understand what's going on, but you have to abide by the law."

"It'll be fine, Grandma."

Noreen didn't say anything else, and because of the nonchalant look on his father-in-law's face, Curtis knew Joe didn't blame Matthew, either, especially since they all knew Racquel and her mother were innocent.

Charlotte still wouldn't leave it alone, though. "Okay, fine, Matt, but I'm going with you."

"No, we'll be fine by ourselves."

"Matt, why are you doing this?" Charlotte said, standing up and walking closer to him. "You know MJ is only six weeks old."

"He'll be seven weeks tomorrow." Matthew stared at her, and Curtis could tell Charlotte wasn't amused.

"He's still too young," she said.

"Why?"

"Because you don't have any experience with taking care of babies."

"Racquel's mom taught us a lot when MJ first came home. Plus, Dr. Anderson definitely knows how to take care of a baby. There's really nothing for you to worry about, Mom."

Charlotte stared at Matthew, likely wishing she could shake some sense into him, so Curtis said,

"To keep everyone happy, why don't you let me go with you?"

Matthew hesitated at first but finally agreed. "If you want to."

The more Curtis thought about it, Matthew was too upset to drive MJ anywhere. He was also inexperienced with babies the way Charlotte had said. But he'd made it clear that he was going no matter what, so Curtis had no choice but to go along with him. It was better to do that than it was to take a chance on his having an accident.

When Matthew secured MJ in his car seat, he went around to the other side of the truck, opened the back door, and climbed in next to him. Curtis was a little surprised that he hadn't gotten in the front, but he was proud of Matthew for being so protective of his child.

As Curtis drove down the driveway and exited onto the street, Matthew said, "Dad, something isn't right."

"With what?"

"This DCFS stuff."

"Yeah, but hopefully the investigation will go quickly and this will be over."

"But what if someone set them up? What if someone hated them just that much?"

Curtis didn't have to question his son's last

comment. He knew immediately what he was in-sinuating. Still, he said, "What are you saying?"

"That I hope Mom didn't have anything to do with this. I haven't mentioned anything to Rac-quel, but the thought crossed my mind."

Curtis tried to keep a straight face, and he made sure not to look into his rearview mirror, because he couldn't take a chance on Matthew reading his mind. Curtis hadn't wanted to think or believe anything so awful about his own wife, either, but truth was, he had. He'd tossed around every thought imaginable, but in the end he'd decided that no matter how low Charlotte had stooped in the past, she would never concoct a scheme like this. She'd always been the kind of woman who was willing to do what she had to in order to get what she wanted, but not this. Not taking her son's baby from his own mother, and not us-ing the State of Illinois Division of Children and Family Services as a way to do it.

"Son, I know your mom has caused a lot of problems for Racquel and her family, but I doubt she would do something this cruel."

"I don't know how you can say that, Dad. She found a way to fix that DNA test when Marissa was born. And didn't you think it was strange that she all of a sudden apologized to Racquel and her

mom? She never admits being wrong about anything."

Curtis wished he could argue with him, but he
couldn't.

"And any woman who could sleep with as many
men as Mom has is capable of anything."

Curtis was stunned. "Matt, I'm really shocked
to hear you speak about your mother that way. I
know you're upset, but you're out of line."

"But it's true, Dad. You've only been married
what, eleven years? And already she's slept with
three other men?"

Curtis flipped on his signal, turned his head, and
checked the traffic behind him, then crossed into
the other lane. "Yeah, but it's not like I've been
the perfect little Boy Scout, either. Your mom and
I have both done things we're not proud of."

Matthew looked out his window, but didn't respond.

"We've both made a lot of mistakes," Curtis
said, now mulling over that thing he'd done so
long ago—that wretched thing that had come
back to haunt him. So far, there had been no
other communication, but he worried that his secret would be publicized any day. "And when I
mean a lot of mistakes," he continued, "I mean a
lot of them."

"But Mom never stops. She's always on a mission to get what she wants."

"She doesn't always handle things the right way, but I still don't think she's involved with this."

"She'd better not be. That's my mom and I love her, but if she had MJ taken from Racquel..." His voice trailed off, and he stared out the window again.

Curtis tried to ease his mind. "Son, I'm sorry this is happening. It's a tough time for all of us."

Matthew looked over and checked on MJ, but didn't say another word. Curtis didn't, either, because as much as he wanted to believe that Charlotte was innocent of all charges, he knew anything was possible. He knew Matthew might be right about everything he suspected. Nonetheless, Curtis prayed that Matthew had never been more wrong in his life.

Chapter 32

*M*atthew rang the doorbell, and Neil opened it instantly. There was no doubt that he'd been waiting and watching for them to drive up.

"Thanks for bringing him, Matt," he said. Thank you, too, Curtis."

"Oh my God," Racquel yelled, hurrying over. She pulled MJ out of his carrier and walked away from them. "Mommy missed you so much, sweetie. And she's so sorry they took you. I promise you, everything's going to be all right, though, okay?"

Curtis, Neil, and Matthew watched in silence, but Curtis couldn't help noticing Racquel's appearance. Her hair wasn't combed properly, her face was pale, her eyes were red and puffy, and she seemed exhausted. This whole ordeal was steadily taking a toll on her, and Curtis hoped things returned to normal soon.

"Hey, Matt," Vanessa said, walking into the living room. "Hey, Curtis."

They both spoke to her, and Vanessa hugged Matt. "I'm so glad you're here. I know it's hard flying back and forth, but Racquel really needed you."

"It's no problem, Mom."

Curtis didn't mind Matthew calling Vanessa Mom, but he was glad Charlotte wasn't there to hear it, because she'd already complained about it before.

"Can we get you two anything?" Vanessa asked.

They both thanked her but told her no.

"You guys have a seat," Neil said, and everyone sat down except Racquel. She stood, holding MJ, rocking him back and forth. She was a lot more distressed than Curtis had imagined, and he hoped she wasn't threatening a nervous breakdown. She seemed almost in her own world, and she hadn't said a word to Matthew. She acted as though he wasn't there.

But then he got up and stood next to her. "You wanna go up to your room?"

Curtis didn't think this was necessarily a good idea, because the last thing he wanted was for him and Matthew to be there for more than a few minutes. As it was, a neighbor of the Andersons had made the accusation against Vanessa, so he didn't want to take a chance that this neighbor had seen them bring the baby into the house. If they reported this to DCFS, they would find Curtis and Charlotte in violation and might place the baby in a foster home. He would allow Matthew and the baby to visit with Racquel for maybe another ten minutes, but then he'd tell Matthew they needed to go.

Neil moved to the edge of the sofa. "We didn't know you were coming, too, Curtis, but I'm glad you did. I'd been hoping to talk to you before now, but I've had back-to-back surgeries for three days. I wanted to thank you for getting here so quickly yesterday."

"It was no problem. We were glad to do it. We're not happy about what this is doing to Racquel or to both of you, but we'll keep MJ for as long as you need us to."

Vanessa nodded. "All I kept thinking last night was what if you and Charlotte lived out of town? Because it's not like we have a lot of family in Mitchell. Poor MJ would have been handed over to strangers."

"Thank God that wasn't necessary," Curtis said.

"We also want to thank you for coming over

with Matt," Vanessa said, "Especially since MJ isn't supposed to be here."

"I didn't want him driving alone, and I also knew Racquel needed to see the baby."

"I just wish we'd hear something," she said, "because I'm not sure how long Racquel can manage. She's terribly depressed, and she cries all the time."

"Have you thought about hiring an attorney?" Curtis asked.

"We called one today," Neil said. "He asked a few questions and then put me in contact with a private investigator. I told the investigator what happened, and he's already working on it."

"Good."

Vanessa's face turned sad. "We really are innocent."

Curtis sympathized with her. "Of course you are. I have no doubt about that."

"But I know this doesn't look good, and that you want the best for our grandson. I just don't want you to think we mistreated him."

"I'm not sure who made these accusations or why, but I know you and Racquel wouldn't hurt MJ. Charlotte knows that and so does Matthew."

Neil raised his right foot onto his knee. "The P.I. will work to find out who called protective services, and then they'll go from there. His plan will be to find out who falsely accused Vanessa and Racquel, and then our attorney will seek criminal conviction."

Curtis tried not to think about his conversation with Matthew, but he couldn't stop himself. What if Charlotte had played even a small part in this DCFS charade? What if she'd wanted to spend time with MJ so badly, she'd gone to reckless extremes? But no, she just wouldn't do that. Curtis was an intelligent man with lots of wisdom and forethought, but he refused to believe Charlotte was capable of such ruthlessness. On the other hand, he wondered if for the first time in years he was being naïve or if he was merely choosing to see what he wanted. Was he purposely protecting the woman he loved along with the rest of his family? Was he giving Charlotte the benefit of the doubt, because last year she'd promised him she was a changed woman?

"I hope they find out who did this and quick," he said.

"So do we," Vanessa added.

Curtis glanced at his watch. "We should probably get going."

Vanessa stood up. "Racquel will hate to see MJ go, but you're right. I'll get them."

Curtis and Neil chatted about MJ and how happy they were to be grandfathers until Curtis's phone rang. It was Charlotte.

"Hey, baby," he said.

"Are you guys on your way back?"

"We will be soon. Are your parents still there?"

"Yeah, and they were hoping to see Matt and MJ before they leave. Not to mention, MJ doesn't need to be out in the cold."

"We'll be there soon."

"I'm sure you can't talk, but are Racquel and Vanessa there?"

Curtis knew this was the real reason she'd called. "Yes."

"This can't happen again," she said. "It's too risky, and you and I could get in a lot of trouble with the State."

"We'll see you when we get home."

"Fine."

Charlotte wasn't happy, but thankfully she'd taken his hint and hung up. Gosh, he hoped she hadn't done anything crazy. But now that he thought about it, Charlotte sure had worked awfully hard over the last couple of weeks getting that nursery redesigned. She'd made it her priority every single day, and once the painter and wallpaper installer had finished up what they needed to do, she'd stocked up on everything. She'd purchased a number of items before MJ was born, but this morning when Curtis had gone in there to wake her up, he'd noticed a lot more. As a matter of fact, she hadn't even had to go out to buy Pampers, because MJ had all that he needed and then some.

Curtis still didn't want to believe Charlotte was behind those DCFS accusations, but now he knew he had to ask her. He wouldn't accuse her outright. He would simply approach her in a non-condemning fashion and wait for a response. He would pray that both he and Matthew were wrong about Charlotte, and that someone else was guilty as charged.

Chapter 33

Curtis climbed the staircase, looked in on Curtina, who was sleeping peacefully, and strolled a couple of doors down to MJ's nursery. Curtis, Matt, and the baby had been home for a while, his in-laws had driven back to Chicago over an hour ago, and now Curtis was beat and ready for bed. Before heading to his own room, though, he eased open the door to the nursery and smiled at Matthew, who was sitting in the rocking chair fast asleep. Curtis could see, too, that MJ was pretty content, and strangely enough, he was resting in his bassinet. The other thing Curtis had noticed was that he hadn't cried during their visit with the Andersons, but maybe it was because Racquel hadn't put him down.

Curtis closed the door and went to the end of the hallway. When he walked inside, he didn't see Charlotte, but he heard water running in their bathroom. Even though he'd made the decision to casually ask her about her possible involvement with the DCFS claim, he'd sort of rethought it on the way home. He knew that if there was a chance Charlotte actually had devised such an awful scheme she needed to be confronted, but he also hated driving a new wedge between them. They'd come such a long way as husband and wife, and it felt good not having to argue—good not walking around for days giving each other the silent treatment. They were in a great place for a change, and people could call him a wimp if they wanted to, but he'd grown tired of all the bickering and no longer had a lot of energy for it. It was so much nicer having peace and tranquility in a marriage than it was dealing with controversy. He'd also be remiss if he didn't acknowledge that dreadful secret of his that might be exposed very soon, because if this happened, he and Charlotte would have more than enough trouble to deal with.

Curtis walked into the bathroom and leaned against one of the vanities. Charlotte saturated her face with moisturizer and looked at Curtis through the mirror.

"We really need to sit down and talk to Matt," she said.

"About what?"

"That stunt he pulled tonight. He's not thinking, and he has no idea how serious those allegations are."

"Maybe, but to me it doesn't matter, because they're not true. They're totally bogus."

Charlotte looked at her reflection and smoothed more product on her face. Curtis wondered why she'd looked away from him until she said, "Are you sure about that?"

Curtis squinted his eyes. "What do you mean, am I sure? We're both sure, right?"

"I wanna be," she said, still facing the mirror. "But this evening I thought a lot more about it, and I don't know what to think. It would be one thing if there was only one accusation, but two are a bit much."

Curtis wanted to believe she was joking, but the tone of her voice was as serious as could be. He didn't even have words.

"That's why I think we should let DCFS do their job," she continued. "We also need to keep MJ away from them until we know more. Matt will never agree to that, but once he goes back to Boston, he won't be able to sneak MJ over there again. He shouldn't have done it tonight."

"Why? Nothing happened, and he was with the baby the whole time." Curtis didn't bother telling her that Racquel and Matthew had taken MJ upstairs so they could be alone with him, because with this latest revelation of hers there was no telling how she might react.

Curtis listened to her go on and on, but just as he was about to ask her flat out if she was behind all of this, his cell rang. It was after ten o'clock, so he wondered who was calling him this late. He pulled his phone from the side of his waist and looked at it, but when he didn't recognize the number, he panicked. His stomach swirled uncomfortably, as he feared this might be the stranger who'd been contacting him. He wanted nothing more than to disregard it and put his phone away, but since Charlotte stood there watching, he had no choice but to answer it. If he didn't, she'd ask questions and wonder why he was ignoring phone calls. He also didn't want to miss anything urgent relating to one of his members.

"Hello?"

"Pastor Black?" the man said.

"Dillon?"

"Yes."

Curtis was relieved it was him, but he didn't like

the desperation in Dillon's voice. "Is everything okay?"

"No, things are a mess, Pastor. I've really messed up this time."

"Where are you?"

"Sitting outside the strip club."

Curtis shook his head. "Dillon—"

"I just can't help myself," he said.

"Well, you did the right thing by calling, and try not to beat yourself up over this."

"I *really* wanna go in there, though. Especially after what happened."

"What?"

"Melissa gave me her ring back and told me she never wants to see me again."

"Why?"

"She followed me . . . to the strip club tonight."

"Oh no," Curtis said.

"She just left, and that's when I called you. I told you, I really messed up. I never should have let her catch me here again."

"You have to find the strength to leave."

"Well, it's not like I have anything to lose. She broke things off for good."

"Actually, you have everything to lose. Starting with your serenity, your self-respect, and more than anything, your soul."

Dillon was quiet.

"Are you still there?"

"Yeah…maybe if I had someone to talk to. I know it's late, Pastor, but can you come get me? I hate bothering you like this, but if I go inside this place, I'm not leaving without one or two of those women. Maybe I'm sick."

"You have a problem, and you need help. Just tell me the address."

Dillon rattled off directions as best he could, still sounding distraught.

"I'm on my way, but don't leave your car. Just stay put, and call me back if you need to."

"Thank you so much, Pastor. I won't forget this. Oh, and I'll be sitting in a white Cadillac."

"See you soon," Curtis said.

Charlotte turned around. "Who was that?"

"The guy I've been counseling. The one with the porn problem."

"What did he want?"

"For me to come meet him."

"Where?"

"At a strip club."

"Excuse me? Can't he meet you somewhere else?"

"Once I find him, I'll have him follow me to a coffee shop."

"I hope so. And you be careful, because a strip club isn't the kind of place you should be going to. Not even the parking lot."

Curtis kissed her, told her they'd finish their conversation in the morning, and left.

Chapter 34

*C*urtis slowed his SUV, turned in to the parking lot of DJ's Gentlemen's Club, and curved around to the rear of the building where Dillon was parked. A few minutes ago, Dillon had called and told him he was moving his vehicle from the front, because he didn't want anyone recognizing Curtis and starting rumors. Curtis hadn't thought much about it, but now that he saw how crowded the strip club was, he was glad to avoid as many people as possible.

He spotted Dillon's vehicle right away and pulled up next to him. They each rolled down their windows.

"Thank you again for coming," Dillon said.

"It was no problem. I'm glad you called. Why don't we find a restaurant or something? That way we can talk privately."

Dillon stared at him and appeared uneasy. Curtis wasn't sure why he seemed anxious and nervous, until Dillon looked toward the back of Curtis's SUV. Curtis glanced into his rearview mirror and saw a large figure rushing toward him, but there was no time to react. A tall, husky man snatched open Curtis's door and yanked him out of it. Then he slammed Curtis to the ground.

"What in the world?" Curtis said, seeing Dillon zoom away in his car. "Are you crazy?

The man stomped Curtis's head and then his stomach.

"Ahhhhhhh!" Curtis screamed.

Now Curtis felt kicking at both his sides. The pain was razor sharp, and he realized a second person was attacking him. His vision was fuzzy, but he definitely saw two different people standing over him.

"Owwwww!" Curtis bellowed. "Oh dear God."

The men never said a word, just kept kicking Curtis with full force in every part of his body. His head, his chest, his stomach, his sides, his legs, his arms. They kicked him over and over and over again until his body fell limp. He struggled to open his eyes, but he couldn't. He tried with everything in him but failed. He lay there until they beat him unconscious.

* * *

Curtis blinked his eyes slowly and then opened them as far as he could. His vision was still blurred, and he had no idea where he was. Piercing, throbbing pain swept through his head, but when he went to raise his hand toward it, he couldn't. He jerked his right hand and then his left, realizing they were tied down. He wasn't sure what they were attached to, but as he gained more of his faculties, he could tell he was sitting in a chair. He also tried moving his legs but couldn't. Finally, he blinked his eyes again, trying to focus them and search his surroundings, but just as his vision improved someone slapped him silly.

"Ohhhhhhhh!" he moaned, seeing stars.

His face stung so intensely, it felt like it was on fire. His attacker had whacked him so hard, his head had jolted to the side, and now his neck ached.

"That's for all the times you grabbed on me and threatened me like I was a child," the woman said, and smacked him again. "And that's for lying to me from the moment I met you."

She lit into him a third time with what seemed like all her might.

"Owwwwww!" Curtis yelled. He took deep breaths and tried to recall the familiar voice.

Kimberla Lawson Roby

"That one was for pretending you loved me, when all along you were sleepin' around with whores whenever you felt like it. You could've given me all kinds of nasty diseases."

Now the angry woman laid into him with her fists. Curtis moaned and groaned from all the pain, but he still concentrated on the woman's voice. Of all the people he could think of, this just couldn't be. There was no way.

"Look at me!" she shouted, grabbing and squeezing his chin and breathing in his face. "Open your eyes and look at me when I'm talking to you!"

Curtis fought to open his eyes again, and as they began focusing, his heart stopped in shock. "Mariah?"

"Exactly."

Streaks of pain ripped through Curtis's stomach, chest, and back, and he wondered if his ribs were broken. Now he struggled to breathe. "Why are you doing this?"

"Because you deserve it," she said.

"But why?"

Mariah laughed like a madwoman. "You know why," she said, and then mocked his words from long ago. " 'I only married you because the church required me to have a wife within my first two years...but I was never in love with you...I could never love you.' Remember that? Remember those cold and cruel words you said to me? Remember how I cried my eyes out when I caught you at that hotel with Charlotte? Remember how you never even told me about Matthew or how you'd gotten Charlotte pregnant when you were married to Tanya? Remember how you started whoring around with that Adrienne woman? Remember that, Curtis?"

Of course he remembered, but why was she dredging all this up now? He hadn't heard from Mariah since she divorced him, and that had been nearly twelve years ago. And when had she become so violent and hateful? The Mariah he'd known had been as meek and naïve as a schoolgirl. She'd never raised her voice to him, and for a long time she'd believed any- and everything he told her, and she would have done anything to make him love her. So he didn't know who this person was standing before him now, dressed in a black button-down blouse with the collar raised up toward the nape of her neck. Curtis wondered where this drastic and bizarre transformation had come from. She'd gone from being one of the most timid and submissive women he knew to being a ruthless gangster? She had to have lost her mind. It was the only feasible explanation.

Curtis scanned the area and saw two huge, muscular men dressed in jeans and leather jackets. He couldn't tell for sure, but one of them looked like the thug who had snatched him out of the truck. Curtis peered through swollen eyes, trying his best to get a better view. It was definitely him. If only the doors to his SUV weren't programmed to automatically unlock when he placed his gear in park, this never would have happened. He'd have been able to drive away in a hurry. But then, Curtis thought about the whole reason he'd been in the back lot of a strip club in the first place. Dillon. Curtis wondered why he'd sped off—and why he'd set him up like this. He'd seemed like such a good guy who just happened to have an addiction problem, but now Curtis knew those counseling sessions had all been part of the plan—part of Mariah's plan.

"You look pathetic," she snarled.

Curtis licked the bottom of his sore lip, tasting dry blood. "What is it that you want me from me, Mariah?"

"This," she said. "I wanted you to see how it feels to be helpless and in pain. I wanted to see you bruised and bloody."

A sharp ache raced through Curtis's side. "After all these years?" he asked, frowning. "After all these years, you're still holding a grudge?"

"Hmmph, I'm over it, but I'm not through with it. You've hurt people, Curtis, and you've gotten away with it. But not this time."

"Look," he said, taking deep breaths. "You've done what you needed to do, so now what?"

"We wait."

"For what?"

Mariah laughed. "Didn't you get my letters?"

Curtis stared at her. "I don't believe this."

"Why, because you didn't think I had it in me? Well, that was the old Mariah; this is the new one. I'm a totally different woman, period. I'm the nightmare you never saw coming."

Curtis's head swirled, and he closed his eyes. He wondered if he had a concussion.

Mariah struck him again. "Wake up!"

Curtis's eyes flew open but his head spun faster. He wasn't even sure what to say to this lunatic anymore, so he just sat there, praying she would let him go. He wasn't sure what time it was, but he knew hours had likely passed, and Charlotte had to be going out of her mind. He also wondered where his phone was, but then he remembered he'd left it on the front passenger seat.

And, now that he thought about it, what had they done with his truck?

"There's something else I wanna say, too," she said, forcing his head back with her hand.

"Oh God!" he shrieked. "Mariah, why are you doing this?"

"I already told you...you deserve it. But like I said, there's something else I wanna say to you. So listen up!"

Curtis twisted his head from side to side, trying to shake off the dizziness, but it wasn't working.

"I told you a thousand times that I wasn't comfortable with oral sex, but you just wouldn't leave it alone. Then when you insisted I do it, I told you I wanted to pray about it. I begged you to give me more time, but all you said was, '*Pray?* As far as I'm concerned there's nothing to *pray* about. Either you're going to do it or you're not.' Then, you threatened to get it elsewhere. Of course, me, being the pathetic thing that I was back then, I hurried and did what you wanted. Especially when you told me you would love me more than you already did and that we would finally bond completely. Remember that?"

Curtis sighed. Why on earth would he remember such a lame conversation? Not to mention, it was years and years ago. Now he *knew* Mariah had snapped. People just didn't change like this otherwise.

She grabbed his chin again. "Well, do you?"

"Do I what?"

"Remember."

"No, but I'm sorry. Is that what you wanna hear? I'm sorry, I regret the way I treated you, and I only want the best for you. Okay?"

"'Sorry' won't help you at this point. You should have said those words when we were married. But no. Instead, you moved to another town with that whore, Charlotte, you married her, founded your own church, and you've been living happily ever after."

"I'm not sure what else you want me to do. I've apologized, and whether you believe it or not, I'm a different man, Mariah."

"I don't think so."

Curtis wished she'd get to the point and stop torturing him with all this chitchat. He truly was sorry for the things he'd done to her, but he couldn't take anything back. If he could he would, but it wasn't possible. Didn't she know that?

"Aren't you even going to ask me about Dillon?" she said.

"Why? It's very clear that he's the one who set me up," Curtis said, but then glanced over at her two thuglike bodyguards, who stared at him like they wanted to trounce on him again. If only D.C. were there to handle this.

"You know that thing you did in grad school? Well, he's Sonya Whitfield's son. Remember her?"

Curtis inhaled and exhaled numerous times, trying to catch his breath. He couldn't speak if he wanted to, couldn't find the words. Still, painful thoughts danced through his mind, and all he could think was, *Dillon Tate, the man I've been counseling and trying to help, is actually Dillon Whitfield? Sonya Whitfield's son? Dear Lord.*

Chapter 35

Charlotte paced back and forth in her bedroom, calling Curtis again. This was her tenth time over the last half hour. Curtis had left to go meet that Dillon guy late last night, but now, it was three minutes before seven, and she hadn't heard a word from him. She'd thought it strange when she'd awakened and had seen that it was three a.m., but now she was worried to death and didn't know what to think. When something like this had happened in the past, Curtis not coming home until the wee hours, it had always been because he'd been out with Tabitha. Charlotte didn't want to believe he'd resorted to having affairs again, but if he wasn't with another woman, that meant only one thing: he was in danger or someone had already hurt him pretty badly.

Charlotte dialed him again and hung up. Earlier, she'd left a couple of messages, but now she didn't see where it would matter. She'd thought about calling the police but she knew that not enough time had passed, and a part of her was hoping she wouldn't have to alert anyone outside of their household. "Curtis, where in the world are you?" she said out loud.

After another twenty minutes, she dialed his number again, but there was still no answer. She wasn't sure what to do at this point, and while she didn't want to alarm Matthew, she had to tell someone. So she went down to the nursery. When she didn't see him, though, she went over to his bedroom and knocked.

"Come in," he said. She'd barely heard him, but he probably spoke low because he didn't want to wake the baby.

Matthew lay in bed with his head propped against two pillows, watching television, and MJ lay next to him with one blanket beneath him and another covering his little body.

"Honey, something's wrong," she said. "I've been trying to call your dad for hours, but he's not answering."

Matthew got up. "When did he leave?"

"He got a call last night from a guy he's been counseling, and he went to meet him."

"And he never came back?"

"No."

Matt pulled his phone from his dresser and dialed his dad. Charlotte looked on, praying he would pick up, but he didn't.

"Hey, Dad, it's Matt. Call me as soon as you can."

"This isn't like your father at all. I'm really worried."

Charlotte's phone rang, so she quickly scuttled out of the room so she wouldn't wake MJ. Matthew followed behind her.

"Hello?"

"Charlotte?"

"Lisa, how are you?" Charlotte said. If there was one person on the outside who had proven she could be trusted, it was Curtis's longtime publicist in New York. So Charlotte was glad to hear from her.

"Not the best. Is Pastor Black there? I tried to call him three times."

"No, he's not. He went to meet one of our members last night, and I haven't spoken to him since."

"Really?"

"Yes."

"Well, I just received a call from the CBS affiliate there in Mitchell."

"Why?"

"They wanted to know if I had any comments."

Charlotte didn't like the sound of this and frowned. "About what?"

"They're going to be interviewing some guy by the name of Dillon Whitfield, and they wanted to know if Pastor Black would like to make a statement."

"Well, that's interesting because Dillon is the guy Curtis went to meet. I don't know his last name, but I doubt this is a coincidence."

"Whenever something like this happens, it's never good, so I was hoping to talk to Pastor Black beforehand. Supposedly, the man is claiming that Pastor Black is responsible for his mom's death. I wish we knew more, but the interview is scheduled for seven-thirty. I wish I were there, but since it'll be streaming live from the station's website, at least I'll still be able to see it."

Charlotte looked at the clock on her nightstand. That was only minutes from now, so she lifted the TV selector and flipped on the television. "Why would they interview someone without hearing both sides?"

"Ratings. The producer told me that this Dillon person offered them an exclusive. So, once they air the interview, they'll post it on the Internet and it won't take long at all to go viral. The national affiliates will pick it up as well."

"Why won't people just leave us alone?" Charlotte said.

"Mom, what's going on?" Matthew asked.

Charlotte looked at him, not knowing how she would explain things. "Lisa, I'll call you when the interview is over, okay?"

"Sounds good. And please let me know if you hear from Pastor Black."

Charlotte hung up and told Matthew all the details, but now she regretted it.

"What?" he said, raising his voice. "More scandalous news about Dad?"

"Honey, try to stay calm. I have no idea what this is about, but I'm sure money is involved. Someone is probably trying to blackmail your dad again."

Matthew didn't seem convinced and reached for the remote. Charlotte had already turned it to the right channel, but Matthew upped the volume. "It's bad enough that everyone knows us, but I have a son now, Mom. I also have to go back to school."

"I'm sure this will be fine," she said, praying her words were true.

When the commercial ended, Candy Hernandez, the picture-perfect, Saturday morning anchorwoman, smiled into the camera.

"As we mentioned earlier, we have a young man here in our studio who says his mother's story is long overdue. He also says that local resident and nationally-known pastor, Reverend Curtis Black, played a huge part in it. Dillon Whitfield first contacted our producers yesterday morning, stating that he wanted to do an exclusive interview, and while we did reach out to Pastor Black, there was no comment." Candy turned toward her guest, and now he appeared in full view. "Good morning, Dillon."

"Good morning, and thank you for having me."

"So, it's my understanding that your mom met Pastor Black many years ago."

"Yes."

"Down in Atlanta, right?"

"Yes."

"And you say he's the reason your mom died in an accident?"

"Yes, and that's not all. Pastor Black is also my biological father."

Candy's face stiffened, and Charlotte dropped down on the bed.

Matthew folded his arms. "Wow."

"I'm not sure I understand," Candy said. It was

clear she'd been blindsided with this "biological father" bit just as much as Charlotte, Matthew, and everyone else who was watching.

"When my mom was in her early twenties, she worked at a strip club in Atlanta, and Pastor Black used to go there with some of his college buddies. He was in grad school, but eventually he and my mom started dating...well, maybe *dating* isn't quite the right word, but you know what I mean. Anyway, not long after, my mom got pregnant, but when she told Pastor Black about it, he said he wasn't the father. She told him that she hadn't been with anyone else for months, but he stopped seeing her and never spoke to her again."

"Before we continue," Candy said, looking directly into the camera, "I just want to clarify to our viewing audience that Pastor Black has neither confirmed nor denied these allegations and that we will do everything we can to obtain a comment from him." She turned back to Dillon. "Even if this is true, what does her having a baby have to do with her death? How is Pastor Black responsible for that?"

"He may not be responsible legally, but he's definitely the reason she's dead. After I was born, she contacted him again, but by then he'd just finished his master's degree, he'd become a minister, and he was engaged to be married. She called him because she wanted him to take a DNA test, but he said she was just trying to ruin his future with lies. Said he had big plans, and she would never be a part of them. But even after that, my mom begged him to see me and when he wouldn't, she filed a paternity claim. Next thing she knew, though, she'd gotten fired from her job, no other strip club would hire her, and when the DNA test came back, she was told Pastor Black wasn't the father."

Candy looked at him in shock. "Then why do you believe he is?"

"Because a few months ago his play brother, Larry, contacted my aunt and told her he was the one who took the DNA test for Curtis. He was also the one who got two of the girls at the strip club to say my mom was stealing money from the owner. That's how she lost her job."

"I'm really sorry about everything your mom went through, but I still don't see how Pastor Black caused her accident."

"Well, I'll tell you. After she lost her job and the DNA test came back negative, she went to Pastor Black again. She begged him to admit that he was my father and to help take care of me, but he told her that if she ever mentioned a baby to him again, she would be sorry. And according to Larry, she confronted Pastor Black one last time and threatened to go to his fiancée. Then, a week later, I ended up missing. But within one hour after I was taken, Pastor Black called my mom and told her that if she ever wanted to see me again, she would have to sign papers. She had to agree to say he wasn't the baby's father and that she would never contact him again. But even though I was returned that same evening, my mom became chronically depressed. According to my aunt, she was like that for weeks leading up to her accident. My aunt never knew about the legal papers or that I'd been taken until Pastor Black's brother called her, but it was common knowledge that my mom had borrowed a friend's car and slammed it into a tree. She did it on purpose and killed herself because of my father."

Curtina pushed her parents' bedroom door all the way open. "Is that man talking about Daddy?"

Charlotte picked up the remote and flipped the channel as fast as she could. "Not really, honey. Just news stuff. You sure did sleep late this morning." Charlotte hoped she wouldn't ask any more questions.

Curtina rubbed her eyes. "I was really tired after Grandma and Grandpa left."

Matthew turned toward the doorway when he heard MJ crying, and Charlotte quickly said, "Honey, why don't you go with your brother to see about the baby?"

"Okay," she said.

Matthew never looked at Charlotte, but left. He was livid, and Charlotte hoped and prayed this Dillon character was lying about everything. Curtis just wouldn't do something so evil. Taking someone's baby from them? Even for an hour, it just didn't sound like her husband. And then disowning a child for nearly thirty years? And pushing the mother so far that she committed suicide?

Charlotte wondered if the interview was still airing, but when she turned the channel back to the CBS affiliate, a commercial for Deliverance Outreach was on. How fitting.

She picked up her phone to call Curtis again, but Lisa's number displayed.

"Hello?"

"Did you watch?" Lisa asked.

"Yeah, and so did Matt."

"Charlotte, this is bad. I'm hoping there's no truth to any of this, but at some point we're going to have to respond. Still no word from Pastor Black?"

"Nothing. Something's definitely wrong."

"Well, I'll see what else I can find out. I'll be in touch."

"Thanks, Lisa."

As soon as Charlotte pressed the button, Elder Jamison called. "Hey, Charlotte, is Pastor there? I just saw some crazy interview."

"No, and I haven't heard from him since last night."

"Why?"

"He went to meet a member named Dillon, and I believe it's the same guy we just saw on TV."

Elder Jamison sighed. He was Curtis's right hand and greatest supporter at the church, no matter how bad things got, but his silence told Charlotte that he was getting a little tired of all these surprise secrets that came out of nowhere.

But just as Charlotte was getting ready to respond, Elder Jamison said, "Oh no, are you still watching the news segment?"

"No."

"You'd better turn it back. They're saying they have an update about Pastor."

Charlotte flipped the channel and saw the words *breaking news* at the bottom of the screen.

The screen was also now split, with Candy Hernandez in the studio displayed on one side and a young male reporter on the other.

The reporter held the microphone closer to his mouth and spoke. "We've just arrived on the scene, but we're getting word that nationally known, *New York Times* bestselling author Pastor Curtis Black was found just behind this popular strip club, beaten and unconscious. The police aren't giving any further details at this time, but we will of course bring you all new developments as this story unfolds."

Charlotte watched the television but couldn't move or say anything. The news was far too devastating.

Chapter 36

*W*ell, the deed is finally done, and I have been feeling on top of the world for hours. All those years of wanting to pay Curtis back for the way he treated me and then finally being able to stare him straight in his face, well, it just feels good. I'd finally stood up for myself the way I should have done the whole time I was married to him, but better late than never. Actually, I'd always been weak, even as far back as elementary school. I'd allowed other kids to bully and walk all over me year after year, until I graduated high school. So, in a sense, tearing down Curtis has also helped me pay back anyone who's ever hurt me. Of course, no one, especially not Curtis, would have suspected me of doing what I did, and this is the very reason doggish men need to be careful who they play with. They should think long and hard before charming, using, and tossing away certain women because they might end up messing over the wrong one just like Curtis did with me. But again, I felt good *about it because I'd gotten a chance to torture the infamous Reverend Curtis Black all while he was tied up and helpless. I felt even more satisfied knowing he'd been beaten to the core right before Tommy and Ronan brought him to me. I'd planned everything carefully and perfectly, even down to renting a small house out in the country and paying two guys I'd grown up with on the South Side of Chicago to teach him a lesson—they'd beaten Curtis to a bloody pulp, and although it may sound harsh, just for a few moments, a part of me had wished they'd killed him. Ended his life so that he would never have a chance to hurt another woman again. I'd gotten Curtis back for me, but I'd also done it for his first wife, Tanya, and also Adrienne, the mistress he'd had two affairs with—one affair while married to Tanya and one while married to me. But the reason I'd felt so sorry for Adrienne was because she had so believed Curtis would eventually marry her the way he'd claimed, that when she'd realized he'd been lying to her, she hadn't been able to take it. She'd shot him and then turned the gun on herself. It had taken a long time for me to get over that, but it was Adrienne's suicide and the fact that Curtis's lies and deceit had caused it—well, this was what had prompted me to help Dillon. To be honest, I had sort of made a decision to forget about Curtis and stop obsessing over getting revenge on him—*

especially since so many years had passed—but when Dillon contacted me and told me about his mother and her death, I'd been pushed over the edge. I'm not sure why, given the fact that I'd never met Sonya, but hearing that Curtis had used and tossed away yet another innocent woman... well, that had been way, way too much for me. Of course, the icing on the cake was the fact that the reason he'd gone to such extremes to get rid of Sonya was simply so he wouldn't jeopardize his new little life, which included entering the ministry and getting married. He'd disowned his own flesh and blood and hadn't thought twice about it. It was as if the man had no conscience, and I'd decided it was time to do something about it once and for all. But interestingly enough, it had been Larry who'd gotten the initial ball rolling in the right direction. Weeks before I'd ever spoken to Dillon or even knew that this young man existed, Larry had chosen me as the one to call with his confessions—something that was a bit strange, since I'd only met Larry a couple of times when Curtis and I were married. I'm sure, though, he'd done it because he still had it in for Curtis (Larry had told me about Curtis having him arrested a few years back), so I just think Larry was hoping he could convince me to help him scheme against Curtis—which he'd quickly been able to do once he told me that Curtis had slept with even more women while I was married to him—women I didn't know about. Anyway, Larry had been looking for an ally, and though I had no interest in Curtis's money, Larry hadn't talked about much else. Money was the reason he wanted to ruin Curtis. Finally, after we'd spoken a few times, though, Larry had called Sonya's sister and told her everything he'd done—how he'd taken the DNA test for Curtis, how he'd gotten her sister fired and blackballed at other strip clubs. Sonya's sister had then contacted her nephew, Dillon. Shortly after that, Larry had given Dillon my number, and Dillon had called me, saying he couldn't let "Pastor Black" get away with what he'd done to his mother. And since I'd been hurt by "Pastor Black," too, he wondered if I would please help him. I didn't even have to think about it, because I'd already started planning the perfect scheme right after talking to Larry. Dillon was living in Atlanta, working at a fast-food restaurant, though, barely making ends meet, so I'd told him that he and his girlfriend, Melissa, could move to Chicago to stay with me and that I would take everything from there. The first thing I did was have them drive over to Mitchell every single Sunday eight weeks in a row, so they could attend service at Deliverance Outreach. I even rented a new Cadillac for them to drive until this thing was over with. Then, I encouraged them to join. Then, once they completed their new membership classes, I had *them make an appointment for martial counseling. With Curtis's congregation growing the way I'd been hearing, I'd called the church to find out whether he met with couples himself or couples met only with the assistant pastors. The woman on the phone had told me that Curtis felt an obligation toward handling marital counseling himself, and this was when I sat down and figured out the rest of the plan. I guess I could have chosen any problem at all for Dillon to be struggling with, but somehow because Curtis had met Sonya in a strip club, I decided that being addicted to porn and strip clubs was priceless. The irony of the whole thing was too much to pass up, and boy did it work. Anyway, my part is done, and I can finally move on. Also, given the fact that Curtis is likely in critical condition—at least that's what it seemed like when Tommy and Ronan took him back to the strip club and dumped his body next to his truck—so yes, given that particular fact, I doubt Curtis will be contacting me anytime soon. I'm also sure he won't be telling the police anything about me, either, because he'll be hoping no one ever finds out about what he did to Sonya and Dillon. I'm sure he has no idea about the interview I just watched on television. He has no clue that loads of websites are already reporting the story. I just Googled it again, and comments are flooding in from many of his angry supporters, too. When I'd told Dillon that he would have to secure a live local interview over in Mitchell, he'd worried that folks might think his story was farfetched. But I had quickly promised him that by now, most people nationwide had heard so much about Curtis's past, they knew he was capable of just about anything. Like I said, though, my part is done, and I finally have the closure I need. Right or wrong, revenge feels good. Especially when it involves a ruthless whoremonger like Curtis. Especially when I'd been able to right a wrong that had been done to me and so many others, namely Sonya Whitfield. She'd killed herself because of Curtis, but her death would now get her the only thing she'd wanted from Curtis in the first place: for him to take care of his son. I'd put forth the effort to punish Curtis physically and emotionally, but Dillon will reap the financial rewards. I know this because Dillon is now the newest heir to the Black Family fortune. He is Curtis's firstborn child.*

Chapter 37

*C*harlotte and Matthew dashed inside Mitchell Memorial and strolled over to the window where less-emergent patients checked in. A woman with salt-and-pepper hair smiled, and Charlotte could tell she recognized her. People had started noticing her more and more as the ministry had grown, but even more so now that they broadcast on television. The cameramen usually made sure to capture a couple of shots of her during each sermon they aired, and now Charlotte didn't know if that was a good idea.

"The doctors are with your husband, but I'll let them know you're here," the woman said. "Someone will be out as soon as possible."

"Thank you."

Charlotte and Matthew went over to the same ER family room they'd sat in numerous times: years ago when Marissa had fallen down the stairs, two years ago when Curtis had gotten hurt in his car accident, and just a few weeks ago when Racquel had gone into early labor. It seemed as though tragedy struck them all the time, but now she wondered if maybe God wasn't happy about her scheming to get MJ and was punishing her. But no...not when God knew MJ was in the best place and that Charlotte had only done what she had to do to protect him. She reminded herself that Racquel was just a child, and that Vanessa was too busy to give MJ the kind of time and attention he needed. Charlotte, on the other hand, wanted to be there for him every waking moment, and she was missing him even now. Just before she and Matthew had driven over to the hospital, she'd called Aunt Emma and then dropped off Curtina and MJ. She hadn't wanted to, but she'd also known a hospital setting wasn't the place for a newborn, and Matthew had agreed.

They sat in the waiting area, trying to stay calm and hopeful. Charlotte prayed that Curtis would be okay. She knew the reporter had mentioned that Curtis had been beaten and was unconscious, however Charlotte hoped this was the extent of it; that all he had were a few bruises and maybe a concussion but would be able to go home with them in a few hours.

In the meantime, Charlotte called her parents to let them know what was going on. Then, she called Janine, Elder Jamison, and Lana. She wanted Elder Dixon to know, too, but she knew Lana would contact him. Matthew called Alicia and Racquel, and while everyone said they were on their way, Charlotte knew from the look on Matthew's face that Racquel wasn't coming.

"Can't you come for just a few minutes?" he said. "I really want you here with me."

Charlotte listened to him, practically begging that silly girl, and she wanted to grab his phone from him. Racquel was so wrong for Matthew. Here her future father-in-law had been rushed to the hospital, yet she wasn't planning to be there for the family?

"I understand," he said, "and I'll keep you posted."

Matthew hung up his phone, and Charlotte looked at him. "Is Racquel okay?"

"Not really. She's so depressed, Mom. She misses MJ, and she got upset when I told her we took him over to Aunt Emma's."

"Well, it's not like we could bring him here."

"She knows that, but she doesn't understand why we couldn't bring him to her."

"Because DCFS doesn't want him there."

Matthew leaned his head back against the wall, closing his eyes. He sighed so loudly, others in the room stared at him.

Charlotte ignored him, though, because Racquel was the least of her worries. Curtis was her priority, and she had to stay focused.

After a few moments, Matthew opened his eyes. "Gosh, I just don't believe Dad. Treating that woman so badly and pretending all these years that they never had a child. What kind of person does that?"

"First of all," she said, "we don't even know if this story is true. I mean, why would your uncle Larry all of a sudden fess up about everything when he could have done it years ago? He certainly could have done it when he was trying to steal money from us."

"I don't know, but I believe that guy."

Charlotte frowned but then looked around and saw people staring again. "Why?" she whispered.

"He looks just like Dad. And why would someone lie about this kinda thing?"

"Money, of course."

Matthew pursed his lips, leaned his head back, and shut his eyes again.

Charlotte left him alone and waited. They both sat quietly until a nurse came and led them down to a meeting room.

"Dr. Mason will be with you shortly."

"Thank you," Charlotte said, realizing Dr. Mason was one of the doctors who'd taken care of Curtis two years ago.

They waited only a couple of minutes before he walked in.

"Mrs. Black, how are you?"

"As well as can be expected," she said. "You remember Matthew, right?"

"How are you son?" he said, shaking Matthew's hand. "Well, I won't try to sugarcoat this. Pastor Black is in pretty bad shape. He was beaten from head to toe. To be honest, I don't believe there's a part of his body that wasn't injured."

Charlotte winced. "Dear God."

"His ribs are broken, his spleen is ruptured, and he has a large contusion on the back of his head. Whoever did this must have kicked him until they were exhausted."

Matthew didn't say anything, but tears streamed down his face. He tried wiping them away as quickly as he could, but they kept rolling. Charlotte latched onto his arm, trying to console him.

"The good news is that we finally got him to

wake up. He didn't stay with us for long, but he was conscious. Anyway, our main goal is to get his spleen repaired. He already has some internal bleeding, but we don't want him to lose a lot of blood. We'll be heading to the OR with him as soon as my partner gets here. The rupture is pretty bad, so he's going to assist me."

"Will we be able to see him first?" Charlotte asked.

"Yes—and one other thing. Because he was beaten so badly, we had to call the police. So I'm sure they'll want to talk to you."

"Thank you," she said again.

"I'm really sorry about this, and I hope they catch the lowlife who did this."

"We do, too," Charlotte said, holding back her own tears.

Dr. Mason stood up. "I'd better get back, but we'll let you know when you can go in for a short visit."

"Thank you again for everything," she said.

As Dr. Mason walked out, Neil walked in.

Matthew got up. "Hi, Dr. Anderson. I'll be back after I call Racquel," he said, and closed the door behind him.

Charlotte didn't like this. Why was Neil in there?

"I'm really sorry to hear about Curtis. What happened?"

"We don't know yet."

"Is it true that they found him behind a strip club?"

"Yeah, but he was only there to help one of our members."

Neil raised his eyebrows.

"What?" she said.

"I guess I find that kinda hard to believe. Most men who go to strip clubs go because they want to."

"Well, not this time. Curtis has been counseling a young man who has an addiction problem."

"Hmmm. But we know he likes strip clubs because I saw that interview this morning. I was making rounds and watched it in a patient's room. I couldn't believe it."

"Curtis has been lied on many times before, and this is no different."

"Well, either way, I'm still sorry he's been hurt so badly. And where's MJ?"

Charlotte hated having to answer this because she didn't want Neil, Vanessa, or Racquel thinking she couldn't take care of MJ. "He's with my aunt," she said in a hurry. "Only because we didn't wanna bring him here around all these germs... but I promise you he's fine. He'll be well taken care of... she's taken care of all my kids."

Neil slightly chuckled and raised his hands. "Whoaaaa. It's no problem at all. You don't have to explain. You did the right thing."

"I didn't want you thinking he wasn't safe."

"I would never think that," he said, eyeing her up and down.

"I'd better go," she said, moving toward the door.

Neil grabbed her hand and drew her back to him. "I hope you know I'm still waiting."

Charlotte hated the way he made her feel and pulled away. "Neil, please don't do this. My husband isn't well."

"I understand that, but I still want you. I've never wanted any woman more... and you want me, too."

"I'm really surprised at you. Your wife and daughter are dealing with some very serious allegations, yet all you can think about is sleeping around?"

"But that's just it—they're completely innocent."

"I hope so," Charlotte said. "We all do."

"I guarantee it," he said. "And you of all people know they never did those things."

"Well, it wasn't like either of us was there. We weren't with Racquel or Vanessa when those witnesses claim they saw them."

"Let's stop playing games, Charlotte. I know you paid to have this done. I found out this morning."

Charlotte's heart thumped against her chest. Still, she played like she was calm and clueless. "Excuse me?"

"I know you're behind all this, but I'm willing to overlook it."

"What are you talking about?"

"I don't know the whole story, but I know enough."

"This is crazy," she said, folding her arms. "Who would do something that jaded?"

"Maybe you're not jaded at all. Maybe you just love your grandson so much you wanted him for yourself. I can't say. But what I do know is that nothing is so bad that it can't be worked out."

"I'm not having this conversation," she said.

"It's not like you really have a choice. I know Curtis is about to have surgery, but I'll expect to hear from you sometime tomorrow."

Charlotte stared at him, speechless, and walked out.

Chapter 38

As soon as Charlotte rushed out of the meeting room, two male detectives strode toward her. One was medium height and pretty average looking, but the other reminded her of Denzel Washington.

"Mrs. Black?" the Denzel-looking one said. "I'm Detective Woodson, and this is my partner, Detective Randall. If it's okay, we'd like to ask you a few questions."

"Of course. I'd like to go get my son as well."

"We'll just wait here," he said, pointing toward the room Charlotte had just walked out of—the room where Neil had come on to her again and then claimed he knew her secret. At first she'd doubted his word, but something told her he was serious. Something inside her screamed major trouble, and she wondered who had opened their big mouth. Everything was always about money, though, and now she was sorry she hadn't paid her helpers a lot more.

Charlotte walked farther down the corridor. As she approached the waiting area, she saw Janine, Lana, both the lead elders, her cousin Anise, Minister Simmons, and Minister Morgan. She spoke to all of them, and then said, "Matt and Janine, can you come with me? You, too, Lana."

Anise looked at Charlotte, probably wondering why Charlotte hadn't asked her to come along since she was family. But it wasn't like they'd gotten close again. Anise did talk to her a little more than she had two years ago, but they still didn't have the best relationship. As a matter of fact, the only time she usually saw Anise was at Aunt Emma's.

When Charlotte, Matthew, and the other two women walked inside the room, the detectives leaned forward, resting their arms on the table.

"So, do you have any idea who would've done something like this to your husband?" Detective Woodson asked.

"Not really," Charlotte said. "But there was some guy named Dillon Whitfield on the news this morning, telling a lot of lies about Curtis."

"We were told about that."

"My husband also left to go meet someone

named Dillon last night. He called Curtis shortly after ten, saying he was having some trouble."

"Is it common for your husband to go meet someone that late?"

"Yes, especially when a member needs him."

"Your husband was tossed next to his vehicle, but his door was wide open. So what we're trying to figure out is whether he was moved or he remained there the whole time. We'll also have his vehicle checked for fingerprints. But it really would help if we knew as much as possible."

"For example," Detective Randall said, "has he been receiving any threatening phone calls, letters, e-mails?"

"Not that I know of," Charlotte said.

"Actually, there is something you might want to know," Lana said. "Pastor Black never told me himself, but one of our new assistants, Shelia, says two urgent overnight envelopes came for him. She only told me because when she took him the second envelope, he seemed nervous. To her, something wasn't right, and she got worried."

Charlotte wasn't positive, but she fully believed this Dillon character was behind all this. He was trying to bully his way into their lives for financial reasons, and Charlotte couldn't wait for Curtis to demand a DNA test.

"We'd really like to talk to your husband," Detective Randall said.

Detective Woodson nodded. "Yes, that might help a lot. Especially if he saw faces."

"It sounds like he's very weak, but I agree that you should talk to him," Charlotte said. "Do you mind if I listen in?"

"No problem," Detective Woodson said.

When they left the room, Charlotte asked to see Dr. Mason, and he authorized the detectives to question Curtis. He was still in the ER area, but thankfully, he had a closed-door room. But as Charlotte moved closer to his bedside, her knees buckled.

Detective Randall grabbed her. "Are you okay?"

Charlotte wanted to respond, but all she could think about was how pitiful Curtis looked. Of course, there was an IV inserted in his vein, a heart and blood pressure monitor, and just about everything else he'd been hooked up to when he'd had his accident, but nothing could have prepared her to see what she was looking at now. His face was so swollen that she barely recognized him, and his arms and hands were covered with multiple lacerations. She wondered what the rest of his body looked like, but she was glad his hospital gown and blanket were disguising it. If it were anything like what she *could* see, she didn't as much as want to think about it.

Curtis's attending nurse smiled at Charlotte, and then moved to the other side of the bed, adding medicine to his IV, but Charlotte could tell she wasn't leaving. Seconds later, Dr. Mason entered the room, too.

"I'm sorry to have to hurry you along, but the other surgeon is here, and we need to get Pastor Black down to the OR."

Detective Woodson moved toward the head of the bed. "Pastor Black, can you hear me?"

Curtis slightly moved his head to the side, but never opened his eyes.

Charlotte touched his shoulder. "Honey, are you awake?"

He moved his head again and moaned, but that was it.

"He's in a lot of pain," Dr. Mason said, "so this may have to wait."

Detective Randall wanted answers now. "Pastor Black, can you tell us who did this to you?"

This time Curtis mouthed the word *No.*

"Did you see the person's face?"

"No," he struggled to say.

"Have you been threatened by anyone?"

Curtis tried to part his lips again to speak, but he couldn't.

"I think that's enough for now," Dr. Mason said. "Maybe once he's out of surgery, and he's rested for a few hours. Or possibly tomorrow."

Charlotte looked at the nurse, who was now disconnecting the monitor, but suddenly a piercing alarm went off.

Dr. Mason pushed past Charlotte and the detectives. "Everyone out!"

Charlotte backed away in terror, watching the nurse pass Dr. Mason a syringe different from what she'd used on Curtis just minutes ago. Charlotte had no idea what was going on, but she stood there, stuck in her tracks... until Dr. Mason yelled at all of them again. "I said, everybody out! Now!"

Chapter 39

*P*astor Black," one of the nurses said. "Are you awake?"

"Yes," he said, but his tone was groggy and his throat was sore.

"You're in recovery, but your surgery went well."

Curtis lay there, thanking God for bringing him through it. He didn't remember everything, but he did remember those detectives asking him questions. He'd heard every word they'd said, but he'd answered no to every one of them. He'd done so because if he could help it, no one would ever know about Dillon or his mother. Ever since Curtis had received those taunting letters, he'd dreaded the idea that word might get out, but never in his wildest imagination had he counted on Mariah being involved. Even now, he had no idea how she'd found out about Dillon and Sonya, or how Mariah and Dillon had met. It didn't make

322

a whole lot of sense, and he was also stunned by Mariah's new personality. Her behavior was scary, to say the least, and her character was as different as Miami and Little Rock. She was a completely changed woman, and Curtis wondered what had happened to her. He didn't want to believe that his past treatment of her had anything to do with it, but when she'd slapped him over and over, all she'd talked about was how bad their marriage was. She'd gone on and on about the terrible things he'd done to her, so the more Curtis lay there thinking, he wondered if he *was* the reason she'd turned bitter. Although *bitter* wasn't the best word to describe her, because the woman he'd seen was vicious. She didn't seem to care about what she said or did, and it had sounded as if she'd taken a lot of time planning a most brutal attack. Until the day he died, he would never forget those thugs snatching him from his vehicle, beating him unmercifully, tossing him in the back of a van, and then driving him out to some empty house in the country. Then, although he'd screamed out in pain, they'd dragged him by his legs up to the front door. That was when he'd passed out. But when he'd awakened, he'd found that he was sitting in some chair with his arms and legs tied down like a prisoner.

Now, though, as much as that awful incident would forever haunt him, he had to figure out a way to make things right with Dillon. He still wasn't positively sure that Dillon was his son, but if he was, Curtis would treat him as such. If he was struggling financially, Curtis would help him in that way, too. If he simply wanted Curtis to take responsibility for the malicious way he'd treated Sonya, he would do that as well. Anything, if it would stop Dillon from going public. He also didn't want to take a chance on Mariah tattling things the way she'd promised in those letters, so he would have to locate her and apologize profusely. He'd been wrong for marrying Mariah, a woman he didn't love, and then treating her with such total disrespect. And there were no words to describe the horrendous thing he'd done down in Atlanta during his grad years. He'd been very young, but he'd been selfish and had known full well what he was doing. He hadn't been in love with Sonya, either, but the first night he'd seen her at the strip club, they'd made eye contact and he'd taken her home with him. She'd given him the best sex of his life, and he hadn't been able to get enough of her. It was true that she wasn't the kind of woman he would have ever considered marrying, but he hadn't seen anything wrong with enjoying himself. From the time he'd been a teenager, he'd loved sex, and since Tanya had been set on remaining celibate until they were married, he'd had to find pleasure elsewhere. But then, Sonya had dropped that baby bomb on him and he'd gone ballistic. He'd had such high aspirations, and he wasn't about to let some unwanted pregnancy, with a stripper no less, ruin his bright future. He just hadn't seen how he could do that. He'd also blamed Sonya for not taking precautions, but now that he was older, he knew birth control had been just as much his responsibility.

He'd thought denying the baby and cutting her off would be the end of it, but then she'd threatened to tell Tanya, and he'd had to do something. He'd had to go to extreme lengths to stop her once and for all. Now, though, he regretted every bit of it, because Dillon hadn't deserved to grow up without a father, Sonya hadn't deserved to be blackmailed into signing papers and forced into a state of depression. Curtis hadn't wanted to admit it, but in a sense, he *had* indirectly caused her death. He'd read about the accident in the newspaper the day after it had happened, but he'd been so egotistical back then, he'd hardly thought twice about it. For maybe a week, the thought of her dying had tugged at his conscience, but then he'd moved on. He'd forgotten about it as much as he could and focused on the woman he was marrying.

"Pastor Black, it's Dr. Mason. How are you feeling?"

"Okay," he said, frowning. "My stomach hurts, though."

"I'm sure. We're going to up your pain meds, so you should feel better soon. We had a bit of a scare with your blood pressure right before surgery, but we got your spleen all fixed up, and you're going to be fine. You'll stay here for a while longer, and then we'll get you settled in a room so you can see your family."

Curtis coughed for a few seconds and took a deep breath. "Thank you, Doctor."

He coughed more and wondered how he was going to explain this beating incident to Charlotte. Worse, if those detectives questioned him again, God forgive him, he would have to lie the same as he had earlier. He'd already told them that he didn't know who'd attacked him, that he hadn't seen any faces, and that no one had threatened him. But he had a feeling those one-word answers he'd given weren't going to be enough. The job of a detective was to find out as much as he could about any crime, so Curtis knew they would definitely be persistent.

He would be persistent, too. They could ask him a thousand questions if they wanted, yet he would never tell them about Mariah, Dillon, or Sonya. He would never help put his own son in jail. He just wouldn't.

Chapter 40

Charlotte, Matthew, and Alicia slowly filed into Curtis's room, and though Charlotte had already seen Curtis before his surgery, she was still stricken by the way he looked. Matthew and Alicia cringed in shock, and to Charlotte, Curtis's face seemed more swollen. He'd been beaten nearly to death, and for the life of her she couldn't fathom why anyone would want to do this to him. Curtis wasn't perfect, and he certainly had enemies from the past, but this was unthinkable. Over the years, people he'd hurt or those who were envious of him had tried to embarrass him publicly with exaggerated statements or lies—the way that Dillon person had done earlier this morning—but for the most part, folks only tried to hurt Curtis financially or reputation wise.

Charlotte moved toward the head of Curtis's bed on the right side and Alicia did the same on the left. Matthew, however, stood as far away as possible by the door.

Charlotte grabbed Curtis's hand. "Baby, can you hear me?"

Curtis opened his eyes, forcing a smile onto his face. "Hey."

Charlotte smiled back at him. "Dr. Mason said your surgery was a success, and that you're going to be fine."

"God is good," he said with a raspy voice.

"Hey, Daddy," Alicia said.

"Hey, baby girl. I'm glad you came."

Alicia swallowed hard, and tears filled her eyes. "I'm so sorry, Daddy. And is it true that you don't know who did this?"

"Yes. It was dark, and it happened very quickly."

"And then they just left you there?"

"I guess so."

Matthew sighed and leaned against the wall, and Charlotte could tell he didn't want to be there. There was no doubt that seeing his father covered in bruises and lacerations wasn't easy for him, but Charlotte also knew the whole Dillon interview hadn't set well with him. Unlike her, Matthew believed Dillon was telling the truth, and he was upset with Curtis.

Curtis looked over at Matthew. "Son, why are you standing over there? What's wrong?"

"Nothing."

"I know this looks bad, but I'm going to be fine. I don't want you worrying about me, okay?"

Matt stared at him but didn't respond.

Charlotte and Alicia still weren't on the best of terms, but they were a lot more cordial than they'd been last year. They were certainly in agreement today, too: they didn't want Matthew or anyone else telling Curtis about that television interview.

Curtis closed his eyes, seemingly resting them, but then he opened them again. "How's MJ?" he asked Matthew.

"He's with Aunt Emma. I'm gonna leave in a few minutes, though, so I can check on him." His tone was dry, and Charlotte hoped Matthew wouldn't say anything out of the way.

"You're such a good father, Matt," Curtis said, coughing a bit. "Here MJ is only a few weeks old, yet you're already worrying about his well-being. This is how every father should be, and I'm very proud of you, son."

Matt shook his head in disgust. "Wow. Well, if that's true, Dad, then why haven't you worried about Dillon? Why haven't you tried to see him?"

Curtis gazed at him, but Charlotte glanced over at the monitor. Curtis's heart rate shot up noticeably.

"Son, what are you talking about?"

Matthew raised his eyebrows. "So, you're still gonna deny him? Even after he went on TV this morning?"

Charlotte had to stop him. "Matt, honey...not now."

Matthew gazed at her, turned around, and walked out.

Alicia stood in silence and Charlotte knew why. Just before walking into Curtis's room, they'd agreed not to talk about anything that would upset Curtis. Alicia and Charlotte had discussed how it wouldn't be good for him, given the fact that he'd experienced so much trauma. They had stressed this very thing to Matthew, too, and though he'd seemed okay with it, apparently he wasn't.

"Baby, what was Matt talking about?" Curtis asked, slightly repositioning his body and frowning in pain.

"Nothing. You just rest."

Curtis turned to Alicia. "Tell me the truth. What interview?"

"Daddy, this can wait. Right now, we just want

you to get better. We don't want you worrying about anything."

Curtis's heart rate climbed higher, and he looked at Charlotte again. "Tell me. Baby, please."

Charlotte wished he would leave this alone, but it was obvious he wasn't planning to. She had no choice but tell him what he wanted to know.

"Some guy named Dillon did a live interview with Candy Hernandez. He claims he's your son, and that you're the reason his mom died some years ago. No one knows why he's doing this, but Lisa is working to get to the bottom of it."

Charlotte waited for his response, but surprisingly, all Curtis did was look toward the ceiling. Tears streamed down both sides of his face and onto his pillow.

"Oh my God," she said. "Baby, please tell me this isn't true."

She waited again for him to say something, but all he did was gaze at her and then shut his eyes, weeping.

Charlotte and Alicia looked at each other in shock. Why hadn't he told Charlotte about this long-lost child of his? Would he really deny his own son? Not that she wanted this to be true, because she certainly didn't, but this seemed totally out of character for him. Curtis was the first person to admit that he'd done a lot of things he wasn't proud of, but the one thing he'd always been was a good father. He loved his children as much as any parent could love a son or daughter, so she didn't want to believe he'd known about Dillon all along.

What a secret to hide for decades, she thought. Then for some reason her thinking switched to Neil. Maybe he crossed her mind because earlier Neil had claimed that he'd uncovered the secret *she* was keeping. He'd talk about that whole DCFS investigation and how he knew she was behind it.

Charlotte replayed his words and the look on his face, but then her thoughts fell back on Curtis. She didn't know which was worse: finding out you had a stepson that your husband had ignored for years, or discovering that the wrong kind of person had the goods on you. Both scenarios were distressing, but for now she would have to focus on the latter. Curtis was her priority, but it was crucial that she determine just how much Neil truly knew. She had to find out so she could fix things.

Chapter 41

*C*harlotte dragged her body into the house, keyed in the security code to disarm the system, and shut the door. She dropped her handbag on the island and sighed. She'd spent the night at the hospital and had never been more exhausted. Her parents had driven home around midnight, and Janine and some of the others had left before that, but she and Alicia had camped out between Curtis's room and the family waiting area. Thankfully, he'd slept very well throughout the night and without much pain, so she'd told Alicia she was going home to shower and change. Mostly, though, she'd wanted to check on Matthew and MJ. She had hoped they would be there when she arrived, and she'd been disappointed when she'd seen that Matthew's car wasn't in the garage. When Matthew had stormed out of Curtis's room yesterday afternoon, Charlotte had given him a couple of hours to cool down, and then she'd called him. He'd still not been in the best mood, but she'd tried to explain that everything was going to be all right and that it might be best for him to stay at Aunt Emma's. But, of course, he'd resisted the idea altogether and had told her he and MJ were going home. She'd then wanted to know if he was taking Curtina with him, too, but he'd responded by saying, "No, she wants to stay with Aunt Emma, so I'll just let you pick her up."

Charlotte had listened and gotten nervous all at the same time. She knew the reason he didn't want to take Curtina was likely because he was heading over to Racquel's. So, Charlotte had waited another couple of hours and called him again. But this time he hadn't answered. Finally, though, when she'd left a voice mail, saying how worried she was, he'd called her back. Still, when she'd asked where he and MJ were, he'd said, "Just out and about." Charlotte had known he was lying, but she hadn't wanted to argue with him.

Now, it was seven a.m., and she dialed him again.

"Hello," he said in a rough whisper. Charlotte could tell he'd been asleep.

"Where are you?"

"Racquel's."

Charlotte was furious. "Who's there with you?"

"I don't know. Dr. Anderson said he had early rounds this morning, but I'm sure Racquel and her mom are here. I'm in the guest room."

"Uh-huh, and where's MJ?"

"Mom, what's with all the questions?"

"Matt, why can't you see how serious this is? Why can't you see that DCFS took MJ away so they could protect him?"

Matthew didn't respond.

"Are you there?"

"Yep."

"I know you think this is a joke, but what if DCFS finds out MJ is over there?"

"Who's gonna tell them, Mom? You?"

"Anyone could! And if they find out, they can take him away from all of us."

"Well, I'll just take my chances."

"Matt, please. I know you don't understand any of this, but you have to think about MJ. You're trying to keep Racquel and her mother happy, but MJ has to be your focus."

"He *is* my focus. He's here with me and his mother where he belongs, and he's happy. He hasn't even been crying as much as he used to."

"I'm really concerned, Matt. DCFS left MJ with

me and your dad, and I'm terrified of what might happen."

"Shouldn't you be more worried about Dad than MJ?"

"I'm worried about both of them. I'm worried about you, too."

"Well, don't. MJ is fine, and nothing's gonna happen to him."

He wasn't hearing anything Charlotte said, so it was time to stop being nice. "I want you to bring him home, Matt. Enough is enough."

"Mom, I love you, but please don't try to control me. Please don't make me say or do something I'll regret."

Charlotte could tell he wasn't playing and had to change her tune. "Okay, look. I've had a long night and I just got home, so I'm a little tired. I'm sorry. But can you at least bring him home so I can see him before I head back to the hospital?"

"I'll bring him when it's time for me to pack."

Charlotte wanted to object but realized it was better to simply go along with his crazy thinking. He'd be flying back to Boston in a few hours, anyway. She loved her son and loved having him home, but today she couldn't wait for him to leave. When he was gone, she'd have total control of MJ again, and she wouldn't have to deal with

Matthew's immaturity. Although, she wondered what she would do when he came for another visit, because he'd surely want to pack up MJ and whisk him over to the Andersons again. She didn't want to report Matthew to the caseworker, but if he pushed her she wouldn't have a choice. She would do what was necessary to keep MJ away from Racquel and Vanessa.

Charlotte went into the family room and plopped down on the leather sofa. She closed her eyes and took deep meditational breaths. Her nerves raced, but she needed to calm herself before making her next call. She dreaded it, but if she didn't call Neil she wasn't sure what he might do or who he'd give critical information to. She also knew that now was a good time, since Matthew had told her Neil was at the hospital.

She breathed in and out one more time and dialed his number.

"Good morning," he said. "I've been waiting to hear from you."

"Is this a good time?" she asked.

"Perfect. I just pulled into the parking lot."

"I was hoping to continue our conversation," she said. "You really caught me off guard yesterday."

"I can imagine. I was just as shocked."

"But that's just it. I haven't done anything, so there's nothing for you to be shocked about."

"Maybe you still don't understand. Charlotte, I'm not guessing or wondering—I know for sure that you put this thing together. I have proof, and while I don't want my daughter to endure any more pain than she has to, I'm willing to work with you on this. I'm willing to give you two days to get the investigation dropped and have MJ returned to her."

Charlotte wasn't going to admit anything until she knew more. "You've got the wrong person, Neil. I would never do something so foolish."

"You're just not going to admit it, are you?"

"No one should admit to something they didn't do. That would be insane. Especially when your words are based on hearsay."

"Oh, I see—it's proof you want. Well, according to my source, you paid four different people to carry out this scheme of yours. It's also my understanding that with the exception of the caseworker, you never met any of them and you coordinated everything through some friend of yours."

Charlotte sat quietly but could no longer deny her involvement. Neil knew everything.

"I only did this for my grandson," she hurried to say, forcing the sound of tears into her voice.

"All I wanted was to protect him. I knew Matt and Racquel were too young to take care of MJ. They were too young to be parents."

"Still, what you did was wrong. But like I told you yesterday, I'm willing to overlook it. What you did would be unforgivable by most people's standards, but we can handle this quietly and discreetly."

"I'm not sure what you want me to do."

"Let me explain something. I love my daughter, and there's no doubt that I should have told her everything as soon as I found out. But I'm also a man who has certain needs. I'm married, but I haven't loved Vanessa in years."

Charlotte already knew what he was hinting at, but she still asked, "Okay...but what does that have to do with me?"

"I want to be with you."

Charlotte closed her eyes, partly because she didn't want to betray Curtis and partly because hearing Neil's voice was stirring the wrong kind of feelings in her.

"I can't do that," she said.

"Why?"

"Because I love my husband."

"I'm sure you do, but I know when a woman wants me."

"You're picking up the wrong signal."

"No, you're definitely attracted to me, and you can't control it."

"I have to go," Charlotte said, standing up.

"Why don't you just think about it and call me back?"

"I'm not sleeping with you, Neil."

"Well, then I guess I should tell you."

"What?"

"I'm one of the best neurosurgeons in the Midwest and one of the nicest men you'll ever meet...but I'm also used to getting what I want."

"And?"

"You know the old saying, 'If you scratch my back, I'll scratch yours.' If you make love to me, your secret will be safe. I'll never tell another living soul."

Charlotte couldn't believe he was capable of this. "So, you're going to use your own grandson to try to blackmail me?"

"Let's not turn this into something ugly. All I'm saying is that we're in this thing of yours together now."

"No, we're not. I'm not sleeping with you, Neil. So, please don't ask me about this again."

"I know you have a lot on your mind, so let's talk again tomorrow."

He was totally ignoring her, but she couldn't do this with him and hung up. Still, she knew this wasn't over and that it would have to be dealt with. Only thing was, she had no clue how she was going to get herself out of this mess.

Chapter 42

*C*urtis nestled his head further into his pillows and felt a slight bit of discomfort. His nurse had raised his bed so that he was in more of a sitting position, but he wasn't sure how much longer he'd be able to remain there. Maybe just until he finished his phone conversation with Elder Jamison, and then he'd ask Alicia to lower him a little.

"So is everything good to go?" Curtis asked.

"Yes, no worries. The service will go on as usual."

"Who's delivering the message? Minister Simmons or Minister Morgan?"

"Minister Simmons, of course. While we were waiting for you to come out of surgery yesterday, we discussed it. Minister Morgan was more than willing but said he wasn't fully prepared. You know Minister Simmons was sort of glad to hear that, though."

Curtis chuckled. "He always is. And let me ask you something. I mentioned this to Lana, but do you think Minister Simmons can be trusted?"

"Why, because of how ambitious he is?" Elder Jamison asked.

"Yes. I think he's just determined and has a strong passion for the ministry, but Charlotte has always been a little hesitant toward him."

"I really do think he means well, and I have to say, while you were in surgery, he was just as upset as your children. He loves and admires you that much. His sadness and concern were genuine, and he did a lot of praying for you."

"That's great to hear. I'll have to tell Charlotte about it."

"Well, I'd better get going," Elder Jamison said. "Need to get over to the church. I'll be out to see you this afternoon, though."

"Thanks for everything. You're the reason I'm able to rest. And let me just say this now: I'm very sorry for this thing with Dillon. I promised you and the rest of our members that there wouldn't be any more drama, and I've let you down again."

"If everything Dillon shared is true, then it's very unfortunate, but we'll make it through this. I do think you should make things right with that young man, though."

"I'm going to very soon."

"You take care, Pastor."

"You, too."

Curtis laid his phone at his side on the bed.

"So everything okay, Daddy?" Alicia asked.

"Yep. Sounds like everything's under control."

"Good."

"So when are you going home?" he asked.

"I'm not. When Matt called and told me what happened to you, I packed a bag. And as soon as Charlotte gets back, I'm going over to Melanie's to change." Melanie was Alicia's best friend, who lived there in Mitchell.

"I'm so glad you're here. I know I don't deserve it, but I really need your support."

"We've been through tougher times than this," she said.

"I know that, too, but it just seems that my past keeps causing problems for all of you. I've done so many things that sometimes I literally forget about them. I worked hard to push certain incidents out of my mind because it was easier. Selfish...but easier."

"So what are you going to do about Dillon?"

"I've gotta try to find him. I have to talk to him."

"Do you think he's going to make trouble? Charlotte thinks he just wants money."

"There's a chance he does, but I'm not worried about that. My concern is trying to do right by him. I'm not sure I'll be able to, but I'm going to try. That's the least I owe him. Then, there's Matt and what I'm sure this whole thing has done to him."

"He's not happy at all, Daddy. He's angry at the world right now."

"I could tell. Plus, he has all this madness going on with MJ. That baby never should have been taken from Racquel."

"You don't think any of those allegations are true, do you?"

"Not at all."

"Then why would someone say such things?"

"I don't know, but I believe we'll find out soon."

Alicia shook her head. "Poor Racquel."

"She's been through a lot, but God will be the Finisher of all of this. She'll get MJ back, and life will be good for her again."

"Oh, and by the way, Mom said to tell you that she's thinking about you and praying for you."

"How is she?"

"Fine."

"And James?"

"He's good, too. They're going on a cruise in a couple of weeks, so they're pretty excited about that."

"Good for them," Curtis said. He thought about his marriage to Tanya, and how even though she'd been the reason he'd railroaded Sonya and denied Dillon, he hadn't treated Tanya like the wonderful wife she was. He'd been unfaithful to her on more occasions than he could count, and when she'd finally gotten the courage to leave him, he'd moved on to Mariah—a naïve woman who knew her place and how to stay in it. He'd treated her worse than Tanya and hadn't felt a lick of remorse. He remembered how, back then, he'd almost felt entitled to do whatever he wanted. He'd felt at liberty to sleep with other women and had seen no reason why it should cause any conflict. There were a couple of times when Mariah did complain, but he'd set her straight, and she'd learned not to question him. His grandmother used to say, though, that time had a way of bringing about change, and Mariah had proven that fully. She'd spent twelve years obsessing over the terrible way he'd treated her and had somehow found a way to get revenge. He still wasn't sure how she'd connected with Dillon, but it didn't matter. She'd done what she'd done because of all the emotional pain and head games Curtis had inflicted upon her. She'd turned so bitter that she'd become spiteful and vindictive, and Curtis would never reveal her name to the police or press charges. He'd already decided that when they'd originally questioned him, but now as he lay there thinking, he was positive. He did hope he never had to see or hear from her again, but he wished her well and wanted her to be happy.

Charlotte knocked and then walked in. Dr. Mason strolled in behind her.

"So, how's my patient this morning?" Dr. Mason asked.

"Still some pain from the surgery, and of course my body is sore, but I'm not complaining."

"Things could have turned out a lot worse," the doctor said. "You were kicked and punched in every place imaginable, and other organs could have been damaged. It's bad enough that you have broken ribs and had a ruptured spleen, but again, it could have been worse."

"I'm very blessed," Curtis said. "I had God and you, and I'm thankful. I appreciate everything, Doctor."

Dr. Mason read through Curtis's chart, lowered his hospital gown from his neck down to below his chest and examined him, and then pulled his gown back up.

Curtis fixed the gown so that it was comfortably covering his shoulders again, even though he didn't have it tied in the back. "So when are you going to let me out of here? I've got places to go and people to see."

They all laughed.

"Maybe in a couple of days or so. Tuesday or Wednesday."

"That's an awfully long time from now," Curtis said, joking with him.

"Well, I just want you to get some real rest, because I know what a busy man you are. If I send you home too quickly you'll be back preaching or writing."

"Exactly," Alicia said. "You're doing the right thing, Doctor, and I hope you keep my dad for as long as possible."

Curtis frowned at her playfully. "Whose side are you on?"

"We're both on Dr. Mason's side," Charlotte added. "You know how hardheaded you are when you get sick. You always try to do too much."

"You're healing up fine, though," Dr. Mason said, smiling, "and I'll stop by tomorrow before my first surgery."

"Thanks again, Doctor," Curtis said. "Enjoy the rest of your weekend."

When Dr. Mason left, Alicia grabbed her black leather shoulder bag and kissed her father on the cheek. "I need to freshen up, so I'm gonna head over to Melanie's. But I'll be back."

"Thanks for everything, baby girl. I love you."

"I love you, too, Daddy. See you, Charlotte."

"See ya."

When the door closed, Curtis smiled at his wife and said, "Come here."

Charlotte walked closer, and he grabbed her hand. "I'm so, so sorry."

"For what?" she asked.

"For keeping yet another secret from you. Alicia found the interview with her iPhone and played it for me."

"She really shouldn't have done that. You don't need that kind of stress."

"She didn't want to, but I insisted. I was wrong, baby, for what I did, and I'm ashamed. The way I bullied Sonya was just plain evil, and I understand why Dillon went public. Imagine how you would feel if you'd lost your mom when you were a baby and then discovered your father had something to do with it. What if your dad had forced your mom into a severe state of depression and then never had anything to do with you?"

"I still say he could have handled things privately. I mean, what's with this 'going public' thing? Why do people feel like they have to put us on blast all the time?"

"Because of my position, and that will never change. But I'm telling you, that was the only thing I hadn't told you about. No more secrets between us."

Charlotte smiled, but she seemed nervous. Curtis wondered why but went on with his conversation. "I've decided to contact Dillon, so we can talk."

"I don't think you should do that," she said. "At least not until you've been out of the hospital for a while."

"I feel bad enough as it is, and I need to apologize to him."

"I still say you should wait. You've been through a lot, and I'm still worried about what happened to you. Someone attacked you, and we need to find out who did it."

"That's the other thing I wanted to talk to you about. I'm not going to pursue that. I just want to move on." Curtis had been serious when he'd told her that there would be no more secrets, but with the way Charlotte was sounding, he didn't think he could tell her about Mariah yet.

"Why?" she asked, looking frustrated with him.

"It's just not worth it. It happened, and it's over."

Charlotte tossed Curtis a strange look, but he ignored it.

"So has Matt calmed down any?" he asked.

"I see you're changing the subject, but no, not really. He's at Racquel's, and he's not listening to anything I say."

"He's young, and he doesn't understand why MJ was taken from Racquel. Just this morning, I said a long prayer for her and Vanessa to be vindicated. It'll happen soon, especially now that Neil has hired a private investigator."

"Oh, really? Who told you that?"

"He did. Friday night when Matt and I were over there."

"Well, I still say Matt needs to follow rules. He needs to keep MJ away from Racquel and her mother."

Curtis didn't bother commenting because he could tell Charlotte didn't want to hear about them being innocent—which was more reason for Curtis to believe she knew more than she admitted. She was hiding something, the same as he'd done with Dillon. But secrets always had a way of coming out. The truth would eventually be exposed, and it would be hard for Charlotte to recover. She would regret her actions from now on. Curtis knew this because he was proof of it.

Chapter 43

As soon as Alicia returned to the hospital, Charlotte kissed Curtis on the lips and started toward the cafeteria. She wasn't thrilled at all about Curtis wanting to talk to Dillon. And now he also wanted to forget about the thugs who'd beaten him up? It just didn't make sense, but Charlotte had been too preoccupied with her own problems to debate him. There was a chance he'd eventually tell her his reason for making such foolish choices, but at the moment, she couldn't stop thinking about something else he'd said.

Neil had hired a private investigator. She'd been splitting her brain, trying to figure out how Neil had busted her, and now she knew. It explained everything, and sadly, Charlotte hadn't counted on this. She'd just assumed everyone would take DCFS's word and then wait for the investigator's findings. But no such luck. Neil had meddled with her plan, and she had to rethink her options. She had to figure out something else, because she didn't want to give MJ back. She also didn't want anyone to know what she'd done, though, so God forgive her, she wondered if Neil would let her keep MJ if she went ahead and slept with him. Maybe this would keep him quiet. She didn't want to cheat on Curtis, Lord knows she didn't, but she also couldn't help how she felt about MJ. She'd said she was willing to do whatever she had to, so if she slept with Neil, it would be for good reason. It wouldn't be about her marriage; it would be for her grandson. She knew she'd promised Curtis she would never be unfaithful again, but it was clear she didn't have other alternatives.

Although maybe Meredith could help her think this problem through, the same as she had with other issues. The other day, Meredith had sounded a little strange on the phone, as if she was plagued with remorse, but Charlotte knew Meredith would always have her back. Meredith had a remedy for everything, and Charlotte was sorry she hadn't called her back from yesterday. She'd called Charlotte four times but hadn't left a message. Charlotte had thought about answering every one of her calls, but she also hadn't wanted to hear any guilt trips. Not that this was the reason Meredith had called, because she was likely calling about Curtis, but Charlotte hadn't wanted to chance it—she hadn't wanted to talk to anyone who thought she should give MJ back.

Charlotte walked further down the atrium corridor and dialed her number. It rang a few times until her voice mail picked up. She wondered where Meredith was, although, now that she'd become a lot more spiritual than Charlotte could ever remember, maybe she'd gone to church.

Now Charlotte called her mother.

"Hey, honey," Noreen said.

"Hey, Mom. How are you?"

"Good. How's Curtis?"

"Doing pretty good. Dr. Mason said he'll be able to go home by Wednesday."

"Wonderful. I'm so happy he's doing well."

"I am, too, but I still have bad news."

"What?"

Charlotte walked toward a corner and looked around, making sure no one was within earshot. She still spoke softly, though. "Neil knows what I did."

"What? Wait a minute. Your dad's downstairs watching a game, but let me close my door."

Charlotte didn't even want to think about what her father would do if he heard any of their conversation.

"So what exactly did he say?" Noreen asked.

Charlotte filled her in with all the details, and it was then that Charlotte realized how serious this was. When Neil had approached her, she'd known his discovery was critical, but now reality slammed her in the face.

"This is awful," Noreen said. "How do you think he found out?"

"Curtis told me he hired a PI, so maybe somebody got scared and told everything."

"So Curtis knows, too?" Noreen asked.

"No, not about me and the DCFS thing. Neil just told him he hired an investigator."

"Have you called Meredith?"

"Just now, but there was no answer. I'll call her back, though."

"I'm sure she'll know what to do."

"Still, I'm really nervous because Matt and Curtis can never know about this, Mom."

"Is Matt still leaving this evening?"

"Yeah, but that's a whole other story. He and MJ spent the night at Racquel's."

"That's too bad, and you know what bothers me about that? What if these accusations were real?

What if Racquel and Vanessa were guilty? I wonder if he's even considered that."

"I doubt it. That's why I know both of them are too young to care for a baby."

"Well, at least he'll be gone in a few hours and you'll be able to take over. And if I were you, MJ wouldn't go near those people."

"He won't. I've already decided that."

Charlotte chatted with her mother and got a bite to eat in the cafeteria. She'd also tried calling Meredith again, and this time she'd left a message. Now she walked through the long corridor and stopped at the elevator. When the doors opened, however, Charlotte looked toward the main waiting area and thought she saw a photo of Meredith on television. Then, after waiting too long to step inside, the elevator doors closed and Charlotte walked closer to the huge flat-screen on the wall. A commercial aired, so she turned to a seventy-something, silver-haired woman. "Excuse me, was that Meredith Connolly Christiansen I saw?"

"Yes, it was a tribute photo," the woman said.

"Tribute?"

"Uh-huh. She passed away this morning."

Charlotte gasped.

"I know," the woman said, seeming to share

Charlotte's disbelief. "She did so much for the community, and she was an inspiration to women everywhere."

Charlotte heard the woman talking, but she slowly tuned her out. She didn't want to hear any more; not when her wonderful friend was gone— not when Merideth Connolly Christiansen was gone for good.

Charlotte was getting tired of this. She'd just left the hospital, and though she'd called Matthew three times, he hadn't answered. He was making a bad habit of this, and though she was trying to be patient and tread lightly because of all that he was going through, he was starting to annoy her. He was blatantly disrespecting her, and she didn't appreciate it. She and Matthew had their issues and there was a lot they didn't agree about, but she was still his mother.

Charlotte turned onto the street they lived on. She wasn't sure why he wasn't answering, especially with his plane leaving in three hours. Charlotte tried Racquel's cell number, something she hadn't wanted to do, but the call went directly to voice mail. *Where in the world are they?*

Charlotte drove up the driveway, into the garage, and went into the house. Naturally, Matthew and MJ weren't there. She hoped Racquel hadn't talked him into going out somewhere, because now he would be late for his flight.

Charlotte sighed in anger and dialed her son again. Thank goodness, he finally answered.

"Hello?" he said, but his disinterested tone irked Charlotte.

"Matt, where are you? Do you know what time it is?"

"I'm at Racquel's."

"Why didn't you answer my other calls?"

"Sorry."

"Are you on your way home?"

"I changed my flight."

"To when?"

"Tomorrow evening, and the only reason I'm going then is so I can withdraw."

Charlotte could hardly breathe. "What? Matt, you're really messing up. Getting your degree is extremely important."

"Are you saying my son and his mother aren't? Are you saying they shouldn't matter to me?"

"No, of course not, but you need an education."

"And I'll get it."

"Is this because of what happened to your dad?"

"Nope."

"I know this has been a tough weekend, but

Matt, you've got to hang in there. You've got to keep pushing forward."

"I'll go back in the fall. That way I can be here for MJ until this DCFS junk is cleared up."

"But Matt—"

"Mom, please. I'll talk to you later. Good-bye."

Charlotte removed the phone from her ear. What if he *never* went back to school? What if he was so caught up with that silly girl that he forgot about college altogether? For the first time, Charlotte sort of regretted taking MJ. Maybe she should have thought about this a little longer and figured out a better way to handle things. What she should have done first was broken up Matthew and Racquel and turned Matthew completely against her. But she'd figured she would work on that after the fact. Now, though, she thought differently. Things were backfiring very quickly, and sadly, she didn't know what to do about it—except (1) beg Matthew to change his mind about withdrawing from school, (2) sleep with Neil, and (3) contact the caseworker to see what else could be done to keep MJ away from Racquel. Maybe it was just a matter of paying Linda Jacobs more money. Or maybe there was some other perfect resolution Charlotte hadn't thought of. Either way, she had to sit down and evaluate the situation—then proceed very quickly.

Chapter 44

Charlotte had barely been able to sleep last night, but she'd made her decision. Just as soon as she left the hospital later this afternoon, she was calling Linda, MJ's caseworker. She knew money didn't solve everything, but she didn't know how Linda would be able to turn down twenty-five thousand dollars in cash. That was the amount Charlotte was willing to pay her if she could keep that investigation going. Charlotte had also taken care of something else. She'd had to think about this decision a lot longer than she had about the money, though. Because as much as she wanted to do this for MJ, if Curtis ever found out she'd had another affair, he would divorce her. There wouldn't be any talking about it; he'd simply file the papers and that would be the end of it. But she needed Neil to keep his mouth shut, and he wasn't willing to accept anything else in exchange. She'd already left him a message and was waiting for him to get back to her.

Charlotte walked into Curtis's room, and though he was still badly bruised, she could tell he felt better than yesterday. Or maybe his bright spirits had nothing to do with how well he felt and everything to do with Dillon. Charlotte had adamantly advised Curtis against it, but Curtis had asked Dillon to come see him. Charlotte hadn't even known about it until Curtis had phoned last night to speak to Curtina. Curtina had been at Aunt Emma's all weekend, but once Charlotte had learned that Matthew wasn't flying back to Boston, she'd gone to pick up Curtina so she could get ready for school today. But when Curtis had called to tell Curtina he loved her and to say good night, he'd also dropped this Dillon bomb on Charlotte. He'd told her yesterday that he'd wanted to speak to him, but Charlotte hadn't expected it to happen so quickly. She'd also hoped that if Curtis did invite him for a visit, Dillon would decline. But Curtis's publicist, Lisa, had called the local TV producer, the producer had called Dillon, and Dillon had called Curtis within the hour. A few minutes ago, Curtis had talked about how cold and curt Dillon had been on the phone, but Curtis hadn't seemed bothered by that and felt obligated to meet with him. He thought it very necessary to make amends. Still, Charlotte prayed that at the last minute, Dillon would change his mind and wouldn't show. But just then, someone knocked on the door. Sure enough, it was him, and Charlotte hoped the media hadn't gotten wind of his being there.

He slowly walked in with some woman at his side. He acted as though he didn't know what to say, so, finally, Curtis spoke up:

"Thank you for coming."

Now Dillon stared at him, but he seemed mortified. Shocked, even, and Charlotte knew it was because of the way Curtis looked. The woman next to him cringed also.

"Thank you for coming, too, Melissa," Curtis said, and now Charlotte realized this was the so-called fiancée Curtis had told her about. She'd been the woman who'd come to the counseling sessions with Dillon, pretending they were a real couple who was about to get married and needed Curtis's help.

"I first want to say," Curtis said. "I'm sorry for everything. I know my apology must mean very little to you, but I'm being sincere. I honestly couldn't be sorrier about anything, and I hope one day you can forgive me."

Dillon leaned against the wall, listening.

"I know I'll never be able to rid you of the horrible pain you've felt all these years, but I'm going to do whatever I can to make things up to you. I'll spend the rest of my life doing it if I have to."

Melissa pushed her bag farther up on her shoulder and leaned against the wall next to Dillon.

Dillon folded his arms. "I almost didn't come here."

"I don't blame you," Curtis said.

"For years, I've been sad and angry about never knowing my mother, but when I found out you were the reason she died, I hated you. I wanted to kill you."

Curtis nodded, almost as if he understood and agreed, and Charlotte wondered if he was losing his mind. There was no denying that Curtis had done a terrible thing, but there was no way Charlotte would let anyone tell her they'd wanted to kill her and get away with it. This whole meeting was ludicrous, and Charlotte wished Dillon would leave. She wanted him to slither back to Georgia or wherever it was he'd said he'd come from and never contact them again. Until now, Matthew had always been Curtis's only son, and as far as Charlotte was concerned he still was. Curtis was doing all he could to accept this so-called child of his, but Charlotte wasn't interested. If he'd come to them privately and explained who he was, Charlotte might feel better about things, but because he'd chosen to go on television, snitching all their business to the world, she didn't like him. She had no respect for him, and she didn't want him talking to her. He hadn't spoken to her, anyhow, him or his sneaky-looking fiancée, and Charlotte wanted them to keep it that way.

"I'm also going to contact my attorney," Curtis said, and Charlotte thought she would choke. Maybe Curtis's nurse had given him the wrong medication, because he was clearly out of his head. "I'm going to provide for you in my will and have one of my banks cut you a check. I realize no amount of money will bring your mom back, but I'm hoping five hundred thousand dollars will help in some way."

Charlotte tossed Curtis a wicked look. "Curtis?" she yelled.

"Baby, I'm sorry I didn't discuss this with you, but God has led me to do this. I owe this young man, and until I do right by him, I won't rest."

"And you can't think of any other way besides giving him a half a million dollars?"

"I'm sorry," he said again.

Charlotte was outraged. Who did Curtis think he was giving away this kind of money to a stranger? What was wrong with him?

Dillon stared at Curtis like he'd just won the lottery. "Don't you even want a DNA test?"

"Just for our own peace of mind, but I know Sonya wasn't sleeping with anyone else. At least not when she was with me. She was a stripper, but your mom was a good person with a big heart. She just wasn't the kind of woman who would lie about paternity."

"Can I be honest?" Dillon said. "I don't know why, but seeing you in person isn't what I expected."

"How so?"

Dillon turned to Melissa and then back to Curtis. "I only came here to tell you that I was filing a lawsuit against you. My plan was to sue you for everything you have."

"I don't blame you for feeling that way, but I'm hoping you'll give me a chance to get to know you...and to maybe be the kind of father you deserve."

Charlotte wanted to punch Curtis, but then she looked over at Dillon. Was he crying? He was! This whole father-son charade wasn't turning out nearly the way Charlotte had wanted it to. She had prayed that Dillon wouldn't show up, but now that he had she'd spent the last few moments hoping he would go ballistic, hoping he'd demand an astronomical amount of money from Curtis—much more than five hundred thousand—and then go storming out of Curtis's hospital room. Then, Curtis would call his attorney so they could prepare to fight Dillon in court.

But not only had Curtis offered Dillon six figures, Dillon acted as though he wasn't all that angry anymore. He seemed as though he was relieved and was thankful to be in Curtis's presence. She could look in his eyes and tell he no longer wanted to be enemies the way he'd planned. He wanted a father, and that unnerved Charlotte—made her sick to her stomach, because it was like she'd been thinking before—she would never accept him. She'd once felt the same way about Curtina, but that was for good reason and the scenario had been different. Dillon, on the other hand, was an outsider who was only trying to latch onto a wealthy family, and Charlotte would never make him feel welcome. MJ was the new addition and priority in this family, and nothing was going to change that.

"I'm really glad I came," Dillon said. "And while I never thought I'd be saying this, I'm sorry, too. If I had it to do over again, I would've just called you. Actually, that was my first thought. But then your brother told me that you deserved a lot worse. I was so angry and hurt, it wasn't hard for me to listen to him."

"I'm not surprised," Curtis said.

"Then as time went on, he seemed more upset than I was. He kept saying I deserved millions."

Curtis shook his head in disappointment. "And I'm sure he's expecting some sort of payoff."

"He talked about it a couple of times, but I haven't heard from him in three weeks."

"He's probably out on a drug binge, but you'll hear from him. You can count on it."

Charlotte almost wanted to laugh. Even after going to jail, Larry was still trying to swindle money from Curtis. He hadn't been successful the first time, but he'd done a pretty good job with this Dillon fiasco. He had exposed old secrets that had been buried for nearly three decades, and now Curtis was left picking up the pieces. There was no doubt Curtis and Charlotte would have to answer to the media and their congregation, and she wasn't looking forward to that. They'd had to answer to their members last year after that Sharon woman had snapped, but this Dillon story wasn't going to be as easy for folks to swallow; not so much because Curtis had fathered a child with a stripper but because of the backstory. People would have a problem with the reason Sonya had died and the fact that Curtis had never tried to be a father to his son.

Charlotte heard her phone ringing and pulled it from her purse. It was Neil, and though she didn't want to miss anything Curtis might say to Dillon, she also wanted to talk to Neil before the day was out.

"Baby, I'll be back," she said to Curtis.

"I'll be right here," he said, smiling.

Charlotte walked out of the room and down to the end of the hallway. No staff members were in the last two rooms, so she knew it was safe to talk there. She hadn't answered her phone in time, though, so she called Neil back.

"Charlotte, I'm glad I reached you," he said frantically. "Something terrible has happened."

"Oh God, no. Is MJ okay?"

"He's fine, but Vanessa went through my briefcase, and she saw the letter."

Charlotte wondered what he was talking about. "What letter?"

"The letter that talked about your connection to DCFS. The one that said you should give MJ back."

"I don't get it."

"I'm really sorry. I should've hidden that letter somewhere else."

"What letter, Neil? You're scaring me."

"From Meredith Connolly Christiansen. She was my patient."

Charlotte hyperventilated and struggled to control it.

"Four months ago," he said, "she found out she had an aggressive brain tumor, and her doctor referred her to me. I eventually determined it was inoperable, but she was admitted on Friday and died on Sunday. But before she passed, she gave me a letter that was addressed to you, and then she apologized. Because of all the pain medicine, she was sort of out of it. But she begged me to forgive her for taking my grandson. Said she didn't want to hurt you, but that she'd tried calling you multiple times on Saturday and you wouldn't answer. She was very weak, but she said she couldn't die in peace without confessing and repenting to someone."

Charlotte's breathing revved up. *Dear God, why didn't I answer her calls? Why didn't I call her back?*

"I'm really sorry," Neil said.

"Why didn't you tell me?" she spat. "How could you let this happen?"

"I messed up. Even though Meredith had told me part of the details, I had no right opening your letter. But my curiosity got the best of me."

"I can't believe you let this happen! How stupid of you to leave something like that in your brief-case!" Charlotte was livid, and she couldn't have cared less about those nosy nurses huddled together a few doors down, staring at her.

"And there's something else," he said.

"What?"

"Vanessa called the police."

"Why?"

"She wants you arrested. I've been trying to talk her down for two hours, but she wouldn't listen. She's so through with me for not doing something about this."

"*You?* You're worried about Vanessa being mad when the police are probably camped out in front of our home?"

"Like I said, I'm sorry. I never meant for this to happen."

"Whatever, Neil," she said, ending the call. She threw her phone inside her purse, and tried to think. She thought of several different possibilities, but nothing seemed feasible. *Oh God, what if they arrest me?*

Charlotte hurried down the hallway, nearly

knocking over one of those nosy nurses, and jet-
ted past Curtis's room. When she turned the corner and stepped in front of the elevator, the doors
opened and her heart stopped. Matthew glared at
her like he hated her, and tears rolled down her
cheeks.

"Matt, please let me explain."

"Explain what, Mom? That you're so evil and
selfish that you would pay thousands of dollars to
take MJ away? You paid people to lie on Racquel
and her mom for no reason? Are you really that
crazy?"

"Matt," she said, tears pouring down her face.
"I wasn't myself. I wasn't thinking."

"You never do. You just do whatever you want.
I've been saying that all along, but I always forgive you. But I'm done this time, Mom."

"Sweetie, please," she said, grabbing him with
both hands.

Matthew pushed her away from him. "No,
Mom! You're gonna pay for this one. You're
gonna pay for what you did to me, Racquel, and
her mother, and you can forget about ever seeing
MJ."

Charlotte wept like a five-year-old. "Matt, I'm
begging you. Please don't do this. Please don't
turn your back on me."

Matt threw his hands in the air, sighing loudly. Then he turned toward the elevator, pressed the button, and wiped his face. "Why?" he yelled out, crying, and faced her again. "Why can't you and Dad just be normal? Why do you both always have to ruin everything? Here I was feeling bad about embarrassing you with MJ, when my whole childhood was a total embarrassment. Do you know how many nights I cried myself to sleep and sometimes wished I were dead? Do you, Mom? And all because of the sleeping around, the lies, and everything else you and Dad have done for years. Well, I'm tired of pretending like I'm happy, Mom, and like you and Dad are such great parents. You're not...and I'm done with both of you."

When the elevator opened, Charlotte saw the two detectives who were working on Curtis's case. They both stepped out, and the Denzel-looking one walked closer to her and pulled out his handcuffs. "Charlotte Black, you're under arrest for conspiring to defraud a state agency and for conspiring to obstruct justice. You also have the right to remain silent..."

He went on with the rest of the Miranda statement, but all Charlotte could think about was Matthew. He stepped into the elevator, stared at her with no emotion, and the doors shut. She was going to jail, but no matter how bad things got from here on out, it would never be worse than losing a child. Matthew was alive and well, but he wanted nothing else to do with her.

Epilogue

Three Months Later

C harlotte looked on as Curtis took a deep breath and smiled at his congregation. It had been three months since he'd stood in the pulpit, preparing to deliver his morning message, and the sanctuary was filled to capacity. Just about every seat was taken, meaning two thousand people had been kind enough to support their pastor's return. And this was only the early service, so Charlotte had a feeling the later service might have standing room only.

It had been a long, tough road of recovery for Curtis. He'd ended up getting a bad infection and having a second surgery, something that had sent him back to the hospital for a seven-day stay. At first, his primary-care physician had ordered him an oral antibiotic, but when it hadn't worked, he'd sent Curtis back to his surgeon, Dr. Mason. This had all been quite unexpected, and ultimately, Dr. Mason had discovered another rupture in his spleen and an infection so severe they'd had to administer his antibiotics intravenously. Thankfully, though, with the exception of the few scars and bruises that were still visible, he was just like new.

This, of course, was a far cry from what Charlotte had suffered through, and she wasn't sure she'd ever recover from that DCFS stunt she'd pulled. She'd been arrested for the first time in her life. The detectives had handcuffed her in front of hospital staff members, escorted her down to the main floor where all visitors entered and exited, and then ushered her out to an unmarked police vehicle. Everyone, including children, had stared at her like she was a murderer, and she'd never felt more humiliated. She'd also been able to tell from the loud gasps and stunned looks that many of them knew she was Reverend Curtis Black's wife, so some had taken photos with their camera phones and submitted them to the media. Then, a few days later, Charlotte had read one article online that said, "The Black family is the epitome of total dysfunction, so how could they possibly set examples for anyone, let alone their congregation? How could Pastor Black and his wife even consider calling themselves Christians?" She remembered being angry, but then, as she'd sat thinking, she'd realized the words in the article were justified. She and Curtis had done a lot, the same as Matthew had pointed out right before her arrest, and she'd been ashamed.

But even once her parents had bailed her out—since Curtis had been in the hospital—things had only tumbled farther and farther downhill. While she'd hired a top defense lawyer who was known for getting charges dropped, he had soon advised her to make a deal with the state's attorney's office: she would plead guilty to both counts of conspiracy, which meant she'd have a record for the rest of her life; she would be sentenced to two years of supervised probation, do two hundred hours of community service at an orphanage just outside of Chicago, and she would pay fines that totaled fifty thousand dollars. Charlotte hadn't wanted to plead guilty to any charges, but because the prosecutor had been given that letter from Meredith and he'd made deals with the four others who'd been involved, she hadn't had a choice. Sadly, Linda, the DCFS caseworker; Linda's supervisor; and the two women who'd made false allegations against Racquel and Vanessa had all agreed to testify against Charlotte. All four of them had done what they had to to lessen their punishments. Charlotte's attorney had recommended she take this route because the evidence and witness depositions were so damaging, she would of course be found guilty. He'd also told her that no judge or jury would be lenient on any woman, let alone a wealthy one, who'd taken a child from his mother for personal benefit. So Charlotte had done as she'd been told, but her guilty plea had prompted Vanessa and Racquel to file a civil suit against her very quickly. Charlotte hadn't been all that surprised, but when she'd learned they were suing for ten million dollars, she'd been horrified. There was no doubt that Vanessa had been the one to come up with such a sky-high figure, but Charlotte's attorney had promised he would defend her aggressively. He was also planning to contact Vanessa and Racquel's attorney to discuss settling out of court.

The whole thing was a huge mess, and Curtis wasn't happy. He had gotten past Charlotte's attempt to frame Vanessa and Racquel—at least somewhat—but what he was most upset about was the fact that Matthew hadn't stepped foot in their house in three months. Matthew had declared he was finished with both of them, and he'd meant it. They also hadn't seen MJ for the same period of time, and this made Charlotte and Curtis doubly sad.

But there wasn't a whole lot they could do. That first few weeks, they'd called him dozens of times and then tried him multiple times over the last couple of months, but Matthew had never answered. Then, two days ago, Charlotte had tried calling him again, but a recording had played. She'd then called their cell phone provider and discovered that Matthew had canceled his service. He'd cut Charlotte and Curtis completely off, and he seemed to be eliminating any way for them to contact him. But thankfully, he did talk to his grandparents and Aunt Emma. He also went by Aunt Emma's when he knew Curtina was going to be visiting, and he'd told her she could call him whenever she wanted—just not when Curtis or Charlotte were around. Needless to say, Curtina didn't understand any of what was going on, but she was slowly learning to live with this abrupt change in their family dynamic. They'd been transformed seemingly overnight, and they officially were a house divided. Matt had separated himself and moved in with the Andersons (Charlotte had learned that a June wedding had been confirmed), and though Curtis hadn't realized it, the two of them as husband and wife were at great odds over Dillon. Curtis now went out of his way, trying to stay in touch with his firstborn son—well, actually, his firstborn child, period— and Charlotte wanted nothing to do with him. Even Curtina hadn't taken to her new brother the way she normally did with everyone else she met.

As a family, they were miles apart from where they needed to be, and Charlotte knew she and Curtis were to blame: Curtis because of the secret he'd kept about Dillon and his mother, and Charlotte because of the shameful crime she'd committed. They'd caused a double scandal this time around, and it was the reason Curtis was about to do something he'd never done in the past. He was stepping down as senior pastor of Deliverance Outreach. He'd just announced it to the congregation, and moans of disappointment could be heard throughout the sanctuary.

"I know this isn't what most of you came to hear," Curtis continued sadly, "but I've prayed and prayed and prayed about my decision, and I know this is what I have to do. I've come a long way, and while I thought I had gotten things right with God, I now realize it's time to get them *all* the way right with Him. It's time to take my relationship with God a lot more seriously, and time I listen to *His* voice and direction. I also have to focus on bringing my family back together. I've always known that the Holy Spirit will set your path and guide you, but I haven't always remembered that. So again, if I am to follow God in the best way possible and lead you in the way God would have me to, I must step down until I'm ready to serve in a more spiritual capacity. My wife will also be stepping down as first lady.

"In the meantime, however, Minister Simmons and Minister Morgan will deliver the morning messages, and I'll be attending service, and worshiping and praising God the same as you. In a sense, it will feel as though I'm starting out all over again as a brand-new Christian. I'm going to spend hours studying the Word and doing all I can to learn as much as I can. I'm going to do all that God has expected me to do since the day he called me to minister: teach His Word, follow His Word, and live by His Word, no matter what. But finally, I wanna thank all of you for your genuine love and continued support of the ministry. Thank you for supporting our family in such an amazing way. I love you, I appreciate you, and I pray all the very best for you."

Everyone stood and applauded, and only a handful of parishioners kept their seats. It was good to know they truly cared about their pastor.

They cared about Deliverance Outreach, and they were willing to give Curtis all the time he needed to make his relationship with God much better. They were even willing to wait until he mended things with his family. This was certainly not something Charlotte would have suggested he do—stepping down from his position as senior pastor—but now, as she saw such encouraging smiles on everyone's faces, she knew Curtis had made the right decision.

She would also make important changes, specifically where her own relationship with God was concerned, and with the way she treated people. She'd made this statement many times before, but today she meant it. Matthew had talked a lot about how selfish she was, and it wasn't until she'd been arrested, convicted of a crime, and lost her son and grandson that her eyes had been opened. She'd always been a strong and very independent woman, but ever since the arrest, she cried all the time, and not a day went by when she didn't feel depressed. There were times when she felt so miserable and sad that she'd wanted to take a drink, but she fought the urge for Matthew and MJ, just in case Matthew somehow had a change of heart and forgave them. She prayed, hoped, and dreamed about that day, and when it finally happened she would be ready.

She and Curtis would both be ready to take on the role of being good parents. They were, of course, a little late to be realizing just how much their mistakes had affected Matthew, but now they had to take responsibility. They were well aware of how many times they'd hurt him, but what they hadn't realized was that far too much damage had been done. As a result, Matthew had taken a hard stance against them. He was tired of talking, begging, and pleading to have a normal life, and he was willing to move on without his parents. This was the last thing she and Curtis wanted, though, and now it was up to *them* to talk, beg, and plead. Instead of focusing on themselves, they would make Matthew, Curtina, and MJ their highest priority. They would sacrifice whatever was necessary. They would turn their broken house into a loving home—the kind of home where parents rarely hurt or disappointed their children; a home where love, trust, happiness, and peace were at the core.

They would do what they should have done from the very beginning, and Charlotte had faith that it wasn't too late. There was still a chance for all of them, thanks to a kind, merciful, and forgiving God, and it was this reality that would see them through. She was sure of it.

Acknowledgments

s with every book I've written, I thank God for absolutely everything. You have given me more grace and mercy than I could have ever imagined, and I am eternally grateful.

To my wonderful husband, Will, for being the best husband ever. You are my soul mate and best friend, and I love you with everything in me. Also, thank you for making me smile and laugh *every* single day of my life. To my brothers, Willie Jr. and Michael, and each of your children—I love all of you so very much; to my stepson and daughter-in-law, Trenod and Tasha, and your children—I love you dearly; to the rest of my loving family—I love you all: Tennins, Ballards, Lawsons, Stapletons, Youngs, Beasleys, Haleys, Romes, Greens, Robys, Garys, Shannons, Normans, and everyone else I'm blessed to be related to! To my first cousin and fellow author, Patricia

Haley-Glass, whom I grew up with and who is more a sister to me than a cousin—I love you so very much; my girls/friends/sisters for life, Kelli Bullard, Lori Whitaker Thurman, and Janell Green—I love you all; to my spiritual mother, Dr. Betty Price, for all your unwavering love, kindness, and support—I love you dearly; to everyone at the best publishing house ever—Grand Central Publishing—thank you for everything! To the best freelance team ever: Connie Dettman, Shandra Hill Smith, Luke LeFevre, Pam Walker-Williams, and Ella Curry—thanks a million! Then, to every bookseller who sells my work, to every newspaper, magazine, radio station, TV station, and online website or blog that supports me as an author year after year, and to every book club that continually chooses my work as your monthly selection—thanks for all that you do!

Finally, to the folks who go out of their way to make my writing career possible—**my wonderfully kind and supportive readers**. Years ago, I never imagined that I'd be writing the 10th title in my Reverend Curtis Black series, and it certainly couldn't have happened without all your encouragement. I love you, and I am forever grateful to **ALL** of you.

Much love and God bless you always,

Kimberla

E-mail: kim@kimroby.com
Facebook: www.facebook.com
        /kimberlalawsonroby
Twitter: www.twitter.com/KimberlaLRoby

Reading Group Guide

1. Can you understand Charlotte's frustration with Vanessa? Is Vanessa intentionally trying to exclude Charlotte, or is Charlotte imagining things? If Vanessa is trying to exclude her, why do you think she is doing that? Is she jealous as Charlotte says, or just trying to protect her daughter?

2. What should a grandparent's role be in raising a child? Do grandparents have rights? What kind of boundaries, if any, should exist?

3. Is Curtis right to agree with Vanessa that Charlotte needs to calm down, or, as Charlotte's husband, should he be on her side no matter what?

4. Do you think Matthew should have stayed at Harvard, or should he have stayed in Chicago to take care of his child?

5. How do you feel about the way Matthew treats Charlotte in the story? Is his anger justified, or, as her son, should he have been more sensitive to her feelings?

6. Was Curtis right to keep the threats he was receiving a secret from his family? Is there any way he could have handled the situation differently to make things better?

7. Have you ever had a family member you couldn't get along with? How does the relationship impact your family? Do you have any advice on how people can deal with difficult relationships?

8. Curtis is able to forgive those who have hurt him, but for some people forgiveness isn't so easy. How important is it to forgive others? Is what Charlotte did at the end of the story forgivable? Do you believe Matthew will ever forgive his parents? Have you ever been in a situation where you found it difficult to forgive someone for something? Or have you ever had to ask for someone else's forgiveness, and what did you do to earn it?

CONELY BRANCH
055174339